Apostle's Cove

ALSO BY WILLIAM KENT KRUEGER

THE CORK O'CONNOR SERIES

Spirit Crossing

Fox Creek

Lightning Strike

Desolation Mountain

Sulfur Springs

Manitou Canyon

Windigo Island

Tamarack County

Trickster's Point

Northwest Angle

Vermilion Drift

Heaven's Keep

Red Knife

Thunder Bay

Copper River

Mercy Falls

Blood Hollow

Purgatory Ridge

Boundary Waters

Iron Lake

OTHER NOVELS

The River We Remember

This Tender Land

Ordinary Grace

The Devil's Bed

Apostle's Cove

A Novel

William Kent
Krueger

ATRIA BOOKS
New York Amsterdam/Antwerp London
Toronto Sydney/Melbourne New Delhi

ATRIA BOOKS

An Imprint of Simon & Schuster, LLC
1230 Avenue of the Americas
New York, NY 10020

First Atria Books hardcover edition September 2025

ATRIA BOOKS and colophon are trademarks of Simon & Schuster, LLC

Manufactured in the United States of America

1 3 5 7 9 10 8 6 4 2

Library of Congress Cataloging-in-Publication Data
Names: Krueger, William Kent, author.
Title: Apostle's Cove: a novel / William Kent Krueger,
Description: First Atria Books hardcover edition. | New York: Atria Books, 2025. |
Series: Cork O'Connor mystery series
Identifiers: LCCN 2025009163 (print) | LCCN 2025009164 (ebook) | ISBN 9781982179304 (hardcover) |
ISBN 9781982179311 (trade paperback) | ISBN 9781982179328 (ebook)
Subjects: LCGFT: Detective and mystery fiction. | Paranormal fiction. | Novels.
Classification: LCC PS3561.R766 A86 2025 (print) | LCC PS3561.R766 (ebook) |
DDC 813/.54—dc23/eng/20250310
LC record available at https://lccn.loc.gov/2025009163
LC ebook record available at https://lccn.loc.gov/2025009164

ISBN 978-1-9821-7930-4
ISBN 978-1-9821-7932-8 (ebook)

To my father,
the high school English teacher,
who taught me a love of words and
of the stories we create with them.

Apostle's Cove

PROLOGUE

The best of autumn was past, color fallen from the trees, branches gone bare and black against a sky that had been overcast for days. This was always an unsettled time, after the flow of leaf peepers had dried up and before the snowmobilers arrived. Halloween was only a few days away. In the week following that celebration of ghouls and goblins, Cork O'Connor would close Sam's Place for the winter.

Nine p.m. and it had already been hard dark for more than an hour. Cork prepared to bag the day's take for the drop at the First National Bank on Center Street. He was alone. The high school kids who'd been his crew that evening had finished up the cleaning and gone home. Cork sat in the back of the old Quonset hut where he conducted both the business of Sam's Place and his occasional work as a private investigator. He'd pulled a Leinenkugel's from the fridge and sat sipping the beer and looking at the numbers he'd entered on his laptop. It had been a slow day. In a slow week. In a slow fall.

He felt old.

He had a birthday coming up in November, one he didn't feel

at all like celebrating. He'd recently added cholesterol and blood pressure medications to his daily dose of multivitamins. He'd begun wearing glasses for reading. He couldn't remember the last time he'd gotten out of bed in the morning without feeling pain somewhere. He played basketball regularly at the Y with the Old Martyrs, a bunch of guys who had gray hair or no hair at all anymore. When each spring came in full, he biked a good deal, on road and off. He could still paddle for a week in the Boundary Waters and portage a fifty-pound pack and canoe across several hundred rods. But the prospect of an upcoming birthday, of yet another step toward the inevitable decline of everything, weighed on him heavily and caused him, as he sat alone in Sam's Place, to consider the future darkly and ruminate, with many regrets, on the past.

He thought of himself as a man of few words, well chosen and unrevealing. He didn't want people worrying about him. So he hadn't shared with anyone—not his wife, Rainy, or his children or his friends—the depth of his dark considerations. It was his struggle alone, and he would get through it.

He sat in a circle of harsh light from the overhead bulb. A stiff autumn wind blew outside, and occasionally a branch from one of the pines that grew next to the old Quonset hut scraped against the metal siding, a sound like the scratch of some wild creature trying to claw its way in. Otherwise, the place was deathly quiet. So when Cork's cell phone rang, that shattering of the stillness startled him. He fumbled the phone from his pocket and saw on the display that it was his son.

Stephen currently lived in Saint Paul with his wife, Belle, and was in his second year of law school. He'd secured an internship working for the Great North Innocence Project, an organization whose aim was to analyze old cases to determine if new evidence might overturn a wrongful conviction. Stephen was passionate about this work, and Cork was proud of him. But he missed his son. And maybe that was a part of the darkness he felt.

"Hey, kiddo, what's up?" Cork said.

"Still at Sam's Place?" Stephen asked.

"Just closed up. In the counting house now, counting out my money."

"And the queen is in her parlor?"

"Rainy's at home. Only me here."

"Drinking a Leinie's, I'll bet."

"Good call, Counselor."

"Not a counselor yet, Dad."

"All in good time."

"So," Stephen said, then paused.

Cork sensed in that momentary silence at the other end of the line the seriousness of what Stephen was about to say. He set the bottle of Leinenkugel beer on the table.

"Do you remember a case you handled a long time ago? Axel Boshey?" Stephen finally asked.

"Of course," Cork said. "Impossible to forget. The first major crime I investigated after being elected sheriff. A particularly brutal murder. Why do you ask?"

There was another pause, another plunge into an unsettling silence.

Then Stephen drove home the painful point of his call, the nightmare of every man or woman who'd ever worn the badge of a sheriff and had taken to heart the solemn pledge to protect and to serve.

"Dad, I'm pretty sure you sent an innocent man to prison."

- PART I -

25 YEARS AGO

CHAPTER 1

In those days, the Tamarack County Sheriff's Department was located on the first floor of the courthouse. The hands of the clock in the clocktower on that grandiose county structure hadn't moved in more than twenty years, having been significantly damaged during an exchange of gunfire in which Sheriff Liam O'Connor, Cork's father, had been killed. Cork was thirteen years old at the time. The clock had never been repaired. Some folks said it was because the cost was too great, others that it was a fitting memorial to a good and brave lawman. Only a few months had passed since Cork O'Connor had been sworn in as sheriff of Tamarack County and had pinned to his own uniform the same badge his father had worn. Every day, when Cork showed up for work, the paralyzed clock face looked down on him, a stern reminder of the shoes he had to fill.

That morning, Cork walked into the sheriff's department and said hello to Bos Swain, who was dispatcher, clerk, public greeter, and sometimes mother hen to the small cadre of Tamarack County law enforcement officers. Her real name was Henrietta, but in her youth, she'd had a fascination with the American Revolution and her greatest desire had been to live in Boston, the center of all that history. She'd married instead and stayed in Aurora, but she'd seen to it that one of her daughters fulfilled the passionate dream. That daughter had graduated from Boston College and was on the school's faculty now. Bos, who'd worked for the sheriff's department for years, had been saddled with her nickname as far back as Cork could remember.

"Banana nut muffins," Bos said, nodding toward a plate on one of the three desks in the open area behind the contact counter. She stood at a filing cabinet, top drawer open.

"Ed Larson in yet?" Cork asked.

Bos's thin eyebrows arched a bit and she gestured an empty hand across the department, every inch of which, except for Cork's office, was visible. "See him anywhere?"

"Could've checked in and gone out," Cork said.

"Well, he didn't. Just you and me here, pumpkin."

Before being elected sheriff, Cork had been a deputy for several years. He'd served under Bill Gunderson, who'd been less a lawman and more a politician. Gunderson had no law enforcement experience before he was elected, but he'd been a popular civil attorney, a regular figure in the county courthouse, and had curried the favor of the local party machine. He knew the law, more or less. Often, in Cork's experience, a bit less than more. He was a sympathetic figure, a widower who'd raised his daughter alone after his wife died in a boating accident. He was big and flamboyant. As soon as he was sworn in, he took to wearing a sidearm everywhere and encouraged the nickname "Wild Bill" Gunderson. For the most part, he'd let his officers perform their duties without a lot of interference. The previous summer, a county commissioner who'd been away on business had returned early and discovered Gunderson in bed with his wife. Although it had been a huge scandal, Wild Bill refused to resign his public office and chose to run for another term. Cork, who was a solid family man, an Aurora native with lots of law enforcement experience, and son of a legendary father, had been encouraged on all sides to run against Gunderson. Cork had won the badge handily.

"The specifics of the next budget request are on your desk," Bos said. "Good luck convincing our county commissioners."

"How about you bake them some snickerdoodles before I argue my case?"

"Happy to do whatever I can to help."

Cork stepped into his office. When his father was sheriff, Cork had been in that room many times. Although small, it had seemed to him almost a sacred place and his father's duty there to be a kind of high priest of the law. Cork had a more human and informed understanding of the job now, much of which was simply mundane and far too political in nature for his taste. Before coming back to the place of his birth, he'd been a Chicago cop for several years. On the whole, law enforcement in Tamarack County tended to be on the quiet side.

He'd only just seated himself and prepared to bend to the budget document in front of him when the 911 call came in.

"Slow down," he heard Bos caution. "I can't understand what you're saying." He stepped from his office and saw her with a pencil poised above the log sheet beside the phone. She glanced up at Cork and shook her head. "Try to stay calm. Where are you?" She wrote something down. "Are you in danger?" She listened. "All right. We'll have officers there in a few minutes. I'm going to stay on the line until they arrive. What's your name? No, wait, don't hang up." She set the phone in the cradle and read from the note she'd written. "Timber Lodge and Resort. One victim, multiple stab wounds. The caller was female, hysterical, didn't give her name. And, Cork, I heard a baby crying in the background."

"Who's out on patrol?"

"Cy Borkman west county, Rocky Martinelli east county."

"Radio them both. Have them meet me there. Get hold of Ed Larson. And get the paramedics on it."

In a heartbeat, he was in his cruiser, siren blaring, light bar flashing, racing down Center Street toward the outskirts of Aurora. He listened to the chatter on his radio, Borkman and Martinelli reporting their locations and ETAs, Bos confirming that paramedics were about to roll. As he drove, he was trying to wrap his thinking around a homicide with a baby somewhere on the scene.

The Timber Lodge and Resort had been officially closed for the season. Although the main lodge and most of the cabins had been winterized and locked, the caretaker's cabin was occupied year-round. When he pulled up, Cork spotted a familiar pink VW Beetle parked there and saw that the cabin door was wide open. He leaped from his cruiser and hit the open doorway at a run. The moment he entered, he stopped. Before him was a pool of blood. At its center lay the naked body of Chastity Boshey. Beside her sat Aphrodite McGill, her mother, a butcher knife in her hand. From a room out of sight came the constant crying of a toddler.

"Aphrodite," Cork said as calmly as he could.

She didn't respond. Her silky black hair hung long over her shoulders, her eyes were fixed on a point beyond the small lake of blood in which she sat.

"Aphrodite," Cork said again. "Put the knife down."

Now her gaze lifted. She focused on Cork, but he could see the emptiness in her eyes.

"The knife, Aphrodite," he said. "Put it down."

Her eyes shifted to the bloody blade. She stared at it as if she couldn't comprehend what it was doing there in her hand. She looked up at Cork in a questioning way.

"Just set it down and we'll talk, Aphrodite. We'll sort this out."

At last, she lowered her arm and set the knife down beside her.

Cork took a handkerchief from the back pocket of his uniform khakis and, careful not to step into the pool of blood, reached forward, took the big knife gingerly by the handle, and removed it. Next, he pressed the fingers of his free hand against Chastity Boshey's carotid artery. No pulse and her skin was ice cold.

"Wait there, Aphrodite," he said, although it was clear to him she wasn't going anywhere.

He didn't want to leave the knife where she might once again put her hand on it, so he carried it with him as he sought out the room with the crying toddler.

Moonbeam—Cork knew the child's name, knew the whole family well—was standing in her crib, fat little hands gripping the railing, her eyes squeezed shut and her face contorted as she wailed. As far as Cork could tell, she wasn't hurt. His natural instinct was to comfort her, but not with a bloody knife in his hand and a traumatized woman in the other room, where the brutalized body of the child's mother lay. For the moment, he left Moonbeam screaming in her crib.

Off the cabin's main front room and separated from it by a simple counter was a small kitchen. Several doors led to other rooms. One to the baby's room. Another to a bedroom where Cork could see the rumpled sheets of an unmade bed. Another to the bathroom. Cork heard the howl of sirens on fast-approaching vehicles. He set the knife and handkerchief on the kitchen counter, walked carefully around the crime scene. A set of bloody shoe prints lay between the big pool of blood and the telephone on the wall. Cork stepped over the prints and stood at the outside door. Aphrodite McGill still sat in the middle of the room, staring at nothing, her clothing deeply stained with her daughter's blood.

The paramedics were the first to arrive, a team of three men. Cork knew them all. He'd worked with them on the scenes of car wrecks and house fires and sudden deaths. They stepped past him into the cabin, then pulled up short when they saw the body.

"Uh . . ." Brisco, who was the team leader, said. "What do you want us to do, Sheriff? Should we check for vitals?"

Cork said, "I checked for a pulse already. She's gone."

"What about her?" LaForge, another of the paramedics asked, nodding toward Aphrodite McGill.

"Wait until my team arrives. I want photos. Then we'll get her up and you'll probably need to treat her for shock."

"Maybe we shouldn't wait for your team," Dannon, the third paramedic said. "She looks pretty pale."

"She's always looked pale," Cork said. "And see those footprints in the blood? I don't want to lose them in a confusion of other prints. Just a few more minutes."

He heard another siren scream to the cabin, and a half a minute later, Cy Borkman rushed in, almost knocking into the paramedics. Borkman had been a deputy when Liam, Cork's father, was sheriff. He'd also been Liam's good friend. He was a heavy man, in his late fifties, nearing retirement now, but still a good officer.

"Jesus," he said when he saw the scene.

"Get the camera from your cruiser, Cy," Cork said. "I need photos of this, and I need them now."

Borkman spun and took his huge bulk out the door.

"Aphrodite," Cork said, using the calm voice with which he'd spoken to her all along. "In a minute, we're going to help you up, okay?"

She showed no sign that she'd heard him.

"And then I need to know what happened here."

Now she lifted her head. Her face contorted and her eyes became dark slits. In a rasp of a voice that bespoke pure hatred, she said, "He killed her. That son of a bitch Axel butchered my little girl."

CHAPTER 2

Aphrodite McGill sat in an ER room at the Aurora Community Hospital. She'd been examined by a doctor, who'd given Cork an okay to question her. The doctor had wanted to administer a sedative, but Cork asked him to hold off until he'd had a chance to question the woman. She wore clean clothing. All her bloodstained things had been taken away as evidence. Her tan slacks were particularly soaked from sitting in the pool of her daughter's blood. She'd asked for a cigarette, which was against hospital policy, but Cork had arranged for it anyway. Now she smoked, her hand quivering each time the cigarette rose to her lips.

She was an astonishingly attractive woman, raven-haired and emerald-eyed, sensual lips, perfect symmetry in every feature of her face. She was only a year or two older than Cork, not even forty yet, but she was already a grandmother. She'd had her daughter when she was little more than a child. And her daughter had done the same.

"What made you think something was wrong?" Cork asked.

She took a moment, stared out the window through the smoke she'd just exhaled, then said, "I talked to her on the phone yesterday evening. She was upset. Then last night I had a dream that scared me. A nightmare."

"Nightmare?"

"Of Chastity dead. I tried calling her this morning, but she didn't answer."

Deputy Marsha Dross was in the room, taking notes on the interview. Dross had been the officer Cork sent to Aphrodite's home to bring a change of clean clothing. She was the first female deputy ever hired by the Tamarack County Sheriff's Department, and it had been Cork's doing. She came from a family of cops, had majored in criminal justice, and had been at the top of her class when she graduated from the law enforcement program at Hibbing Community College. She'd interviewed first with Wild Bill Gunderson, who'd joked after she left that it would be nice to have a woman under him in the department—and on top of him sometimes, too. When Cork was sworn in as sheriff, he'd invited her to come in for another interview and had hired her on the spot.

"When you talked yesterday evening, what was the problem?" Cork asked.

"Axel," Aphrodite said. "It's always Axel. Drinking again."

"What time did she call?"

"Around seven, I think."

"Did you go over there?"

"I told her I was coming. She said she could handle it. I told her it was time to kick that son of a bitch out."

"Did she seem afraid?"

"No. Just pissed."

"When she called, was Axel there with her?"

Aphrodite took another draw from the cigarette, then sent a stream of smoke from between her lips and across the room. In that moment, she reminded Cork of a dragon spreading its cloudy breath. "He left. Took Sundown with him."

"But left Moonbeam. Why would Axel take his stepson but leave his daughter?"

"God only knows what goes on in that Indian's head."

"Did Chastity say where Axel was going?"

"Where does he always go? The rez."

Cork let a few moments pass, then said, "Aphrodite, you were holding a knife when I got there."

"It was lying beside her. I . . . I don't know . . . I just . . ." She leaned forward and bowed her head. Cork thought she might puke. Instead she sobbed uncontrollably.

The cigarette was singeing a strand of her loose-hanging hair. Cork eased it from between her fingers. She didn't seem to notice.

"I'm sorry, Aphrodite," he said. "Take a few minutes. It's okay."

Cork spotted Cy Borkman at the door. The deputy crooked a finger, beckoning.

Cork handed the cigarette to Dross and silently indicated for the deputy to keep an eye on Aphrodite, then joined Borkman in the hallway.

"Ed and the team have finished up at the cabin," Borkman said, speaking quietly. "Wasn't the knife killed her, Cork. She was stabbed with the fireplace poker. Stabbed a bunch of times. Her body's been taken to the mortuary. Sigurd Nelson says he'll do the autopsy this afternoon."

"Thanks, Cy."

"What now?"

"We need to locate Axel. Aphrodite believes he went to the rez, took his stepson with him."

"His mother's place, you think?"

"My best guess. It's where we'll begin."

"You want to be there when we search?"

Cork glanced back at Aphrodite McGill, who was still bent over and sobbing. "Yeah. But give me a few more minutes here."

When Cork reentered the exam room, Aphrodite sat up. "Where's Moonbeam? Where's my granddaughter?" she said, as if it had only just occurred to her.

"At the moment, she's with some folks from Child Protection Services," Cork said. "They're good people, Aphrodite. She's fine."

"I want to see her."

"You will. In due time. But I need to ask you a few more questions first. Can you tell me exactly what happened when you got to the cabin? Can you take me through it step by step?"

"I don't want to do that. I don't want to have to remember."

"I understand. But it's important if we want to find out who did this to Chastity."

"I already told you who did it. Axel, goddamn him."

"When you got to the cabin, was the door closed?"

She squeezed her eyes shut and thought. "Yes."

"Locked?"

"No, otherwise I couldn't have gone in."

"When you stepped inside, that's when you saw Chastity?"

"Yes."

"No one else?"

"No."

"What did you do then?"

"I ran to her . . . tried to talk to her . . . called you . . . then I just . . . sat with her. What else could I do? Christ, I need a cigarette."

Cork saw that Dross had used the sole of her boot to stub out what little had been left of the earlier smoke. He nodded to her, and from the pocket of her uniform blouse she pulled another of the cigarettes she'd bummed earlier from an orderly. She handed it to Aphrodite McGill, then used the lighter the orderly had given her as well. Between sobs, the woman took a couple of draws on the cigarette.

"Okay, that's all for now, Aphrodite. Deputy Dross will see you home when you're ready to go. I'll need to talk to you again. All right?"

Aphrodite gave a nod. Cork signaled for Dross to follow him from the room. In the hallway, he said, "I'll let the doctor know she can have the sedative now, if he still wants to give it to her. When she's ready, take her to her house. I'll have Azevedo drive her car there."

"We'll need her fingerprints, Sheriff."

"I know. We'll do that later."

Dross eyed the woman, who was alone in the room now, smoke rising above her head in a funereal gray haze. "She shouldn't be alone."

"I'll get in touch with Father Monroe at St. Agnes. Aphrodite's not a parishioner, but Chastity was. Maybe he'd be willing to sit with her, help calm her. Until he gets there, I want you to stay with her. Be sure you make notes of anything else she tells you."

"Will do," Dross said and turned back to the exam room.

CHAPTER 3

Cork drove. He'd opted for his Bronco rather than his department vehicle. Captain Ed Larson sat in the passenger seat.

One of Cork's first actions as the newly elected sheriff of Tamarack County had been to elevate Deputy Ed Larson to the position of captain and place him in charge of all major crime investigations. Larson was a decade older than Cork and looked more like a college professor than a cop, eschewing the khaki uniform in favor of a sport coat, white shirt, and tie. Wild Bill Gunderson would never have stood for this, but Cork was fine with it. Larson was good at his job, thorough and organized, and he'd earned the respect of his fellow officers early on by talking a distraught father out of a house where he'd barricaded himself, his wife, and his young daughter. The man, Daryl Carville, had lost his job when one of the iron mines closed and he'd been out of work forever and way over his head in debt. For a long time, he'd been spiraling downward into a black pit of despair. Wild Bill Gunderson had been the sheriff when this occurred and had wanted to have a sniper shoot Carville through the living room window. Larson, who knew the man and knew about his circumstances, had advocated for trying a different approach first. He'd talked his way onto the front porch, where, using both reason and empathy, he'd convinced Carville to put down the shotgun he held. In the process, Larson had put himself at great risk. But the affair had ended without bloodshed.

Cork had been in the Twin Cities at a law enforcement conference when all this went down. Wild Bill Gunderson had, of course, taken the credit for suggesting reason over a sniper's bullet, and Larson had never contradicted the sheriff's version of the incident. But the other officers who'd been there made sure that Cork knew the truth.

"Axel Boshey," Larson said. "Trouble and that man are brothers."

"It's the booze," Cork said. "When he's not drinking, he causes no trouble."

"Must've had been drunk out of his mind this time," Larson said. Then he said, "He's a cousin of yours, yes?"

"Second cousin technically. His mother was my mother's cousin. There's a big web of family relationships on any reservation."

"You know that puts you on the outside of this investigation," Larson said. "Family connection."

"Let's wait to see what Axel has to say. And you're going to need my help with any part of your investigation that takes you to the rez."

Larson gave a grunt of what sounded like begrudging acknowledgment of this truth.

"Still, I'm only part Anishinaabe," Cork said. "And I wear a badge. So I may not be much help either, but I'm probably your best bet for getting some answers out there."

"We'll see," Larson said. "If Axel's still drunk, we might need backup."

"We'll cross that bridge when we come to it. I don't want to stir things up on the rez any more than I have to. A lot of cop cars and everything could get way more complicated. That's why I'm driving my Bronco. Less conspicuous."

Patsy Boshey's house was on a dirt road at the edge of Allouette, the larger of the two communities on the Iron Lake Ojibwe Reservation. It was BIA housing, a simple prefab with gray siding. To one side was a vegetable garden, the plants empty after harvest, except for the kale, which still grew in deep green profusion.

The woman who answered Cork's knock was stocky, with long graying hair, and deep brown eyes. She wore a knitted red sweater, gray sweatpants, and fluffy white slippers.

"*Boozhoo,* Auntie," Cork said, using a traditional Anishinaabe greeting.

"Good morning, Corkie," Patsy said brightly. Then she looked at Larson. "I know you. You investigated my son when Clyde Greensky was killed."

"Yes, ma'am," Larson said. "And cleared him."

"No," she said. "The truth cleared him. What do you want?" she said, looking at Cork, her demeanor not so friendly now.

"We need to talk to Axel."

"He's not here."

"Do you know where he is?"

She shook her head. "He came yesterday. Asked me to watch Sunny, then left. He said he would be back, but he hasn't come yet."

"Sundown's here now?"

She nodded. "Sunny's inside watching television."

"Any idea why he'd bring his stepson but not his daughter?"

"He didn't say."

"When Axel came last night, had he been drinking?" Larson asked.

Patsy crossed her arms over her chest, her dark eyes bored into Larson and she didn't reply.

"Auntie, there's been trouble," Cork said.

"What kind?"

"Chastity is dead."

Her face, which had been like stone when addressing Ed Larson, showed her great surprise. "Dead? How?"

"I can't go into that," Cork said. "But it was last night."

"Oh, dear God." Patsy put her hand to her mouth. She glanced back over her shoulder into her house, where Cork could hear that the television was on, and he imagined little Sundown sitting in front of it. "Oh God, no."

"I'm afraid so," Cork said. "We've been told that she and Axel had a fight last night."

She nodded. "He told me. But . . . that's nothing new. They fight all the time."

"We were told he'd been drinking."

She let out a sigh. "Also nothing new." Then she seemed to get the drift of Cork's questioning. "You think Axel killed her."

"We need to talk to him."

"No," she said. "No way."

"No way he killed Chastity, or no way we can talk to him?" Cork asked.

"Both." Then she said, "It was her."

"Her what?"

"That woman could drive any man to murder."

"Be careful what you say," Cork cautioned. Then he said, "May we talk to Sunny?"

"No."

"We'll have to talk to him eventually."

"I . . . I need to tell him about his mother."

"All right. Then I'll come back and talk to him. And you and me, we can talk more. In the meantime, if you hear from Axel, tell him it would be best for him to get in touch with me. All right?"

She said nothing but did give a nod.

"*Miigwech,* Auntie," he said, thanking her in her Native tongue.

He walked with Ed Larson back to the Bronco, where they stood for a moment before getting in.

Larson said, "This is my investigation, Cork. You made it sound like I was going to be no part of it."

"Do you think you'd have got anything from her?"

"Did you get anything useful?"

"Not this time maybe. But in Indian Country, patience is the rule of thumb."

"You called her Auntie. I thought she was a cousin."

"A respectful term. On the rez, everyone my mother's age is "Auntie" to me. Everyone my grandmother's age is "Grandmother." My contemporaries are "Cousins." In its way, it's an acknowledgment that we're all family regardless of bloodlines. So what now, Captain?"

"Drop me back at the department," Larson said. "I'll take a look at whatever evidence we got from the cabin this morning. And I've got a couple of deputies canvassing the neighbors in case someone saw something."

"Nearest neighbors are a quarter mile away."

"Due diligence," Larson said. "And the press'll be coming, Cork. Hell Hanover will be breathing down our necks for sure. City papers, too, soon enough."

Helmuth (Hell) Hanover was the editor of the local newspaper, and a man Cork was never happy to have to deal with.

"If Hell's at the department, I'm sure you can handle him,"

Cork said. "Me, I'm going to have some lunch. Then I'll see if I can find Axel."

"Where?"

Cork swung his hand in an arc that included the reservation land all around them. "It's like Aphrodite told me this morning, Ed. He's got nowhere else to go but here."

CHAPTER 4

During World War II, German prisoners of war were trucked to Aurora, Minnesota, and housed in several Quonset huts on the shore of Iron Lake. There'd been no barbed wire to hold them in the compound. If they escaped, where would they have gone? Because American men were off fighting overseas, the German POWs supplied important labor for harvesting lumber from the great Northwoods. They were treated humanely, even earning a wage for the work. At war's end, they were returned to their homeland, and the compound was abandoned. All but one of the Quonset huts was disassembled, the last one kept standing for reasons unknown. It sat idle for several years, just beyond the town limits. In the early fifties, an enterprising member of the Iron Lake Band of Ojibwe purchased the structure and spent a year repurposing it. He divided the Quonset hut into two sections. In one, he installed a big griddle, large freezer, deep-fry well, ice-milk machine, and a prep area with a stainless-steel sink. He hung a sign outside that proclaimed the new food enterprise was called Sam's Place. The back section of the hut housed a little bathroom, into which were crammed a shower, stool, and sink. There was a living area with a bunk, dining table, two chairs, and a file cabinet. It was where Sam Winter Moon kept his business records, ate his meals, and sometimes slept in the months his burger joint was open.

Sam had been a good friend of Liam O'Connor. They were both veterans of World War II, both men of deep conscience and few words, and both believed profoundly in the idea of justice for all, White and Ojibwe alike.

After Liam O'Connor was killed, Sam Winter Moon, in many ways, took on the role of surrogate father for Liam's son, Cork. He tried to pass on to the adolescent the lessons he believed Liam would have taught his son and also his own take on the world through the eyes of the Anishinaabe people. Every summer when he was in his teens, Cork earned money working at Sam's Place, learning how to run the business and manage others, opening and closing, and banking the day's take. Some of what Cork earned was spending money. Some went into a bank account for college. Some went to his mother to help with the bills. Sam Winter Moon and Sam's Place were responsible in many ways for Cork's understanding of what it meant to be a responsible human being.

When he reached Sam's Place that day, it was half past noon. There were several folks in line at the serving window. Cork parked his Bronco and waited until the last of the customers had been seen to, then he got out and went to the serving window. The face of the young woman who peered out at him was familiar—Roxanne Bloom, who went by Roxie. Her mother, Mary Bloom, had been Cork's fourth-grade teacher. Her father, an Iron Lake Shinnob, had worked for the lumber mill in Brandywine, the other small community on the reservation, and had been on the Tribal Council. Roxanne was attending Aurora Community College, hoping to become a physical therapist.

"*Boozhoo,* Roxie. Busy lunch hour."

"Fridays are always busy. Just wait until this evening when the leaf peepers arrive."

Another young face appeared beside her, a face also familiar to Cork. Tamara Larson, daughter of Captain Ed Larson. "We heard about Chastity Boshey. My God," Tamara said.

"Is that Cork?" Sam Winter Moon spoke from somewhere out of sight.

"Yep," Cork called through the serving window. "Need to talk to you, Sam, if you've got a moment."

"Come on in," Sam said. "You two kids see to our customers. And let's try to stay away from any talk about killing, okay?"

"But Mr. Winter Moon," Tamara said. "It's what everybody's talking about."

Already? Cork thought.

"Stick to the weather," Sam said.

Cork walked to the door on the side of Sam's Place, which opened onto the back section of the Quonset hut.

"*Boozhoo,* Cork," Sam greeted him. "Coffee? And would you like a burger? I'll have one of the kids whip up a Sam's Special."

"Thanks, I could use a bite. Been a rough morning."

"I can only imagine. Sit. I'll be right back." Sam stepped into the prep area and spoke to his workers, then came out with a disposable cup filled with coffee. He set the coffee in front of Cork and took a chair at the table where Cork sat.

Sam Winter Moon was nearing seventy. He was medium height and stocky, in the way of many Ojibwe men. His hair was white and he wore it in a crew cut. The irises of his eyes were the warm brown of creamed coffee.

"So, a friendly visit?" he said. "Or is this about Chastity Boshey?"

"It's about Axel. I need to find him."

"You think he killed his wife?"

"I don't think anything at this point, Sam. I'm trying to gather all the pieces. Axel's a big one. And I don't know where he is."

"You've already talked to Patsy, I imagine."

"Just came from there."

"Told you nothing, I'll bet."

"That's right."

Sam nodded to himself. "I'd be worried sick, I was her."

"Because you think he might have done it?"

"Because he's the first one everybody'll think of," Sam said, then added, "And not just white folks. Heard it was brutal."

"Pretty vicious."

"Axel's got a lot of anger in him, especially when he's been drinking. True of a lot of our vets."

"So, you think he could have done it?"

"I've seen enough in this life to think anybody's capable of anything. I guess what I'm saying is that I understand why you have to talk to Axel. You just need to clear your head before you do."

"Clear my head?"

"Despite what you told me a minute ago, I'm guessing that the white voice inside you is already saying Axel did it. Quiet that voice, if you can, and listen to the Shinnob inside you."

"If I was a hundred percent Anishinaabe, what would my voice be saying?"

"It might say, 'Listen to the owl.'"

"What does that mean?"

"The owl only asks one question. *Who?* Don't stop asking yourself that."

"Right now, the question I need an answer to is *where*. I think Axel's got only one place to hide. He's somewhere on the rez."

"If you already know that, what are you doing here?"

"Like I said, I talked with his mother this morning."

"And got nowhere. So?"

"I'm going back out to the rez. I was wondering if you might consider going with me."

"Going back to the rez?" Sam said. "Is that why you're not wearing your uniform?"

"I changed at the department. I'd rather not go out in my regalia."

Sam swung a hand toward the prep area. "I've got a business to run."

"The kids can handle it for a couple of hours."

"A couple of hours? You really think that's all it'll take?"

"That's all I'm asking. Because, as you say, you have a business to run."

"And you have a job to do. I don't ask you to flip burgers. At least, not anymore."

"Sam, I need your help. A white woman's dead. Murdered. And a Shinnob is the most obvious suspect. This is a fire just waiting for a match to get it started."

They were interrupted by Roxie Bloom, who came from the prep area carrying a basket that held a Sam's Special and fries. "Here you go, Sheriff."

"*Miigwech,* Roxie."

After she'd returned to her work, Sam was quiet for a long moment, his warm coffee eyes considering Cork. Finally he said, "Eat your burger. Then we'll go."

CHAPTER 5

Cork O'Connor was one-quarter Ojibwe. He'd grown up in Aurora, the son of a white man of deep Irish heritage and a woman who was half Ojibwe. As a kid, he'd spent a good deal of time on the reservation, where his grandmother, a true-blood Iron Lake Ojibwe, had lived. He'd played with other kids there, gone to school with them in town, even attended church at St. Agnes with some of their families. He had friends and relatives on the rez. But he'd always been different from them, both because he was of mixed blood and because his father wore a badge.

He still had relatives on the rez and people he counted as friends. But since he'd put on the same badge his father had worn and now represented in such a visible way an arm of white society that had often handled Native people unfairly, brutally even, his visits had become less frequent.

"Doesn't matter you're not wearing your uniform," Sam said as they headed up the east side of Iron Lake toward Allouette. "Everybody'll already've heard about Chastity. Rez telegraph. You think anybody's going to tell you anything, even with me along, you're barking up the wrong tree."

"I need to hear Axel's side of the story, Sam. I can't do that if I don't talk to him. And I can't talk to him until I find him. Simple equation. I'm hoping you might help folks understand that."

"Am I going to help them understand that you're not taking Axel straight to jail?"

Cork didn't respond.

"So you are going to take him to jail," Sam said.

"I'll probably take him in for questioning."

"You have any idea how often one of our people has been taken in for questioning and come out beat to hell?"

"Not on my watch, Sam."

"Or your dad's either. But there've been some pretty bad hombres in charge between his tenure and yours. Our people, we've got long memories. And, Cork, on the rez, the jury's still out about you."

Which was something he'd felt, but it had never been said to him out loud.

"I'm just trying to get to the truth," Cork said.

"Truth is a tricky critter. Not always what it seems."

"I don't agree. A woman's been killed. I'm trying to get to the truth of who killed her. And that truth is going to be solid as a rock. You'll see."

"Oh, Cork," Sam said, in the same way he used to say it when Cork was a kid and still had so much to learn.

They pulled up in front of Patsy Boshey's house. Cork killed the engine and started to get out.

Sam put a restraining hand on his arm and said, "Let me."

"I don't think . . ."

"You already tried once and got nowhere. You come in with me, it'll be the same result."

Cork studied Sam, then the small house, and finally gave a nod. "All right."

Sam got out and walked to the front door. Patsy Boshey answered his knock. He spoke to her for a moment and then was let inside.

Cork sat back to wait.

Allouette was a quiet town, a grid of a dozen streets, most with BIA houses or old cabins or trailers up on cinder blocks. The main drag had a few businesses, among them a Mobil gas station and garage, the Nanaboozahoo Cafe, a small thrift store called the Beaver's Tail, and LeDuc's General Store, which doubled as the post office. A bit farther down was the old community center. Around the corner from the café was the largest structure on the rez, a building that housed most of the tribal offices. To the casual eye, it appeared to be an economically depressed town, which was true. But the casual eye didn't see the true spirit of the Ojibwe who lived there, a people who, though they'd been lied to by politicians and cheated by developers and beset by demons that came with multigenerational cultural trauma, still held tenaciously to their traditions, their language, and their sense of hope. Cork's grandmother Dilsey, a fierce and eloquent defender of her people, had given her grandson an abiding respect for that part of his heritage. And although folks on the rez didn't always welcome him with open arms, Cork still held them firmly in his own heart.

An old pickup passed him, stopped, and backed up. Cork saw that it was Leroy Beauchamp, a mechanic at the Mobil station. He was another distant relative, a cousin a couple of times removed.

Leroy rolled down his window and eyed Cork. "Sheriff," he said.

Not Cork. Not Cousin. Which meant that Leroy knew why Cork was on the rez that day and probably wasn't going to be helpful.

"Looking for my homie Axel, I expect," Leroy said.

"That's right. Seen him?"

"Nope. But I'll tell you one thing. If he killed that wife of his, he had good reason."

"You hear how she died?" Cork said. Then added, "Cousin."

"Didn't hear that."

"Stabbed with a fireplace poker, a bunch of times."

That made Leroy sit back. "Shit."

"No one deserves that," Cork said.

"Look, I heard she was running around behind Axel's back. Just like she did with Clyde Greensky."

"You hear who she might have been running around with?"

"Nope."

"You mind asking around? Might help Axel. Especially if he's a homie."

Leroy thought about it. "I'll see what I can do."

"*Miigwech,*" Cork said. "Cousin."

Leroy rolled up his window and drove on.

Sam Winter Moon was inside Patsy Boshey's house for fifteen minutes. When he came out, Patsy was with him, but she didn't accompany Sam to Cork's Bronco. She just stood in the doorway, scowling at Cork as if he were the enemy. And Cork understood that, in a way, he was.

"Still no idea where Axel might be," Sam said. "But I can tell you what Axel told Patsy. She says he came by last evening, brought Sundown along with him. Asked if she could keep the child for a while."

"Because?"

"Him and Chastity had a fight. Big blowup, sounds like. Axel was pretty upset."

"Did he tell her what the fight was about?"

"He wanted to divorce her. She told him to go to hell. One thing led to another. Pretty soon they're ready to kill."

"Is that how Patsy put it?"

"Axel put it that way. Told Patsy that's why he left. He was afraid of doing his wife harm."

"Why'd he take Sunny?"

"Chastity insisted."

"So he drops Sunny here. Then what?"

"Patsy didn't know. But she was afraid that . . ."

Sam didn't finish, so Cork did. "That he went somewhere to drown his sorrows in booze. Did you talk to Sundown?"

"Sunny was taking a nap. Patsy wouldn't wake him. And she's worried sick about little Moonbeam. Wants the child to be with her."

"Moonbeam is with Child Protection Services."

"That baby needs to be with her grandmother."

"We'll see if we can make it happen."

They sat in silence for a bit.

"A man drunk out of his mind, full of anger, who left his house because he was afraid he'd do his wife harm," Cork said. "Not looking good for Axel, Sam."

"We don't know for a fact that he went drinking."

"But if he did, where would he go?"

They looked at each other and Cork said what he believed they both were thinking. "North Star."

"Damn," Sam said.

CHAPTER 6

The North Star bar stood at a crossroads just outside the reservation boundary. Most folks in Tamarack County referred to the establishment as "that Indian bar." White faces were a rarity, usually hunters or snowmobilers who stumbled in, unaware that they weren't particularly welcome. It didn't take them long to figure that out, and they generally left before they'd even ordered a drink. From Allouette, the road to the bar, all crushed gravel and oil, cut back and forth between woodlands and marshland and had long ago been dubbed Waagikomaan, which meant "crooked knife." The building itself was two-story, old wood, and peeling paint, with windows that hadn't been washed in forever and were plastered with signs advertising the booze inside, which completely blocked any light that might come through. As a result, it was perpetual night in the North Star.

Cork pulled into the dirt lot, where a half dozen other vehicles were parked. They all had reservation license plates and were spattered with dried mud and covered in a thick coat of road dust. Which reminded Cork of that old western saying about mistreated horses: "Rode hard, put away wet."

Sam said, "So what's your strategy? You know they'll be as tight-lipped with you as Patsy was. And they've been drinking, so anything that does come out of their mouths when you talk to them is likely to be unpleasant."

"You're not going in alone, if that's what you're getting at."

"Your funeral," Sam said and stepped from the Bronco.

They went in together, Cork in the lead. The place was as dark as a bear's den with not much conversation going on. What little talk there was ceased as soon as those inside recognized who'd just arrived. Cork's eyes hadn't fully adjusted to the dark when he heard someone give a clear "Oink, oink!"

Behind the bar, in the glow of a neon Budweiser sign stood Will Fineday, who owned the joint. He was wiping the inside of a shot glass with a rag and looking at Cork with a face as hard as granite. In truth, that face was a frightening thing to behold, not because of the hard look but because of the enormous scar that ran like a white snake across his left cheek, nose, and right eye before it ended halfway up his forehead. It was the result of a blow from a hockey stick in a fight on an ice rink during his brief career playing for the Toronto Maple Leafs. He was pretty much blind in that right eye. Cork had played hockey with him in high school, when Fineday had been a standout and had taken the team to the state playoffs, where sportscasters were all abuzz about the Indian phenom. Although Cork and Fineday hadn't been exactly friends, they'd been on good terms. But a lot of water had passed under the bridge since. Fineday had come back to the rez and used the money from the insurance settlement to buy the bar. He'd somehow got hold of the stick that had done the fateful deed, and it hung on the wall behind him, blood red in the neon glow from the Budweiser sign.

"O'Connor," he said when Cork stepped up to the bar.

"Will."

"*Boozhoo,* Sam."

"*Boozhoo,* Will."

Fineday's good eye focused on Cork. "You here to drink?"

"Just looking for some information, Will. You've heard about Chastity Boshey?"

"All anybody's talking about."

"I heard that Axel might have been here last night. That true?"

"I don't keep track of my customers."

"I just need to know if he was drinking here."

"No. You're trying to find out if he was drunk enough to do what was done to his wife."

"Yeah, pretty much."

"I don't recall seeing him last night."

"Will, if he was here and you're not telling me, I might construe that as obstructing a lawful investigation."

"And you'll what? Arrest me?"

"No, but it could, I suppose, cause problems the next time your liquor license comes up for renewal."

"Oink!" someone from a back corner said. Cork didn't turn to find out who.

Sam said, "Axel needs to tell his side of the story, Will. Maybe what he has to say'll clear him."

"And maybe it'll get his neck put in a noose. And just what the hell do you think you're doing, Winter Moon? Playing Chester to O'Connor's Marshal Dillon?"

"I'm trying to help Axel. Me, I think he had nothing to do with his wife's death. But if a bunch of uniformed white guys track him down, could be he'll never have the opportunity to clear himself."

"Yeah," Fineday agreed. He eyed Cork again. "Shoot first, ask questions later."

A door to the right of the bar opened and a woman, Fineday's wife, stepped out. Celine wasn't Ojibwe. She was French-Canadian, had married Fineday during his time with the Maple Leafs. She was a pretty woman, small and dark-haired, with emerald eyes. She'd stood by her husband as he recovered from the blow of the hockey stick and now helped him run the bar. She walked to Fineday and put her hand on his arm.

"Good afternoon, Sheriff O'Connor," she said with a hint of a French accent.

"Celine," he said.

"It was a vicious killing, yes?"

"Pretty brutal. Look, all I'm trying to do is locate Axel so that he can clear his name."

"We don't know where he is and that's the truth."

"Told you," Fineday said to Cork.

"No, you told me you didn't remember if he was drinking here last night."

"He was," Celine said. "But he left. Called someone on the pay phone there and took off."

"Any idea who he called?"

"No, but it was woman."

"How do you know?"

"I heard him say, 'I need you. Please.'"

"Could have been anyone. Why do you think it was a woman?"

"Because I know how a man talks to a woman. Especially when he's desperate."

"Was he drunk?"

"He had quite a bit to drink," Celine said. "He was clearly upset about something."

"What time did he leave?"

"We close at midnight. He left just before that."

"You're sure you didn't hear a name when he was talking on the phone?"

"I didn't."

"What about you?" Cork asked Fineday.

"Saw nothing, heard nothing."

"Oink, oink!"

Celine looked past Cork, peering into the corner. "Another one of those and you're out of here."

"We should leave," Sam said to Cork. Then to Celine he said, "Before you lose any customers."

Cork said, "If Axel shows up again, will you let me know?"

Celine glanced at her husband, who gave her no sign. "We'll see if that happens."

"Come on," Sam said. "*Miigwech*, Will."

Back in the sunlight, Cork said, "What the hell, Sam? If a bunch of uniformed white guys track him down? Shoot first, ask questions later?"

"It was what he was thinking. What most Shinnobs would think. And I needed to get him away from believing I'm your gimp deputy. You were lucky Celine showed up."

"So, he talks to a woman and takes off. I'd love to know who that was."

The door of the bar opened and Celine stepped outside. She glanced back, as if to make sure she wasn't followed or could be overheard. "There's one more thing. I wasn't fond of Chastity. She came in a couple of times with Clyde Greensky and then with Axel, acted pretty high and mighty. But she didn't deserve what happened to her. No woman deserves that. So here's something to think about. When he was talking on the phone, Axel said he hated the bitch and wished she was dead. Now get out of here before you scare away all our clientele."

After she'd gone back into the bar, Sam asked, "What's next?"

"Let's go back to Aurora. Sigurd Nelson should be working on the autopsy by now. And I want to check in with Ed Larson, see what he's got from the evidence his team gathered at Axel's cabin. Maybe that'll give us more direction."

"Not me, Cork. I've got a business to run, remember?"

"Sam, I really appreciate your help today."

"Not sure I got you anywhere. And, listen, you get Moonbeam to her grandmother pronto, understand? I promised Patsy."

"I'll make it happen, Sam. If I need your help again?"

"I meant it. I'm not your gimp deputy."

Cork waited a moment, then said, "There is one more thing."

CHAPTER 7

Cork didn't go directly back to Sam's Place. He and Sam Winter Moon made an important stop on the way.

In those days, Jo O'Connor operated her law practice out of a small office above Swenson's Scandinavian Bakery. The place often smelled of freshly baked bread or pastries. She had told Cork that the comforting smell alone was helpful in getting clients to relax and share their concerns and secrets. She had a general law practice, everything from wills and divorces to criminal cases, on occasion. She did some work for the Iron Lake Ojibwe, much of it pro bono. That relationship had begun shortly after she came to Aurora with Cork, when, on behalf of an Ojibwe woman named Lizzie Favre, she'd brought an important and successful lawsuit against the Great North Development Company for discriminatory hiring practices. As a result, although she had no Native blood in her, she was viewed more positively by a lot of folks on the rez than was her badge-wearing husband.

Sam accompanied Cork inside. As they walked up the stairs, Sam lifted his nose and said with pleasure, "Rye bread."

"Lovely aroma. Maybe that'll help our cause," Cork said.

The law office was at the end of a hallway whose doors led to other small businesses—a State Farm insurance agent, a psychologist, and a chiropractor. Cork opened the door with JO O'CONNOR, ESQ. printed on the glass. Fran Edelman, who was Jo's secretary and paralegal, looked up from her desk.

"Cork," she said and smiled. "And Mr. Winter Moon."

Fran was young, a recent graduate of Aurora Community College, and wanted very much be a lawyer herself one day.

"Is the counselor in?" Cork asked.

"Nose to grindstone, as always."

"Okay if I go in?"

"I don't imagine she'll mind."

Cork gave a light tap on the door to Jo's private office and opened it. "Got a minute?"

Jo eyed him over the rim of her half-glasses. She held a pencil in her hand, which was poised above a legal tablet. She was slender, with hair so blond that in bright sunlight it looked nearly white. Her eyes were glacial blue. She was only just beginning to show with her third pregnancy, a little rounding to her belly. Her demeanor as she looked at her husband was not particularly welcoming. Then she saw Sam and her face changed.

"*Boozhoo,* Sam."

"*Boozhoo,* Jo. Hope we're not interrupting."

"Just working on a brief for an easement dispute."

"Still mad at me?" Cork said.

Jo considered him, then said to Sam, "We had a disagreement this morning concerning waffles versus pancakes."

"Like 'em both," Sam said.

"There, you see," Jo said, holding out her hand toward Sam as if that settled the argument.

"I'm willing to admit I might be wrong. I need a favor, Jo."

"Ah, that's why you yielded so easily. What favor?"

"You've heard about Chastity Boshey?"

She sat back now, and her face softened. "Terrible news. And you've been working on it all day, haven't you?"

"I have." He glanced at Sam. "We have. And we need your help."

"In what way?"

"The Bosheys' child, Moonbeam, is in the care of Child Protection Services. We need to get her to her grandmother's house as soon as possible."

"I'm not authorized to act on the family's behalf."

"No, but JoEllen Ambrose is in charge of CPS. You've worked with her a lot. And you and JoEllen play bridge together. If anybody can spring that little girl, it's you."

"End run on the system, is that it?"

"For a good cause," Sam said. "This whole thing's traumatic for everyone. The child needs to be with family."

"Did Patsy Boshey ask for Moonbeam?"

"She did," Sam said. "I spoke with her this afternoon."

Jo nodded. "I'll do what I can. But, Sam, it might help if you were with me to explain it from a cultural point of view."

"I can do that."

Jo shifted her attention back to her husband. "How's the investigation going?"

"The most likely suspect at the moment seems to be Axel Boshey, and he's nowhere to be found."

Jo frowned. "If that man didn't have bad luck, he'd have no luck at all."

"I don't think luck has anything to do with the trouble Axel gets himself into. You ought to know that. You represented him the last time he was suspected of murder."

"Circumstances, Cork. That situation was all about unfortunate circumstances."

"I'm pretty sure this one's different."

Jo let that pass and said to Sam, "We should go. Get that little girl to her grandmother." Then to Cork she said, "Will you be home for dinner?"

"No guarantee. I'll let you know."

"Rose said she's making fried chicken."

Cork allowed a smile to spread across his lips. "In that case, I'll do my best." He shook Sam Winter Moon's hand. "Thanks for your help."

"Innocent until proven guilty," Sam said.

Cork gave him a puzzled look.

"Just reminding you how the law works. Because when it comes to Indians, sometimes white people forget."

"I'm not all white, Sam. And I won't forget," Cork promised.

When Cork walked into the department, Bos Swain looked beat to hell.

"Phone hasn't stopped ringing," she said. "Media people in and out. It's been a zoo today, Cork."

"Captain Larson?"

"In your office."

"Thanks, Bos."

"Don't thank me. Just give me a raise."

"Noted," Cork said and went into his office.

Ed Larson was sitting in the chair opposite Cork's desk, leafing through the pages of a notepad. He looked as weary as Bos.

"Next time you give me a promotion, remind me to turn it down," he said.

Cork sat at his desk. "Get me up to speed."

"We found bloody clothing hidden in the woodshed at Axel Boshey's place. A man's shirt, pants, shoes, gloves. We got Chastity Boshey's blood type from her physician, and I sent a blood sample over to the hospital lab for testing. But it's got to be her blood."

"And it's Axel's clothing? That's certain?"

"Sizes matched everything in his closet and bureau."

"How about prints?"

"Lots of latents. Two sets of prints on the knife. One set belongs to Chastity. Pretty sure we'll find that the other set is Aphrodite's. But here's the odd thing. Although there's blood all over the poker, there are no prints. And no prints on the front doorknob."

"Someone wiped them clean."

Larson closed his notepad. "Any luck locating Boshey?"

"He dropped his stepson at Patsy Boshey's house last night, then went to the North Star to do some drinking. Called a woman from there and took off."

"Took off where?"

"No idea."

"The woman?"

"Again, no idea. But apparently he told whoever it was that he hated Chastity and wished she was dead. We should check the records for the pay phone at the North Star. Also, check the phone records for Boshey's house, see what calls came in or went out yesterday evening."

Larson opened his notepad again and wrote something down.

There was a tap at the doorway, and Marsha Dross stepped in. "Father Monroe is with Aphrodite, Sheriff. Out at Shangri-La on Apostle's Cove."

"Good. Did she tell you anything more?"

"She rambled some. The sedative, I suppose. Did you know that she changed her name to Aphrodite? Her given name was Lois Jean McGill."

"I did know that. A flower child," Cork said. "Came here when she was barely eighteen. Gorgeous, free-spirited. Left everything spoiled by the modern world behind, including her name. Took up with the architect who built Shangri-La and all those back-to-nature disciples who lived with him then. Had a child. Named her Chastity. A little ironic when you think about it."

"Was the architect the father?" Dross asked.

"Never really clear. She married him but never took his last name. When he died, she got everything. She's continued to live a pretty free lifestyle. String of men, no one for very long."

"You seem to know a lot about her," Larson said.

"When she first came here, I was a senior in high school, and she was like no girl I'd ever seen. Every boy in town lusted after her. A lot of grown men, too, I'm sure. So, Aphrodite's been a topic of conversation ever since she arrived. But also, Jo and I worked with the youth group at St. Agnes for a while. Although I'm pretty sure Aphrodite has no love for the church, Chastity sometimes participated in the group when she was a teenager. Not with any real enthusiasm. I could tell she was troubled."

"In what way?"

"Way too focused on the boys for one thing."

"Isn't that natural for a teenage girl?"

"I thought maybe there was something more complicated going on. With the reputation that Shangri-La has, I wondered what might be going on out there."

"Did you ever try to talk to her about it?"

"Jo did but didn't get far. There was a lot of anger in Chastity, directed mostly at her mother. Then she stopped coming to youth group."

Larson mulled that over then said, "What about Chastity's death, Marsha? Did Aphrodite offer anything?"

"Nothing useful," Dross said. "She kept coming back to Axel Boshey."

Cork thanked her, and she left the office to finish her shift.

When she'd gone, Larson said, "Hell Hanover's been hounding us. And we've had some reporters from Duluth here already. Calls from the Twin Cities. The brutal nature of Chastity Boshey's death is drawing them out of the woodwork. I've scheduled a press briefing for five. You'll be there?"

"Of course. And that'll give us time to check with Sigurd Nelson on the autopsy. Ready to roll?"

Larson stood. "I'll drive."

CHAPTER 8

Sigurd Nelson was both mortician and county coroner, which wasn't unusual in rural Minnesota. Since Cork had been elected sheriff, he'd been pitching to the county commissioners the possibility of a real medical examiner, but so far the idea hadn't gotten any traction. Nelson had been coroner forever, and his father before him. It wasn't that Sigurd Nelson was inept. He simply wasn't a doctor, and so his pathological skills were limited.

Nelson's Funeral Home was a Victorian, one of the oldest and finest houses in Aurora. The first-floor rooms were for viewing and for smaller memorial services. Nelson and his wife lived on the second floor. The prep rooms were in the basement.

Cork had called ahead, and Nelson met them in his office. He was a man in his mid-fifties, balding, and with a large, dark mole to the right of his nose that, as he talked, moved about like a busy beetle. When conversing with the man, Cork had always found it difficult not to focus on that restless blemish.

"She sustained a blow to the left side of her head, which cracked her skull but didn't kill her," Nelson said. "There are seven wounds to her body, all to her thoracic cavity and abdomen. Consistent with the sharp end of the poker you found."

"Did she die from one of the wounds or bleed to death?"

"Two of the wounds were to her heart. That would have done the trick. But one severed her aorta as well. She would have bled out quickly after that."

"TOD?" Cork asked.

"I'd say time of death was somewhere between ten p.m. last night and two a.m. this morning."

"She was naked when she was found. Any sign of sexual activity prior to her death?" Larson asked.

"I didn't see any obvious sign of assault, but I did take a vaginal swab, as you requested, Ed."

"You say it looked as if she'd sustained a blow to the head."

"Yes. I'd say consistent with being hit by that poker."

"Aphrodite was holding a knife when I found her with the body. Any evidence of knife wounds?"

"None."

Larson closed his eyes, slipped his thumb and index finger under his glasses, and massaged the bridge of his nose as he thought out loud. "She's being threatened. She grabs a kitchen knife to protect herself but gets hit with the poker and goes down. Probably drops the knife. Her assailant moves in. He uses the poker to finish her off. But, Jesus, seven wounds. He must've been out of his mind."

"Wasn't necessarily a *he* that did this," Cork said.

Nelson, a man who'd seen death in so many forms, seemed to have paled. "Surely this couldn't have been done by a woman."

Larson said, "When will we see your official report, Sigurd?"

"I'll have it to you tomorrow. But there's one more thing."

"What's that?"

"She was pregnant."

* * *

The press briefing Ed Larson had scheduled was held on the steps of the courthouse. It was short but heated, due mostly to the peppering of questions that came from Hell Hanover. Hanover's given name was Helmuth, although that wasn't what most people called him behind his back. Hell knew this and reveled in the epithet. As publisher and editor of the weekly *Aurora Sentinel,* he was certain to cover all the community events—bazaars, fundraisers, commissioners' meetings, births, deaths—but he also prided himself on delivering hard news. His op-eds were notorious for their vitriol. He'd been a crony of Wild Bill Gunderson, and when the shit hit the fan because of Gunderson's trysting with a commissioner's wife, Hanover continued to support the lawman despite the tarnished badge. When Cork ran for sheriff, Hell Hanover had done his best to cast aspersions, but none of the mud he slung had stuck. Once Cork was sworn in, Hanover continued to do his best to find fault with Cork's oversight of law enforcement in Tamarack County.

The one issue Hanover kept hammering on at the briefing was why hadn't they located Axel Boshey.

"You're Indian yourself, Sheriff," Hanover said more than once, and in a way that made it sound as if Cork might be covering for the man because of that connection of heritage.

"Boshey is certainly a person of interest in the case," Ed Larson, who was in charge of the briefing, responded, more than once. "As I said, we've put out an APB, as well as notifying law enforcement in the adjacent counties. We've also canvassed the reservation"—which was not quite true—"and we continue to pursue all relevant leads."

"Boshey got away with murder once," Hanover said. "Will this make twice that he's escaped the noose?"

"I remind you that Axel Boshey was cleared in the incident you've referred to," Larson responded.

Following Hanover's revelation of the earlier lethal incident involving Boshey, it became clear that many of the news people present were unaware of that history, and Larson was besieged with questions, which Cork thought he handled well.

Larson ended the briefing, promising to keep the press duly informed as the investigation proceeded.

When they entered the sheriff's office, Deputy Cy Borkman was waiting for them. He was eating a burger whose wrapper indicated to Cork that it had come from Sam's Place.

"Listened out of sight," he said. "Good job, Ed."

"What are you still doing here, Cy?" Cork asked. "You were off duty hours ago."

"Had a thought about Chastity Boshey I wanted to share with you two."

"Let's go into my office."

Cork sat behind his desk. Borkman took the larger of the two chairs. Because he was a man of great size, there was always a chair in the sheriff's office that would accommodate his bulk. It had been that way since Cork's father had been sheriff.

Larson took the remaining chair and said, "What've you got, Cy?"

"I patrolled west county last night," Borkman said.

Tamarack County had always been divided east and west for law enforcement purposes, at least one cruiser assigned to each section every shift. Because things were quietest on the graveyard shift, there were usually only two officers patrolling in those dark hours. Normally, deputies were rotated so that all officers took a turn on graveyard, but Borkman had no family and preferred the shift. He also had seniority, so the job had been his for years. He claimed his sleep schedule had long ago adjusted him to being a night owl.

"Did you see something?" Larson asked.

"Yeah. A pink VW Beetle."

"Aphrodite McGill's car?" Cork said.

"Yep. Hard to miss, especially with all those flower decals. And her vanity plate is LUVBUG."

"Old hippie and proud of it," Larson said. "So what about it?"

"She passed me last night around eleven, heading into Aurora. May be nothing, but might be worth asking her about it, particularly since that seems to be the general time frame of her daughter's TOD."

"Thanks, Cy." Cork thought a moment, then said, "Rocky Martinelli was patrolling east county last night. Might be good to see if he spotted the pink bug anywhere near the Boshey cabin."

Bos Swain stepped into Cork's office. It was clear she'd overheard some of the conversation. "You're not suggesting Aphrodite McGill had something to do with her daughter's death, are you? That woman is as freaky as a two-headed calf, but she's no murderer."

"What is it, Bos?" Cork said.

"Hanover's out front. Says he's got a follow-up question for Ed."

"Ask him to write it down and I'll get back to him," Larson said.

"Oh, he'll swallow that one easily." She turned to leave.

"Bos," Cork called to her. "We're not saying Aphrodite had anything to do with the tragedy at the Bosheys' last night. But due diligence requires that we check it out. Okay?"

"You don't think that woman has suffered enough?"

"Thanks for your concern, Bos. Noted," Larson said. "Hell Hanover's waiting."

As she left, Bos made a noise in her throat, a grumble familiar to Cork, which he knew was the voicing of her disapproval.

"She's right," he said. "I can't believe Aphrodite had anything to do with last night."

"But I have to ask her," Larson said. "We still need to get her prints. I'll do a follow-up round of questions then."

Cork nodded to Borkman. "Thanks, Cy. Now go on home, get some rest. You've got a shift coming up tonight."

When Borkman had gone, Larson asked, "What now for you, Cork?"

"Home. Dinner. Then I'm heading back to the rez."

"Staking out Patsy Boshey's place?"

"Best shot of nabbing Axel at the moment."

"You're not going alone, are you? If Axel's responsible for the murder, he's one dangerous man."

"I won't go alone," Cork said.

Larson studied him a long moment and must have guessed Cork's intention. "Walking a thin line, Cork, taking a civilian with you on a stakeout like this."

"Let me worry about that, okay?"

Larson took a deep breath, gave his head a small shake, and said, "You're the sheriff."

CHAPTER 9

A person's heart is the treasure chest of their life. It holds all that is dear, all they would fight and die for. Although it's not much larger than a human fist, it is immeasurable in what it can contain. And if you pay attention, every day you add to it. This is what Cork O'Connor believed, anyway. Even on a day such as this.

He drove home through Aurora just after sunset. The late October sky had been cornflower blue but was darkening now in the east. Above the trees and houses at his back, the light had turned golden. Around him, everything held still, like a sepia photograph that had captured a point in time to be remembered. Except for a few years in Chicago training as a cop and serving in the uniform of the CPD, his life had been spent in this far north town at the edge of a vast wilderness. It was part of all the best memories of his life, kept in the treasure chest of his heart.

But there was another place that held treasure for Cork—the house on Gooseberry Lane where he'd grown up and where now he was raising his own family. He parked his Bronco in the drive and entered the kitchen through the mudroom. The good aroma of fried chicken welcomed him. At the stove, his sister-in-law, Rose McKenzie, said without turning, "I hope you're hungry."

Rose was a plain woman, a little on the heavy side, with a freckled face and arms, and the most genuine smile Cork had ever seen, which she bestowed on him now, turning from the pan where the chicken was frying.

"Table's set, dinner in twenty minutes. Jo's upstairs with the girls."

Rose was a godsend for the O'Connors. His wife's sister had come with them to Aurora to help with the household and the raising of their children as Cork and Jo pursued their careers. She was smart and funny, had at one time seriously considered becoming a nun, and was inordinately fond of the gothic romances she kept stockpiled in the attic, which Cork had transformed into her own living area.

Rose turned again from the stove. "Jo told me about Chastity Boshey. Another terrible tragedy for that poor family. I sometimes ask myself, *What is God thinking?*"

"In my line of work, Rose, I ask myself that all the time. Upstairs, you said?"

"In Jenny's room."

"Smells delicious, by the way."

As he walked down the second-floor hallway toward Jenny's room, he heard Jo talking with the two girls.

"What do you think, Jenny?" Jo said.

"I think Annie should punch him in the face."

"See?" Cork heard his younger daughter say. "Jenny thinks I'm right."

"Brute force never works in the long run," Jo calmly advised.

Cork stepped into the doorway of the room. The two girls and Jo were all sitting on Jenny's bed, cross-legged, as if it were a pajama party, although they weren't dressed that way. Jenny was nine, Annie seven. The two girls were remarkably different in appearance. Jenny resembled her mother, slender and blond. Anne showed her Irish ancestry profoundly in her red hair and tendency to freckle easily in the summer. She was also big for her age and athletic. Already she could hit a softball—and play most sports in general—as well as the boys, even the older ones. Which, Cork was to learn, was the basis for the conversation taking place at the moment.

"Brute force?" Cork said.

"Danny Bassett hit me in the head with a kickball today."

"An accident?" Cork asked.

"On purpose." Annie's dark eyes were aflame with anger. "He told me girls shouldn't be playing with boys."

Cork crossed his arms and leaned against the doorframe. "What did you do?"

"She should have hit him," Jenny said.

"But you didn't?" Cork said.

Annie shook her head. "Mrs. Caldwell saw it and talked to him. It won't do any good. He's always being mean to me on the playground."

"Counselor?" Cork said. "Any advice?"

"I think there might be several possible reasons Danny behaves the way he does," Jo said, addressing her remarks to Anne. "One, he's simply repeating what he's heard others say and acting in a way he thinks is appropriate."

"What others?" Annie said.

"Other boys, other adults, who knows? A lot of people still have outdated ideas about what's appropriate behavior for boys and girls. Two, he may be threatened because you're so good at what you do."

"He's really bad at kickball. He had to get up right next to me to be sure he could hit me."

"That's two reasons," Cork said.

"One more possibility comes to me." Jo put her hand on Annie's knee. "It could be that he likes you and he's really confused about that, and he deals with it by trying to push you away."

"Likes me? Yuck!"

"Boys are pretty stupid," Jenny offered. "I still think a good punch in the nose would set him straight."

"So," Jo said. "What do you think you're going to do?"

Annie considered a moment, then said, "Nothing. Just keep playing like I always do. And maybe he'll be the one who gets a kickball in the head next time."

Jenny grinned at her mother in a triumphant way. "Brute force."

"Would you like me to talk to Mrs. Caldwell about him?" Jo asked.

"Don't do that. I'll be okay."

"Would you like me to arrest him?" Cork said.

Annie smiled big at that. "And put him in handcuffs."

"Rose says dinner's almost ready. You two girls wash up," Cork said. "I need to talk to your mom."

After her daughters had headed to the bathroom, Jo said, "Moonbeam Boshey is with her grandmother Patsy. At least for now."

"Thank you."

"Did you get anything more this afternoon?"

"Sigurd Nelson says Chastity was pregnant."

"Oh, God. That's awful."

"I know. Two homicides. Do the girls know about Chastity?"

"They haven't said anything."

"They've seen the Bosheys at church, so we probably ought to prepare them. They'll be hearing about it soon enough."

"Anything more on Axel?"

"Still missing. I'm going to try to fix that tonight."

"How?"

"Word will have probably got to Axel that Moonbeam is at Patsy's, along with Sundown. I'm thinking that might draw him out from wherever he's hiding."

"And you'll be waiting for him?"

"That's the plan."

Jo gave him a stern look. "Was this the reason you wanted that child with her grandmother?"

"No. Or not completely. Moonbeam needed to be with her people."

"Are you doing this alone?"

"I don't think so."

She eyed him as if she knew perfectly well what he was planning. "Pass along my thanks to Sam. Sometimes I think he's a better friend than you deserve."

Cork said, "Sometimes, so do I."

CHAPTER 10

They sat in Cork's Bronco, parked in a grove of birch trees within sight of Patsy Boshey's house on the Iron Lake Reservation. It was nearing ten p.m. The moon was up, a waxing gibbous that gave enough light for Cork and Sam to see the house and anyone who might come there. Lights were on inside, and also in the town of Allouette, visible through the trees, but everything was quiet. There'd been no vehicles on the road for some time. Cork had lowered the Bronco's windows, in case there were any sounds that might be significant in the stakeout, and a cold late autumn night breeze blew across the two men. Cork wore a leather jacket, Sam a heavy, knitted wool sweater. Cork had brought a thermos of strong black coffee, which the two men shared as the hours passed.

"Sat this way with your dad a couple of times back in the day," Sam said. "Had lots of explaining to do on the rez afterward."

"Did it pay off?"

"The stakeouts or my defense of them?"

"Both."

"They haven't run me off the reservation. And both stakeouts nabbed some pretty dark-hearted souls. The rez was better off with them gone."

"I appreciate your help, Sam."

"I gotta tell you, I think you're barking up the wrong tree on this one. Axel's had his struggles, but what was done to Chastity is way beyond anything he's capable of."

"Then two questions come readily to mind. One, why is he hiding? And two, how did his clothes come to be covered in what I'm sure we'll find out is Chastity's blood?"

"I can answer the first one easy. He's a Shinnob. No Indian ever believes he'll get a fair shake in a white courtroom."

"Okay. What about the other?"

"You're the lawman. What do you think?"

"The clearest explanation is that he was in the cabin during or sometime after Chastity was murdered. If it was during, well. that speaks for itself. If it was after, why didn't he call the sheriff's department to report it?"

"Confused, maybe. Or scared. Here's one for you, Mr. Lawman. If he was at the cabin, why did he run without taking his baby girl, leaving her there alone and for God knows how long before Chastity's body would be discovered? Hard to imagine."

"Unless he was drunk and not thinking clearly. And from what we heard at the North Star today, that sounds real plausible."

"Axel's got his problems, but that man has a good heart."

"Mix alcohol and anger, Sam, and what you've got is a human Molotov cocktail."

A truck drove by, the headlights missing Cork's Bronco. It passed Patsy Boshey's house, going slowly, but didn't stop.

"Leroy," Cork said.

"One of your clan, right?"

"A cousin. I talked to him this morning. He said he'd heard that Chastity was seeing someone on the side."

"Did he say who?"

"Claimed he didn't know. But he said he'd heard the same thing about her when she was married to Clyde Greensky."

"Here he comes again," Sam said.

The truck approached once more, moving slowly, but this time it stopped in front of Patsy Boshey's house and someone got out.

"Axel," Cork said. He started to open his door.

"Wait," Sam said.

"Why?"

"Give him a chance to see his kids, see that they're all right with Patsy. It'll go easier for you. And him."

Cork waited, watching as Boshey knocked at the door and was let inside. Then he said, "I'm going to have a word with Leroy."

"Go easy."

"He may be abetting a murderer, Sam."

"And maybe not."

Cork quietly got out of the Bronco. Leroy had left his truck running. Cork could see that Leroy's attention was divided between Patsy's house and the road ahead and behind his pickup. He wasn't looking at all in the direction of Cork' approach. When Cork tapped at the window of the cab, Leroy jumped.

"Ah, shit," Cork heard him say from inside.

"Roll down the window, Leroy."

Leroy complied. "Look, I was just . . ."

"Have you been hiding him?"

"No, no, nothing like that. He called me out of the blue, said he needed a ride."

"Out of the blue?"

"He wanted to see his kids and didn't want to drive his own truck. Afraid he'd be spotted."

"Where'd you pick him up?"

"He told me to meet him in the IGA parking lot."

"You see his truck in the lot?"

Leroy shook his head. "He told me he walked."

"Did he say from where?"

"Didn't. And I didn't ask."

"You told me you heard Chastity was seeing someone behind Axel's back. Was Axel seeing someone, too?"

"If he was, I didn't hear. But hell, who'd blame him, married to that nutcase."

"You're speaking ill of the dead, Leroy. And she died messy."

"You gonna arrest me? I was just helping out a friend."

"Go on, get out of here. But I may want to talk to you later."

"Christ," Leroy said. "Knew this was a bad idea."

He rolled up his window and drove away.

Cork walked back to the birch grove and to the passenger side of his Bronco. "Axel's had a chance by now to check in with Patsy and his kids. Time to bring him in. You coming?"

"That's why I'm here, isn't it?"

"Not officially. But if he tries to run, your help might be necessary."

"Promise me one thing, Cork."

"What's that?"

"You'll keep your sidearm holstered, even if he runs."

"I've got no intention of shooting anyone tonight, Sam."

Winter Moon stepped from the Bronco, and the two men walked toward the house of Patsy Boshey, which, at the moment, was as quiet as death.

CHAPTER 11

Sam stopped on the unpaved street and stood in the dark for a long moment eyeing Patsy Boshey's house.

"What is it?" Cork said.

"Let me go in first. Maybe I can talk some sense into him."

"We go together."

"If he sees you, he's likely to run."

"I'm hoping you'll help me prevent him from doing just that."

"We'd have a better chance if I talked to him first."

"I told you, Sam. We go in together."

"Patsy sees you, she might not let either of us in. What'll you do then? You can't just barge inside. You don't have a warrant, do you?"

On that last point, Sam was right. Axel Boshey hadn't been charged with anything yet. If his mother refused them entry, there was nothing, at the moment, that Cork could do legally.

"All right," he said, giving in but with great reluctance and more than a bit of apprehension. "But if he runs, I'll be waiting for him."

"With your weapon holstered. You promised me."

"And if he has a gun?"

"I'll make sure he doesn't. Stay out here in the dark where they can't see you."

Cork watched as Sam approached the house and knocked. He saw the curtain on the front window pulled slightly aside as someone checked the identity of the person at the door. Half a minute later, Patsy Boshey opened up, spoke to Sam for a moment, then let him in.

Cork stood alone in the dark. A minute passed. Then two. Then three. As the minutes dragged out, his worry increased. Legally, he knew he was in a precarious situation, putting a private citizen at risk. If anything went south . . .

The door of Patsy's house suddenly flew open. A figure burst out at a dead run, coming straight for the road, but stopped when he realized that Leroy's truck was no longer there. In the gray light from the waxing moon, Axel Boshey saw that Cork O'Connor awaited him instead.

"Axel," Cork said. It was all he was able to get out before the man rushed at him, and they both went tumbling into the dirt of the road.

Axel Boshey wasn't a tall man, but he was broad and muscular, like a small bear. He pressed Cork to the ground and got in one good blow to the side of Cork's head before Sam Winter Moon pulled him off. Axel was up in an instant, ready to have a go at Sam, when Cork clipped his knees from behind and the man went down again. This time, both Cork and Sam leaped on him, and their combined weight and Sam's gritted exhortation, "Easy, Axel. Easy. I'm here to help," brought the man's frantic struggle to an end.

That's when Patsy Boshey demanded, "Get off my son."

Cork craned his neck and found himself looking into the barrel of a shotgun.

"Get off him." The woman's voice was quiet but full of intent and menace.

"All right, Auntie," Cork said, lifting his hands free of her son and raising them, as if in surrender. "All right. I'm getting up." He rose carefully, hands still raised.

"You, too, Sam," the woman said.

"Are you really going to shoot me, Patsy?" Sam asked, not moving from where he still pinned Axel to the dirt. Then he said something in Ojibwe that Cork, who wasn't fluent in the tongue of his ancestors, didn't quite understand. But he heard the word *Kitchimanidoo* and knew that Sam was invoking the name of the Creator. And he saw a change in Patsy Boshey's body as the tension began to ease.

"It's all right, Ma," Axel said from the ground. "Put the shotgun down."

Slowly, the barrel lowered as if in the irresistible pull of gravity.

Cork said, "I'm going to take the shotgun, Auntie, just so no one gets hurt, okay?"

She made no attempt to hold on to the weapon as Cork relieved her of that burden.

"It's okay, Sam," Cork said.

Winter Moon rose, and Axel Boshey said, "Can I get up, too, Sheriff?"

"Promise not to run?"

"Yeah."

"All right, then."

"What are you going to do with him?" Patsy asked.

"He just assaulted an officer. I need to take him into custody."

"I didn't know it was you," Axel said. "Look, I just wanted to see my kids, make sure they're okay."

"And then what? You were just going to turn yourself in? Let's go, Axel. And don't do anything that'll make this worse."

"You think I killed Chastity. What's worse than that?"

"Did you?"

Then Axel Boshey said something that surprised Cork. "I don't know. Maybe."

"No," Patsy said.

In the dim moonlight, Axel's face was gray as he gave his mother a long, probing look and said again, "I don't know."

"Who told you about Chastity?"

"Doesn't matter."

"I'd like to know."

"I can't say."

"Was it whoever you've been staying with?"

"I can't say."

"I'd like to know her name, Axel. Maybe she can help."

"She's not . . ." He caught himself and stopped.

Larson was about to ask another question when Cork said, "Axel, word on the rez is that Chastity was seeing someone. Did you know that?"

"I heard."

"Is that what the argument was about?"

"By then, I didn't care."

"Were you seeing somebody?"

"I can't . . . I can't say."

"Maybe she can help."

"No," Boshey said, angry now. "I'm not telling you anything."

There was a knock at the door. Doug Neinhaus, the night dispatcher, poked his head in and said, "Your wife's here, Cork."

Before Cork could respond, Jo pushed past Neinhaus into the room.

"Until I've talked to my client," she said, "this interview is finished."

CHAPTER 13

"You gave him his Miranda warning?" Jo O'Connor asked.

"Of course," Cork replied.

Cork, Larson, and Jo stood together outside the interview room where Axel Boshey now sat alone behind the closed door.

"What are you doing here?" Cork asked.

"Sam Winter Moon called and told me that Axel might be in need of legal counsel. You did give him an opportunity to contact a lawyer, yes?"

"We did," Cork said. "He waived that right."

"Probably because he had no idea who to contact." She eyed Cork. "But you did."

"It's not my responsibility to advise him in that regard, Counselor," Cork said.

"Not legally, maybe." She looked at Larson. "Before you ask him any more questions, Ed, I'd like to speak to my client alone."

Larson looked unhappy with the whole thing, but he gave a nod. "Let us know when you're ready."

"One question. Did you tell him Chastity was pregnant?"

"We hadn't gotten there yet," Cork said.

"He needs to know."

"Go ahead," Cork said.

After Jo returned to the interview room, Cork and Captain Ed Larson stood for a moment looking at each other like a couple of mute monkeys.

"You got a wife with balls, Sheriff."

The comment came from Rocky Martinelli, a deputy who'd come into the department while Cork and Larson were in conversation with Jo. Martinelli walked to Cork and studied his face.

"Got a bit of a shiner there. Wish I'd been with you on that arrest. I'd love a chance to lay into Boshey myself."

Rocky Martinelli had been a deputy long before Cork joined the Tamarack County Sheriff's Department. He was Wild Bill Gunderson's son-in-law, married to Gunderson's only child, Lucy, hired despite never having completed a law enforcement training program. Gunderson said it was because Martinelli had been trained in military policing when he was in the army, a claim that had never been verified. Most of the deputies, Cork included, speculated that Wild Bill looked on Martinelli as the son he never had, and his favoritism toward Rocky was blatant. Martinelli was a sloppy officer. He was also a bully. And a bigot. Cork had heard Martinelli refer to Native women as squaws and Native men as bucks. As a deputy, Cork had called the man on it. As sheriff, he'd officially reprimanded him. Within Cork's hearing, Rocky Martinelli had stopped using offensive epithets, but Cork knew that off duty he still spoke of the Anishinaabeg in Tamarack County in derogatory ways, characterizing them as lazy, drunkards, untrustworthy, dirty.

"What are you doing here, Rocky?"

"Heard you brought in Boshey. Wanted to see for myself." He looked past Cork toward the interview room, his eyes deep wells of hatred. "I also heard he got himself the best lawyer in town. An Indian lover."

"Watch your tongue, Deputy." Cork took a calming breath. "You're patrolling east county tonight?"

"That's right."

"And last night, too."

"Yep."

"Did you happen to spot Aphrodite McGill's pink VW on the road at all?"

"I didn't. And it's hard to miss that bug."

"Did you see anything unusual at all?"

"Yeah. Saw Boshey's pickup passing Grady's truck stop at two a.m. I was ten-seven and sitting by the window, eating a cheese omelette."

"How'd you know it was Boshey's?"

"It's a reservation beater. The truck's red except for that white door on the driver's side. Like Aphrodite McGill's bug, hard to miss."

"How was he driving?"

"Like shit. Like all Indians."

"I already warned you once. Any idea where he might have been going?"

"Not a mind reader. But I can tell you this. It was Boshey killed his wife. We all know it. Right, Doug?" He looked toward the dispatcher for confirmation but got nothing except a hard stare in return.

"We don't know anything for sure, Deputy," Cork told him.

"We found Boshey's bloody clothes in his woodshed this morning. It's gotta be Chastity's blood that soaked 'em."

"I think you'd best get back out on patrol, Deputy. And I'd appreciate it if you kept your speculations about Chastity Boshey's death to yourself."

"Whatever you say." The look Martinelli gave Cork oozed

with insubordination. "Sheriff." That last word like phlegm spit from his throat.

A woman stepped into the department and said, "Rocky?"

Martinelli turned. "Jesus, Lucy, what the hell are you doing here?"

"He left me all alone," she said as if lost.

"Hello, Lucy," Cork said to Martinelli's wife. Then, seeing the expression of distress on her face, he said, "Are you all right?"

"She's fine," Martinelli said.

"He left me all alone," she said again.

"Who left you?" Cork asked.

"I'll take care of this." Martinelli grabbed her arm roughly. "Come on, let's get you back there."

"Where's there?" Cork asked.

"Things are confused at home, okay? She's staying with her dad for a bit. This is none of your business."

After they'd gone, Neinhaus said, "She didn't look so good. But being married to Rocky, that's got to be one of the circles of hell."

Cork said, "What I told Martinelli about speculations? That goes for everyone, understood, Doug?"

"Ten-four, Cork."

Jo stepped from the interview room. "We're ready."

"Did you tell him that Chastity was pregnant?"

"I did. But he already knew it. He says the child wasn't his."

Larson looked at Cork and said one word. "Motive."

"Again, Axel, I'd like to know where you've been hiding," Larson said. "I'd like to know the woman's name."

"I can't tell you that."

"Because you blacked out? Or because she's involved with you in the murder of your wife?"

"My client hasn't been charged with that crime," Jo said.

"But he admitted that he knew he'd be arrested for it and that's why he was hiding."

"Axel?" Jo said, as if cuing him.

"I was gonna turn myself in as soon as I knew my children were safe."

"Then why did you try to run when I showed up at your mother's house?" Cork asked.

"I panicked, okay?"

"Walk us through what you did after you argued with your wife and left the house," Larson said.

Axel looked to Jo, who nodded.

He went through the events—dropping Sundown off at Patsy Boshey's, buying a case of beer, drinking most of it while he drove around.

"Drove where?" Cork asked.

"Just around the rez."

"See anybody? Talk to anybody?"

"Ran into Leroy. I shared a few beers with him. Then I drove around some more and finally headed to the North Star."

"Where you made a phone call," Larson said. "Who'd you call?"

"I don't remember calling anybody."

"Because you blacked out?" Larson said.

"Yeah."

"I have to tell you, Axel, your blackouts seem awfully convenient. What time did you leave the bar?"

"Must've been close to midnight."

"So you do remember that?"

"No. Just know it's when they close."

"Where did you go?"

"I don't remember."

"What do you remember?"

"Waking up this morning—"

"Yesterday morning, you mean?"

"Yeah. Yesterday."

"Waking up where?"

Axel didn't answer.

"And all the time in between is just what? Blackness?"

"Yeah."

Cork said, "Axel, we have a witness who overheard you say that you wished Chastity was dead. We found clothing we believe to be yours hidden near the scene. The clothing was soaked with what I'm sure we're going to find out is your wife's blood. Trying to hide the clothing strikes me as an awfully rational move for someone who was as drunk as you claim to have been."

"Axel," Larson said, "did you kill your wife? Did you kill her because she'd let another man father her child?"

"I told you, I don't remember. God as my witness, I don't remember."

"Okay," Larson said. "Let's go over it all again."

"Are you really going to charge him with assaulting you?"

Jo sat with Cork in his office. The interview had ended, and Axel Boshey hadn't given them any additional information about the night his wife was murdered.

"I need to hold him until we get the result of the blood test on the clothes we found."

"You're sure they're his?"

"The sizes match all the other clothing we found in his house. So, yeah, pretty sure. Look, Jo, I have to tell you, if you represent him going forward, you're backing a loser."

"Even losers deserve their day in court and the best representation possible. Don't you agree? Sheriff?"

"Did he tell you where he's been hiding?"

"You know I can't tell you that. What I can tell you is this. Axel may have a problem with alcohol, but he's no murderer."

"Seven stab wounds with a fireplace poker, Jo. The act of someone out of their mind. Axel admits he was blind drunk. Angry with his wife. Said he wished she was dead. Even if it's true he can't remember, that doesn't mean he didn't do it."

"But you'll pursue other possibilities, right?"

Cork looked at his watch. "It's late. I've got a report to write up." He stood, a signal for her stand as well, which she did. "And thanks again for your help getting Moonbeam to her grandmother."

"Cork, if you charge Axel, you'll be confirming what a lot of white folks think about Native people, Native men especially. And also what a lot of Native folks think about white justice."

"I know, Jo. But I've got a job to do."

"You have yours." She leaned to him and kissed his cheek. "And I have mine. I'll see you at home."

CHAPTER 14

When Cork heard the kids and Rose banging around in the kitchen, he opened his eyes and found that he was alone. He looked at the alarm clock on his bedside table. Seven-thirty. He'd got four hours of sleep. Restless sleep. It was going to be another rough day, he knew, and already he felt exhausted.

He walked into the kitchen and found Rose at the stove making pancakes, Jenny and Annie at the table drinking their orange juice.

"Morning, Daddy," Jenny said, and Annie echoed her.

"Morning, munchkins. Morning, Rose."

"There's coffee in the pot. And the pancakes are almost ready," Rose said. "Hungry?"

"Us first," Annie said. "We have to go to school."

"There's plenty for everyone," Rose said.

Cork poured himself a mug of coffee. "Where's Jo?"

"Left half an hour ago. She said she was heading out to the reservation to see Patsy Boshey."

"Daddy, I'm going to be in the play at school today," Jenny said. "Will you be there?"

"What play?"

"About Columbus discovering America. I'm playing one of the Indians. I say, 'Welcome, white stranger.'"

"Really?"

"I told you."

"You did? I don't remember."

"Mom and Aunt Rose are going to be there. You said you would, too."

"Columbus didn't discover America," Cork said with a little sigh of exhaustion. "It was here a long time before he arrived and was already full of people. And you don't have to play at being an Indian. You have Indian blood in you."

"Will you be there?" Jenny said.

"What time?"

"Two o'clock assembly," Rose said, putting pancakes on the plates of her two nieces. "Then school's out."

"And Monday's Columbus Day," Jenny said. "No school!"

"Can I come to the play?" Annie said.

"Your class will be there," Rose said.

"Goodie!"

The kids drenched their pancakes in maple syrup and chattered while Cork sipped his coffee.

"You're grumpy, Daddy," Jenny finally said.

"Just tired, kiddo. I didn't get a lot of sleep."

"Jo didn't either," Rose said. "She told me about last night. What an awful business."

"What business?" Jenny said.

"Finish your pancakes, then get ready for school," Rose said gently but firmly.

After the girls had left the table, Rose said, "I've seen Patsy and Axel and Chastity and the kids in church sometimes. They're not regulars, but I know them. It's hard to believe something so terrible can happen to people you know."

By then, Cork had been a cop for more than a decade. He'd seen inhumanity demonstrated in more ways than he cared to remember. But the murder of Chastity Boshey was among the worst. And Rose was right in a way. In a place like Aurora and on the Iron Lake Reservation, where folks had known one another all their lives, this kind of heinous crime would be felt as a personal blow, a terrible rending of the communal fabric. Which would put all the more pressure on the whole system of justice to mend things. As he sipped his coffee, Cork wished he could just go back to bed.

The minute Cork walked into the sheriff's department, Hell Hanover pounced.

"So, you caught our killer. It's about time."

"Helm," Cork said after taking a calming breath, "Axel Boshey hasn't been charged with anything yet. I remind you that even if he is, it's not up to you or me to determine his guilt or innocence. I'd be careful how you characterize him, in either your speech or your newspaper. And how'd you know about Axel?"

"I have my sources. Care to make an official statement?"

"Captain Larson's in charge of the investigation. I imagine he'll be scheduling a press briefing this morning. You'll have to wait until then for anything official."

Bos Swain approached, holding some papers in her hand. "Sheriff, I need to see you in your office. Now. It's important."

"I have business to attend to, Helm. I'm sure I'll see you at the briefing."

Cork pushed past him and heard Bos at his back say to Hanover, "Now, go on. You'll get something for your rag later."

In Cork's office, he sat at his desk and waited for Bos. When she stepped through the doorway, he said, "What've you got?"

"Oh, this?" She held up the papers. "The minutes from the county commissioners' meeting. I just thought the last thing you needed this morning was Hell Hanover. You look awful, by the way."

"Long night."

"I figured."

"Has Ed been in?"

She stepped back and looked to her right. "Speak of the devil." A moment later, Captain Ed Larson appeared at her side. "You look awful, too," she told him.

"And good morning to you, sunshine," Larson said.

"I have oatmeal cookies, if you think that'll help."

"I'm okay, thanks, Bos."

"Coffee?"

"Already had some."

"All right, then." Bos went back to her work.

Larson sat in the chair on the other side of Cork's desk. "I stopped by the hospital lab this morning. It's Chastity Boshey's blood on the clothing we found. Or at least the same blood type."

"No surprise there. What about the sample you sent to BCA for DNA analysis?"

"You know they're always backed up. It'll take a good long while. But I'm hoping to get the records today for the pay phone at the North Star. That should give us a good idea who Boshey called."

"And maybe where he's been hiding out."

Cy Borkman appeared, his bulk filling the doorway of Cork's office. "Heard about you and Boshey last night, Cork. You should've asked me to be there with you instead of Winter Moon."

"And who would've been covering west county?"

clamped them on Aphrodite McGill's wrists. Still the woman struggled, kicking at them now.

"Sheriff?" Dross said, dancing a little to keep her shins out of harm's way.

"Let's put her in a holding cell until she cools down."

They battled with Aphrodite all the way to one of the two holding cells, which were just off the common area. It was only after the door was locked that Aphrodite stopped her struggle. She stood behind the bars, breathing hard and fast, eyeing them like a caged wild beast.

"When you're ready to be civil, Aphrodite," Cork said, "I'll take those handcuffs off and we can talk."

"Pig," she said and spit at him, then began to pace.

Ed Larson and Bos Swain stood with Cork and Marsha Dross watching the bizarre antics of the woman in the cell.

"She's been drinking," Marsha said. "Whiskey from the smell of her."

"I'm betting she's on something else as well," Larson said.

Cork said, "Bos, get hold of Father Monroe over at St. Agnes. Ask him to come in. Marsha, keep an eye on her, make sure she doesn't hurt herself. Ed, in my office."

They'd started in that direction when Axel Boshey called out to them. He was currently incarcerated in the main cell block, which was along a corridor that ran off one side of the department. At the moment, he was the only prisoner housed there.

When Cork and Larson stood in front of his cell, Boshey said, "Was that Aphrodite?"

"It was."

"You can't let her near my kids."

"Believe me, I have no intention of doing that, Axel. Certainly not the way she is now."

"I've seen her like this before. Batshit crazy."

"She's high on something," Larson said. "Any idea what?"

"You name it, she's tried it. My kids are safe with my mom. Keep 'em there, okay?"

"For the moment. But she said something, Axel. She said we were just like Chastity. Any idea what that was about?"

"You think Chastity and me argued, you should have seen what went down sometimes between those two. Like she-bears going at one another. Chastity wouldn't let our kids set foot in Shangri-La. Don't let her at my children. Promise me."

"I'll do what I can, Axel."

When they'd returned to Cork's office and had seated themselves, Larson said, "Just like Chastity. What did she mean by that?"

"When she's calmed down, we'll ask her."

"In her current state of mind, she could be capable of anything."

"Like murder, you're thinking?" Cork said.

"Worth considering. Axel just told us they sometimes went at it like she-bears."

"Cy reported her pink VW was heading away from Shangri-La the night Chastity was murdered. But her own daughter?" Cork shook his head. "I'd love to know what she's on right now."

"As you say, maybe when she's calmed down, she'll tell us."

Another scream, as if from a banshee, came from the holding cell. Cork said, "That could be a while."

Father Jude Monroe was a newcomer to Aurora, the first in what would prove to be a long line of young priests brought in by the diocese to help the aging Father Kelsey, who'd been at St. Agnes forever but was showing significant signs of what was kindly termed "forgetfulness." Father Jude had been a star quarterback at St. John's in Collegeville, Minnesota. He still looked the part—chiseled jaw, handsome, athletic. Cork had more than once heard from female parishioners the lament that all his gorgeousness was wasted behind a collar. The young priest's favorite mode of transportation was a 1967 Jaguar XKE, which he worked on whenever his priestly duties would allow. In Tamarack County, he'd earned the nickname Saint Jag, which he happily embraced.

"She's calmed down a bit now, Jude," Cork told him. They were in Cork's office, door closed. "But she's still feeling the effects of alcohol for sure, and probably something else as well. I'm not sure what."

The priest nodded, as if this wasn't surprising news at all. "Aphrodite. Goddess of love."

"She chose the name for herself, did you know that?"

"I did. I learned it when Axel and Chastity were preparing for Moonbeam's christening. Aphrodite came to see me, told me that Chastity didn't want her in the church for the rite. She, um, she told me lots of surprising things. It was clear to me that she grew up in the church but had problems with it. Like a lot of people. The truth is that both she and Chastity were . . ." He paused, as if weighing the advisability of what he was about to say. Then finished simply, "Unique. Also, both of them troubled."

"Anything you care to share?"

"You know better than that."

"Thanks for staying with her yesterday. I'm sure you were a big help."

The young priest shrugged. "As I said, Aphrodite's not a parishioner, but I'm here to serve anyone in need in any way that I can."

"Did she say anything about what happened at her daughter's place?"

"She was pretty well sedated. Mostly she rambled. Talked

about Chastity when she was little, all the good things they'd done together, all the dreams they'd had."

"Anything more recent?"

"She made several unprintable comments about Indians spoiling everything."

"Chastity married two Ojibwe men."

"In the very few conversations I've had with Aphrodite, she's made it clear to me what she thought of her daughter's choices in husbands. Could I see her now?"

Aphrodite was quiet, sitting on the cot in the holding cell, staring down at the concrete floor. From the other side of the bars, Cork said, "Someone to see you, Aphrodite."

She slowly raised her head. She no longer looked batshit crazy. She looked lost. Or, Cork thought, abandoned. Like a woman on a desert island with no hope of rescue.

"Father Jude," she said in a raspy voice.

Cork said, "If I take those handcuffs off, will you behave yourself, Aphrodite?"

She gave a weak nod.

Cork unlocked the cell door and asked Aphrodite to stand. He removed the handcuffs and could see the deep red marks on her wrists where she'd struggled against the restraints. "You can sit back down now."

She sat and looked up at the priest, her eyes rimmed in red. "Sorry, Father."

"That's all right, Aphrodite."

"I . . . I've been a little upset." She spoke slowly, with still a bit of slur to her words.

"It's understandable. How do you feel now?"

"Like crap. 'Scuse my mouth."

Cork said, "You were out of control, Aphrodite. What did you take before you came here today?"

"Just something to calm my nerves."

"What exactly?"

"A little Jack Daniel's, okay?"

"And something more?"

"Just the booze. Just to kill the pain. Jesus, my little girl's dead."

"Did you argue with Chastity the day she was killed?"

"Argue? We never argued. We loved each other. She was my world." She looked at the priest. "I wanna go home."

"Even if the sheriff lets you, you're in no condition to drive," the priest said.

"Please. I'm tired. I just want to sleep."

Father Jude glanced at Cork. "I'll see that she gets home."

Cork considered the woman, who did indeed look ready to collapse. "All right. But, Aphrodite, before you leave, we'll need a urine sample."

"What for?"

"I'd like to know for sure what you took to calm your nerves. It certainly didn't have the desired effect."

"And if I don't want to you give a urine sample?"

"You assaulted two officers of the law. I could arrest you for that. But if you agree to a urine sample, I'll let it slide."

She looked like a candle melting and finally said, "All right."

In the common area, Cork asked Bos to escort Aphrodite to the women's restroom to collect the urine sample.

"I'll wait for them," the priest said. "As soon as Aphrodite's finished, I'll see that she gets home safely."

Cork returned to his office. He sat a few minutes considering the morning, one more bizarre episode in the days leading to the annual celebration of the bizarre and grotesque. He'd just begun to look over the duty roster for Halloween night when he heard an explosion of angry voices. He stepped quickly from his office. Bos hadn't yet returned from escorting Aphrodite, and the department was empty. He looked toward the main cell block, where the clash of voices spilled from the open door, which should have been closed and locked.

He found Deputy Rocky Martinelli inside Axel Boshey's cell. Martinelli had Boshey pinned against the stone of the cell wall, his hands around Boshey's throat.

"You goddamned drunk son of a bitch," Martinelli screamed into Boshey's face.

Cork grabbed the deputy to pull him off, but Martinelli held firm to the Shinnob.

"I should kill you right now."

Cork wrapped an arm around Martinelli's throat and was finally able to pry him loose from the prisoner. He threw the deputy toward the other side of the cell. Bos Swain stood outside the bars, looking on with huge eyes and a mouth opened in shock.

"What the hell do you think you're doing, Deputy!" Cork hollered.

"Hits her with a poker, then commences to use her body like a pincushion. Seven times he stabbed that thing into her. Then he just leaves her there in that puddle of blood. Goddamned butchering redskin."

"Get out of here, Martinelli. Now. You're suspended until further notice, you hear me?"

"Hides his blood-soaked clothes in the woodshed, like we wouldn't look there. How stupid can you get?"

"Out!" Cork said, pointing toward the open cell door.

Martinelli spit on the floor at Boshey's feet, then exited the cell block.

Cork turned back to Boshey, who was rubbing his neck where the deputy's hands had left marks that would probably bruise.

"I'm sorry, Axel. You okay?"

Axel coughed then said, "Yeah, I'm fine."

Cork looked toward Bos, who'd come in and was still standing beyond the bars, looking aghast. "How'd he get the cell key?" he demanded.

"He must have grabbed it while I was in the ladies' room with Aphrodite. I'm sorry, Cork." She looked toward the prisoner. "I'm so sorry, Axel."

"No harm done," Axel said, though the marks on his throat were deepening in color. "He only said what a lot of other folks are probably thinking."

"It should never have happened, Axel," Cork said. "I swear to you, it won't happen again."

Boshey gave him a sad ghost of a smile and pointed toward the cell window. "I think I'm safer in here than I would be out there."

CHAPTER 16

Cork filled Captain Ed Larson in on what had occurred between Boshey and the suspended Deputy Martinelli. He skipped the press briefing, letting Larson deal with the reporters while he took Aphrodite McGill's urine sample to the lab at Aurora Community Hospital himself. Carole Anderson, who was in charge of the lab, was, like Cork, a parishioner of St. Agnes. He explained to her what he wanted, and Carole promised the test results by that afternoon.

He drove to Allouette, to the home of Patsy Boshey, but no one answered his knock. His next stop was at LeDuc's General Store. If anyone could tell him where to find Patsy Boshey and her grandchildren, and maybe Jo as well, it was George LeDuc.

LeDuc was an elder, a bear of a man in his sixties. In addition to running his store, he was chairman of the Tribal Council. He'd been a widower for many years, but he'd recently married a woman half his age, and although he was usually a man reserved in his demeanor, the robust difference Sarah LeDuc had made in his life was evident in the smile that so often graced his lips these days. He'd been a good friend to Cork's father, and now to Cork.

"*Boozhoo,*" LeDuc greeted Cork when he walked in. It was early, the store empty, and LeDuc was sweeping the floor with a big push broom.

"*Boozhoo,* George."

LeDuc set his broom aside. He wore a red apron, which he removed and shook out. He folded the apron and set it on the single checkout counter. "Business or pleasure?"

"Business, George."

LeDuc nodded. "Axel Boshey?"

"I'm looking for Patsy. Tried her house. No one's there."

"She called me. Seems Hell Hanover came this morning, early. Pounded on her door. She sent him packing, threatened him with a rolling pin. Wanted me to do something to keep him and any other newspaper nuisance from bothering her. I told her there wasn't much I could do. I suggested maybe she go somewhere and lie low for a while."

"Where?"

"The Ganschinietz place. You know, out toward Crow Point. Patsy and Lynn, like sisters those two." LeDuc shook his head. "Terrible business, Cork, what happened to Chastity. But Patsy's sure her boy didn't do it."

The store smelled of fresh popcorn, which LeDuc made all day long in a popper he'd bought at auction when a movie theater in Hibbing had closed years earlier. Children came to the store with their parents just to get a small bag of the stuff. Cork couldn't help but note the discordance between that comforting aroma and the brutal nature of his conversation with LeDuc.

"Axel claims he was so drunk he blacked out, has no memory of that night," Cork said.

"He's blacked out before. I've seen him that drunk, but it's been a while. After Clyde Greensky died, Axel shaped up. It was Henry Meloux helped him get off the booze. Sweats, ceremonies, and such, I guess. When he married Chastity, I figured Axel was ready for the responsibility of a family." LeDuc shook his head. "But we all know how things have gone between 'em. Chastity's been pretty hard on him, from what I understand. Maybe the booze has had a lot to do with that. But that doesn't mean he killed her."

"There's strong evidence that points to him, George. I can't go into the details, but it's compelling."

"So what do you want with Patsy?"

"Aphrodite McGill was at the department this morning, out of her mind, screaming for her grandchildren. I came to warn Patsy that Aphrodite might come knocking. I wanted to let her know to call me if there's any trouble."

"I still remember when that woman first showed up around here almost twenty years ago. Flower child. Used to come out to the rez on occasion, wanted to get back to nature the way Indians did. She finally gave up on that notion. Oh, by the way, your wife was here a while ago, looking for Patsy, too."

"You sent her out to Lynn's place?"

"Pointed her in that direction anyway. And look, I wouldn't worry about Patsy. She can handle Aphrodite McGill."

Lynn Ganschinietz's maiden name was Larson, but she was no kin to Captain Ed Larson. In the North Country of Minnesota, the name Larson was as common as ragweed. Lynn's family was Anishinaabe, Loon Clan. For decades, they'd operated a guide service for white folks wanting a deep, true Boundary Waters experience, and Pasty Boshey, who'd been friends with Lynn all her life, was one of their guides. While in college, William Ganschinietz had made his first visit to the Boundary Waters, along with his parents and two sisters. Young Lynn Larson and young Patsy

Boshey had been the ones to lead them into the vast wilderness. After two weeks of sharing the beautiful spirit of that remarkable sanctuary of solace, Lynn and William had found themselves head over heels in love. Ganschinietz abandoned his college plans, married Lynn, and built a business that became one of the most highly sought-after guide services in the North Country. They lived in a cabin home on a small lake only a couple of miles east of Crow Point. Their northern shore provided an easy portage directly into the Boundary Waters Canoe Area Wilderness whenever William and Lynn wanted to get away by themselves for a bit.

Like so many families on the rez, the Ganschinietzes had a dog, both for companionship and as an early warning system regarding visitors. Their animal, a big German shepherd, was named Animikii, which meant Thunderbird in the language of the Ojibwe. As Cork pulled into the drive, the dog rose from the front porch, where it had been lazing in the sun, and commenced to living up to its name, barking up a storm. Which was a relief to Cork. He liked the idea that if Aphrodite McGill came to demand her grandchildren, the fury of this dog would be the first thing to greet her.

Lynn Ganschinietz came from the house and hushed the dog. Cork looked up at her and spoke from the bottom porch step. "Looking for Patsy."

"Not here."

"Her grandkids are here, though?"

"Both napping at the moment."

"And Patsy?"

"She and your wife walked the east path to Crow Point. Patsy wanted to talk to Henry."

"William around?"

"Leading his last group into the Boundary Waters before the snow comes."

"Okay if I leave my vehicle here while I head to Henry's?'

"Be my guest."

Half an hour later, as Cork approached the solitary cabin in the meadow that covered Crow Point, he heard a dog barking inside. The cabin door opened, and a big yellow mutt came bounding out. Cork bent and greeted the dog with "Hey there, Walleye. That's a good boy." He looked up and saw Henry Meloux standing in the doorway.

Meloux had been an important figure in Cork's life as far back as he could remember. He was a Mide, a healer, who lived alone in his small cabin on the shore of Iron Lake. Although he was old, somewhere in his early eighties, his hair white, his face a patchwork of wrinkles, there was something eternally powerful and probing in his dark almond eyes, as if he was looking deep into your soul, not in order to pass judgment but simply because your true self could never be hidden from him. At least, that's how it always felt to Cork.

"*Boozhoo,* Henry," Cork said.

"*Boozhoo,* Corcoran O'Connor."

Meloux didn't seem at all surprised to see him standing there, and Cork suspected it had nothing to do with Walleye's barking. Meloux never seemed to be surprised by his visitors. He maintained that it wasn't the dog who alerted him, that long before Walleye picked up a sound or scent, the woods told him someone was coming. More times than Cork could count, the old man had advised him that if human beings really listened, they would hear the woods speaking.

Jo, on the other hand, was obviously caught off guard. "Cork, what are you doing here?"

She sat at the birchwood table fashioned by the old man's hands many years before. Patsy Boshey sat with her. They were drinking tea the Mide had made.

The inside of Meloux's cabin was a collection of items both predictable and surprising. A pair of ancient snowshoes of bent wood and rawhide webbing hung on the wall, along with a deer-prong pipe. There was a gun rack that supported an ancient Winchester rifle. Near the potbellied stove hung a page torn from an old Skelly gas station calendar showing a buxom woman bent over the raised hood of a car and displaying a lot of the bare, white flesh of her bottom. Cork had never been able to get Meloux to divulge the reason this particular item adorned his cabin. The old man would simply smile and say, "The past is never really about what is behind us." An enigmatic answer whose meaning Cork had never deciphered.

"Lynn told me you and Patsy were here," Cork replied.

"What do you want with me?" Patsy asked, sounding wary.

"Just to warn you. Aphrodite McGill is eager to get her hands on her grandchildren. She may come looking for them."

"That woman's a menace to herself and anyone close to her."

"Tea?" Meloux offered. When Cork said no, Meloux gestured for him to sit at his small table with the others.

"How is my son this morning?" Patsy asked.

"Sobered up," Cork told her. "And worried about his kids."

"He's a good father."

"He has a good heart, Corcoran O'Connor," Meloux said. "His head has sometimes been a problem."

The old Mide sat in a shaft of morning sunlight that came through his window making the long hair that draped his shoulders seem to burn with a white fire.

"You helped him quit drinking, Henry."

"Not completely it seems."

"You haven't questioned him, have you?" Jo asked, a little sternly.

"Not without you present, Counselor." He turned to Boshey's mother. "Aphrodite McGill came into the department this morning, Patsy. She was pretty desperate to see her grandchildren."

"See them? You mean take them. That woman is a wolverine

when it comes to Sundown and Moonbeam. Anytime she hears that the kids have been with me, she does her best the next time she sees them to buy their affection. Toys, candy, you name it."

"I'm just warning you that she may come pounding on your door. And if she does and makes a nuisance of herself, let me know. I'll see what I can do."

"What if she tries legally to get the kids?" Patsy said. "She can't, can she?"

"I'll help you deal with that," Jo promised.

"Can I see my son?" Patsy asked.

"Of course. There will probably be reporters hanging around the department this morning. Ed Larson has a press briefing scheduled. But this afternoon should be clear."

"I don't want to run into that Hanover."

"Nobody does. Jo, I have lots more questions for Axel. Maybe you and Patsy could be there about one o'clock?"

Jo looked to Patsy Boshey, who gave a nod. "One it is," Jo said.

A silence fell over them all, and Cork understood that he'd intruded, interrupted whatever conversation had been going on before he came, whatever advice Patsy—and maybe even Jo—had been seeking from the Mide.

"I guess that's everything." Cork stood. "See you at home, Jo."

"Don't forget Jenny's play this afternoon."

"I'll do my best to be there."

"Let me walk with you," Meloux said.

He accompanied Cork into the sunlight, Walleye trotting alongside. They walked away from the cabin a bit. The October sky was clear, the air crisp. The meadow still held some late-blooming wildflowers. Cork wished he'd come just to enjoy the sense of peace Crow Point usually offered him.

"Healing can take a long time, Corcoran O'Connor," Meloux finally said. "For some, a lifetime."

"Meaning what, Henry?"

"Axel Boshey. There is still much healing to be done."

"Do you think he's capable of what happened to his wife?"

"That is not a question for me to answer. The answer needs to come from here." He reached out and touched Cork's chest where his heart lay beneath.

"The law is about facts, Henry, not feelings."

"Is there not room for both?"

Meloux turned, and he and Walleye headed back to the cabin.

CHAPTER 17

"Bernadette Polaski," Ed Larson said from his desk the moment Cork walked into the department.

"What?"

"Got the records for the pay phone at the North Star. Bernadette Polaski. That's who Boshey called."

"Our librarian?"

"Our librarian."

"Son of a gun. Well, let's go see what she has to say."

The Aurora Public Library was a Carnegie, a cozy dark stone structure where, as a teenager, Cork had often spent evenings either doing schoolwork or hanging out with Ann Browning, his steady girlfriend in high school. These days, his library trips were usually in the company of his children or Jo. But he still had the same reaction whenever he entered, a sense that, steeped in the smell of old paper and bindings, it was a place sacred in many respects.

They found Ellie Roosevelt, who'd been the head librarian for years, sitting at the checkout desk. She was a stately looking woman in her late fifties and claimed to be a distant relative of FDR. She'd often helped Cork track down a book essential to a paper he was writing for school or made her own recommendations for reading material. In his adolescence, she'd turned him on to Arthur Conan Doyle, for which he was still grateful.

"*Bonjour, mes amis,*" she said, eyeing both men over the top of her half-glasses. She was fond of offering her patrons greetings in various tongues. Not just the usual ones—*Buenas dias, Guten Tag, Ciao*. Cork had received greetings in Swahili, Cambodian, Latt, and other far-flung languages. She never spoke above a whisper, which, Cork had always found, added to the sense of the sanctity of her domain. "I haven't seen either of you in here for quite some time. But Jenny has a book long overdue, Cork. *Little Women.*"

"I'll see that she gets it back."

Ellie removed her glasses and brushed a wisp of steel-gray hair from her brow. "What brings you here?"

"We'd like to talk to Bernadette," Ed Larson said.

"She's downstairs in the stacks at the moment. Is there anything I can do for you?"

"Thanks no," Larson replied. "As I said, we'd like to speak to Bernadette."

"Is she in any trouble?"

"We just need to talk to her."

The librarian gave a nod, as if it didn't surprise her. "She's been . . . distracted of late. And not feeling at all well."

"Downstairs, you said?"

"Yes."

"Thanks, Ellie," Larson said.

Like Cork and so many other kids who'd grown up in Aurora, Bernadette Polaski had worked for Sam Winter Moon in her high school years. The summer following her graduation, she'd experienced a significant tragedy. Both her parents were killed in a car wreck caused by a drunk driver. Her grandparents were dead, and because she had no one else to turn to, Sam had been her moral support. She'd gone on to college, earned her degree in library science, and returned to her hometown. She was in her late twenties, a pretty redhead who'd always been on the quiet, studious side. Everyone assumed that when Ellie Roosevelt finally stepped down as head librarian, Bernadette would ascend to that position.

She was doing nothing when Cork and Larson approached her, simply standing beside a cart half-filled with reading materials, staring down an aisle between shelves of books. There were no windows. In addition to stacks of ancient periodicals and newspapers and esoteric reference materials, the basement was where the restrooms were located. The place had a slight musty odor and was lit with the glare of overhead bulbs that cast shadows in the far corners. As a kid, whenever Cork came down to use the restroom, he thought the basement would be a perfect place for ghosts.

"Bernadette?" Larson said.

The woman turned to them, clearly startled, her face looking as if she were seeing the specters that Cork had once imagined resided there.

"I didn't hear you coming," she said, a little breathless.

"Sorry," Larson said. "We need to talk to you."

"About what?"

"Axel Boshey," Larson said.

She blinked twice, then said, "I don't understand."

Cork had been a lawman long enough to know when someone was dissembling. Bernadette Polaski understood perfectly why they were there.

"He called you the night his wife was killed. What did he want?"

She put a hand theatrically to her breast and said, "I don't know what you're talking about."

"We have the phone records."

"There must be some mistake."

"We can talk here, or we can go to the sheriff's department and talk there," Larson offered. "Your choice."

She looked away for a moment, giving Larson's words some consideration. Like those of many redheaded people, her complexion was fair to begin with. Under the glare of the overhead bulb, her face looked washed completely of color.

At last, she said, "He was drunk, okay. He just needed someone to talk to."

"Did he come to your place?"

"Yes."

"What time would that have been?" Cork asked.

"I don't know. One o'clock, maybe a little later."

"How did he seem?" Larson said.

"Upset. He'd argued with Chastity again."

"Again?"

"It had become a fairly regular occurrence."

Cork said, "And you know this how?"

"He . . . we . . . we're friends."

"Just friends?"

"We've been friends since high school."

"What did he tell you that night?" Larson asked.

"Just that Chastity was being hard on him. As usual. They argued."

"Did he tell you what they argued about?"

"He wanted to leave her. Divorce her. She threatened if he did she would make sure he never saw his kids again."

"Why divorce her?"

"She hated him. Ridiculed him. Rode him relentlessly."

"And why was that?"

"She was a profoundly unhappy woman and she blamed him for it. The same way she used to blame Clyde Greensky."

"How do you know that?"

"Axel told me it was what Clyde told him."

"How long have you and Axel been more than friends?" Cork asked.

She looked taken aback by the suggestion, but Cork could see it was just another instance of dissembling.

"How long?" he said.

"A few months." She set her right hand on the books on the cart in much the same way someone might have place a hand on the Bible when testifying in court. Or maybe she just needed to steady herself. As Ellie Roosevelt had said, she didn't look at all well. "We dated some in high school, but he was way more interested in Chastity. He and Clyde both. All the boys, as a matter of fact. Chastity was movie star gorgeous and had quite the reputation. And no wonder, considering who her mother was. When she got herself pregnant and married Clyde, Axel went into the army. When he came back, we started seeing each other again. Not seriously, just getting reacquainted."

"He was drinking pretty heavily then," Cork said. "I picked him up enough times to know. His license was suspended for a while."

"I don't know what he did in the military, but to me, it was clear that he'd been damaged. He was in a lot of pain. He wouldn't talk to me about it. Then Clyde died and he drank even more. He was difficult to be around. It was hard to see him that way. I kept encouraging him to get help. Finally he did. Stopped his drinking. I thought things might be good for him. Maybe for us."

"But he married Chastity."

"He said she was struggling. He claimed he owed it to Clyde to take care of her and Sunny. A noble impulse," she said with bitterness. "And then, of course, there was Moonbeam."

"Not a happy marriage in the end?"

"He told me that at first, she was all sweetness and light. And he said she was really good with Sunny, and Moonbeam, too, when she came along. But by then, things were already strained between him and Chastity. And they kept going downhill from there."

"And Axel sought comfort in your arms," Larson concluded.

"He just needed someone to talk to, someone he could trust."

"How long was he with you the night his wife was murdered?" Cork asked.

"All night. I went to work as usual the next morning and heard about Chastity, that you all were looking for him. I called Axel and told him."

"When he heard about Chastity, did he seem surprised?" Larson asked.

"Absolutely dumbfounded." Then she got the gist of Larson's question. "He didn't kill her. He's not that kind of man."

"What happened after you called him?"

"I don't know. He was gone when I got home. Then I heard today that you'd arrested him."

"Did he tell you that he thought Chastity was seeing someone else?" Cork asked.

"He didn't care. He didn't love her. It was his children he was worried about."

"Sundown wasn't his," Cork reminded her.

"He thought of the boy as his. Loved him truly, like a son."

"So," Larson said, "once he arrived at your place, he stayed there all night, is that correct?"

"He just crashed. He was too drunk to go anywhere else."

Larson gave it a moment, then said, "And what about you?"

She held up her hand, looking distressed, and said, "I'm going to puke."

With that, she headed quickly to the basement bathroom.

CHAPTER 18

"I can't see it," Cork said. "Our librarian a brutal killer?"

"She loves him, wants him, but his bitch of a wife won't cut him loose," Larson replied. "Killing Chastity would certainly clear the way. And like Celine Fineday reported, Boshey told Bernadette he wished Chastity was dead. So maybe she decided it was time to make that happen."

They were headed back toward the sheriff's department. They'd left Bernadette Polaski in the basement of the library, looking ill and frightened, like a desperate little rabbit in a dark hole. She'd insisted that she hadn't left her apartment once Axel arrived and she'd continued to claim that Axel hadn't either.

"What about the bloody clothing in the woodshed?" Cork pointed out to Larson. "That certainly wasn't hers."

"Maybe it wasn't her alone. Maybe they did it together. But one thing's for sure. We can't take anything she said at face value. She started our interview with a lie. Who knows what else she might have been lying about? When we asked permission to search her place, she said no. That should tell you something."

"I think we've got enough for a search warrant," Cork said.

"I'll move on that ASAP."

"Lots more questions for Axel, too. Jo and Patsy Boshey will be coming to see him at one."

At the courthouse, Larson split off and headed upstairs to the chambers of Judge Parrant to see about securing a warrant to search Bernadette Polaski's apartment. Cork found Deputy Marsha Dross at her desk in the common area, sipping coffee and eating one of the oatmeal cookies Bos had brought in that day. She was alone.

"Where's Bos?" Cork asked.

"Went across the street to the Broiler to grab a BLT. I'm holding down the fort. By the way, Jo and Patsy Boshey are here."

"Where?"

"In the interview room with Axel."

"You let them meet with him?"

"Jo insisted we allow her to talk to her client. And Bos told me you were expecting them."

"They're early," Cork said. "How long have they been in there?"

"Fifteen minutes, maybe."

"Any sign of Hanover?"

"Nope. Or any other reporters."

The door to the interview room opened and Jo stepped out. "Oh good, Cork. You're here."

"I thought I said one o'clock."

"Patsy was eager to see her son. Axel has a request, Cork. He'd like to talk to Father Jude."

"I'll call and see if Saint Jag's available. But I have a few questions for Axel before I let him see anyone else."

"I think we're ready."

"Just you and me and your client. I don't want Patsy in there."

"All right. Give me a few minutes." She headed back into the interview room.

Larson returned from his errand. "I caught Judge Parrant eating his lunch. He's amenable to signing off on a warrant. I'll get that put together now."

"It'll have to wait. Jo's here and Boshey's ready for another round of questioning."

It was just Axel and Jo in the interview room with Cork and Ed Larson. Larson had started the tape recorder on the table and had the video camera mounted on an upper wall going.

"Axel, where did you stay last night?" he asked.

"I woke up in my truck this morning. Must've slept there all night."

"Where was this?"

"Grant Park."

"Not Bernadette Polaski's apartment?"

The reaction was short-lived, but Cork could see that Boshey was surprised.

"I told you. My truck. In Grant Park."

"Who did you call last night when you were at the North Star?"

"Nobody."

"It wasn't Bernadette?"

"I told you. Nobody."

"The phone records we have tell a different story," Larson said.

"But you still maintain that you slept in your truck?" Cork asked.

"Yes."

"Think again," Larson said. "Where did you spend the night?"

"He's already answered that question," Jo said. "Several times."

"We spoke with Bernadette Polaski earlier today, Counselor,"

Cork said. "She told us Axel showed up at her place and stayed with her all night."

"I don't remember that," Boshey said, too quickly.

"Because you blacked out?" Larson asked.

"Yeah."

"We know you left the North Star just before midnight and didn't show up at Bernadette's until a little after one. That's nearly an hour and a half. It's maybe half an hour from the bar into town." Larson paused a moment, then said, "So, what did you did do in that other hour?"

"I told you, I don't remember."

"Is it true you wanted to divorce Chastity?"

"How—?" he started, then it dawned on him.

"That's right," Larson said. "Bernadette told us. True?"

"She was impossible to live with."

"But she threatened that if you divorced her, you'd never see your children again, is that right?"

Boshey nodded.

"Could you give me a verbal response?"

"That's right," Boshey said.

"If you wanted to be rid of her and divorce wasn't an option, killing her might be one way out of the marriage."

Boshey made no response.

"Any idea how your clothing—the pants, shirt, shoes, gloves that we found hidden in the woodshed—got stained with your wife's blood?" Larson went on.

"You don't know for sure that they're Axel's," Jo said. "Nor that the blood is Chastity's."

"We'll know pretty soon," Larson said. "Axel, you say you can't remember what happened, so isn't it possible you killed your wife and tried to hide the clothes that got bloodied in the attack?"

"I don't know. I don't remember." He gave Larson a sudden,

CHAPTER 19

"Tell me about that night," Cork said.

He and Ed Larson sat across from Axel Boshey in the interview room. The tape recorder was running. The video camera on the wall was recording as well. Jo sat beside her client.

"It's all pretty fuzzy. I just remember bits and pieces," Boshey replied.

"Tell me what you remember."

"I remember leaving the North Star. I was pretty blitzed. I don't remember much about the drive. I must've gone straight home because the next thing I remember is arguing some more with Chastity. Lots of yelling and screaming."

"What time would this have been?"

"I don't know exactly. I don't have a clear recollection of time."

"Go on."

"I don't remember killing her, not really, but I must've done it. I remember looking at her on the floor, all that blood."

"Do you remember picking up the poker and hitting her with it?" Ed Larson asked.

Boshey thought a moment. "Yeah, I guess."

"And then you proceeded to stab her with it. Do you remember how many times?"

"I don't know. Seven, I think. I had to be out of my mind."

"The bloody clothing we found at your place? Where did you hide those things?"

"The woodshed?"

"That's a question, not an answer."

"The woodshed." Through much of the interview, Boshey had been looking down at the table, but now he looked Ed Larson in the eye. "I swear I didn't go there to kill her. But she was such a monster. Except when it came to her kids, I don't think she had a loving bone in her body."

"Do you remember Moonbeam crying in the other room?" Cork asked.

Boshey had been fairly composed until this moment. At the mention of his daughter, his face fell and his eyes watered. "All alone, my poor little thing. How could I do that? How could I leave her all alone like that?"

Tears began to roll down his cheeks, and once again he stared at the table. "I wanted to divorce Chastity. Mostly for the sake of the kids. All we did, Chastity and me, was fight. I thought if I took Sunny and Moonbeam and raised them on the rez among family, with a sense of their heritage, it could be different for them, better. But Chastity couldn't let go. I understand. She loved those kids more than anything or anyone. She told me I was nothing but a drunk Indian and no judge was going to give her kids to a drunk Indian. She said she'd make sure I never saw them again." Boshey lifted his gaze, and Cork could see all the misery of the man's soul reflected in those eyes. "Nothing but a drunk Indian. She was right."

* * *

"A confession full of holes," Jo said. "He remembers so little."

"He remembers important details, Jo," Cork said. "We'll continue to question him. Sometimes it takes a little prodding before they remember everything."

"Or before they embrace the answers you suggest to them?"

"I don't operate that way."

"He's exhausted. And scared. And still very confused. I wouldn't trust anything he says."

"You'll be there every time we question him. But we have enough to take to our county attorney. You should go to Patsy and let her know what's happened."

"Will I see you at Jenny's school program?"

"I'll be there."

Ed Larson, who was at his desk in the common area, watched her go. "You might be sleeping on the couch tonight, Cork."

"Talk to Ben Shaver. Tell our county attorney what we've got in terms of evidence and give him a transcript of the confession, such as it is."

"All right. Then I'm going to execute the search warrant for Bernadette Polaski's apartment. I'm sure there's more to her involvement in this than she's let on. What about you?"

"I'm heading to St. Agnes. I'd like to talk to our priest about his conversation with Boshey. Then I've got a school program to attend. Keep me posted on what you find at Bernadette's place. And you should schedule a press briefing. Hell Hanover will be delighted with the news."

Cork knocked at the rectory door, which was opened by Ellie Gruber, a stout woman with an ample bosom and graying hair pulled up in a loose bun. She'd been the housekeeper for the rectory since Cork was a teenager and old Father Kelsey was not so old and not so doddering. Cork could hear the television on in a room somewhere behind her. Then he heard the voice of Father Kelsey bellow, "Not another fastball, you idiot!"

"The Twins," Ellie said. "They're playing pretty good today. But the Father, he's never satisfied."

"I'm looking for Father Jude."

"At the church, in his office. I don't know what happened at the jail, but when he came back, he looked like someone had shot his dog."

"Thanks, Ellie."

Cork walked across the street to the church, a tidy stone structure that had been a part of Cork's life since he'd been baptized. He didn't consider himself especially devout. There was a lot of Church doctrine he questioned. And all his life he'd listened to that part of him that was Anishinaabe, that spoke to him in a spiritual way much looser and, in many ways, much easier to embrace than the rigors of the Church. But he appreciated the community of St. Agnes and, when he sat in a pew on Sunday, the same pew he'd sat in with his parents as a kid, he felt the deep thread of history that tied his own family to that part of his past.

He found the priest not in his office but sitting alone in the sanctuary, staring at the crucifix on the altar. Afternoon sunlight slanted through the stained-glass windows on the west side and threw a multicolored blanket across the man. He didn't seem to be praying but was clearly deep in thought. He was startled when Cork stepped up next to him.

"Sorry, Jude," Cork said. "Didn't mean to surprise you."

"Sometimes I get so deep into reverie, I'm in another universe," the priest said.

"Wouldn't happen to be thinking about Axel Boshey, would you?"

"Heavy on my mind. So tragic. Have a seat."

Cork sat beside him in the pew. "Can I ask you what you said to Axel, or he to you, that turned him around?"

"Turned him around?"

"That confession of his seemed to come out of nowhere."

The priest nodded and made a noncommittal sound in his throat.

"So, what did he tell you?"

The priest took a deep breath. "He prayed. That's all. I listened to his prayers."

"What did he pray for?"

"Although he didn't ask for pardon, it felt to me like a confession, Cork. So, I can't really tell you."

"Was it about killing his wife and about contrition?"

"I can't tell you."

"But whatever he said, it's clearly weighing on you."

"So many of the things I hear in confession weigh on me. Part of the job."

"Taking the guilt of others on your shoulders?"

"Not their guilt, Cork. Their turmoil."

"So, Axel is in turmoil. Because of the guilt he feels?"

"No matter how many ways you ask me, I can't tell you anything. But I will tell you this, that man is deeply concerned about those he loves."

"His children?"

"His children are among them."

"Bernadette Polaski?"

"Cork, would you stop with the inquisition."

"So, Bernadette Polaski," Cork said, nodding. "She certainly contributes a lovely soprano voice to our choir. And she's also been contributing comfort to Axel Boshey, probably for some time now. But I'd guess you know that, if she's been honest with you in her confessions."

"We all need to feel loved, Cork."

"In my experience, Jude, love is at the heart of some of the darkest deeds human beings are capable of committing."

The priest settled his soft gray eyes on Cork. "I hear a lot of difficult truths in the confessional. But they haven't yet turned me to the kind of cynicism I hear from you right now. You make me glad I'm a priest seeing to the soul and not a cop seeing to the law."

"We all have our crosses to bear, Jude. Thanks for the conversation." Cork stood and left the priest to the quiet of the sanctuary.

CHAPTER 20

The bleachers in the gymnasium of the Aurora Elementary and Middle School were crowded with kids and parents. Cork knew the gym well from years of PE and playing on the school basketball team in the seventh and eighth grades. He'd been a point guard and a pretty fair shot. Although the Aurora Timberwolves were never the league leaders, they'd won far more games than they lost.

He sat with Jo in the top row, the residual smell of decades of adolescent sweat wafting up through the air. Next to them sat Dean Barstow, whose grandson was in Jenny's class. Barstow had taught industrial arts at the high school. He'd been Cork's shop teacher and the baseball coach as well. Cork had never liked the man much. In the early course of his teaching career, Barstow had lost part of the little finger on his right hand to a band saw. As a result, behind his back, his students called him "Old Four and a Half." A "deano" became a measure of four and half inches, as in "It's about two deanos long." It was cruel, to be certain, but that's the way kids often were.

"Terrible business, what happened to Chastity Boshey," Barstow said. He leaned toward Cork to be heard above the hubbub of the gym. The odor of whiskey ghosted off his breath. Cork had occasionally smelled the same thing back in high school. Which probably went a long way in explaining the loss of half the man's pinkie to a band saw. "Understand you've arrested Axel Boshey. That boy was nothing but trouble in my shop class. Went after another kid with a wood chisel once."

"Why?"

"Kid said something about him being Indian. Got Boshey suspended for a while."

"And the other kid?"

"Don't remember. But I coulda told you back then that Boshey would come to no good. Hell, he killed Clyde Greensky."

"That was ruled an accident, Dean."

"Greensky's still dead." Barstow shook his head. "Was only a matter of time before things caught up to Boshey."

Cork glanced at Jo, who, he could tell, was on the verge of telling Old Four and a Half exactly what she thought of him. Cork said, "Nice talking to you, Dean. Here come the kids."

They paraded out, more than a dozen of them, some in the dress of ancient mariners, others in what passed for Indian costumes, colorful blankets around their shoulders, tourist shop headdresses with dyed feathers crowning their heads. A couple of the boys held rubber tomahawks. Cork cringed.

It was a playing out of all the myths about Columbus and the Native people, the same things Cork had been taught in elementary school. But as a kid, he'd had another source of information on the true history of North America and its indigenous people—his grandmother Dilsey. She'd been true-blood Iron Lake Ojibwe, an educated woman, a teacher, and a staunch advocate for her people. "Lies, Corkie," she would say. "Nothing but lies. Columbus didn't discover America. Our people had been here for thousands of years. We had wonderful cultures, complex languages, beautiful artistry. But let me tell you, from the moment that bumbling sea captain landed on this side of the Atlantic, the European people and their ancestors have done nothing but lie, cheat, steal, and do their best to get rid of us original inhabitants. Columbus Day my ass. They should call it Total Crap Day, Corkie."

So, when Jenny delivered her enthusiastic greeting—"Welcome, white strangers!"—Cork could practically hear Grandma Dilsey turning in her grave.

After the charade was finished, Cork and Jo picked Jenny and Anne up, and they drove home together.

"I want to be in the play next year," Annie said. "I want to be an Indian, too."

"I have some issues with Columbus Day, little pumpkin," Cork said. "It's not everything you think."

Jo said, "I heard that some people in California have started calling it Indigenous Peoples' Day now."

"What's an Indigenous people?" Annie asked.

Cork said, "When we get home, we have a lot of talking to do."

He was back at the department an hour later. Ed Larson and his team had returned from searching Bernadette Polaski's apartment.

"Nothing," Larson said. "But I spoke with Ellie Roosevelt, who said Bernadette left the library shortly after our conversation with her. So she had time to clean the place up, hide anything incriminating. She was looking pretty pale the whole time we were there. Maybe afraid she'd missed something that we'd find?"

"It might be worthwhile bringing her in for a more official

interview. Threaten her with aiding and abetting, put some pressure on her."

Larson glanced at his watch. "I've got the press briefing in an hour. I need to write up an official statement."

"I'll let you handle that solo. You're good in the spotlight."

"Gee, thanks. But I won't be alone. Ben Shaver wants in on this."

"Our county attorney is up for reelection. I'm sure he thinks that if he brings in a conviction, particularly of an Indian, it'll be a cakewalk in the voting booths. While you take care of that, I'll go see about bringing in Bernadette."

When she answered Cork's knock, she was a mess. Her eyes were red, her cheeks tearstained, her hair mussed as if she'd been running her hands through it constantly. Her face was paler than ever.

The first thing Cork said was "You need to sit down, Bernadette."

She didn't object. She stepped back to her small sofa and dropped onto a cushion as if she had no strength.

Cork scooted an armchair near her and sat. "Are you okay?"

"Not at all," she said. "Everything's falling apart."

"What's everything?"

"My whole life." She bent over, holding her stomach as if in pain, and began to cry.

"Hey, Bernadette, it's okay."

"No, it isn't. Nothing's okay. Nothing will ever be okay." She looked up at Cork, her expression pleading. "Axel didn't kill Chastity. I swear it."

"And you know this how?"

"I know him. I know his heart. There's no murder in it."

Cork nodded as if in understanding. "What about your heart?"

Through her sobs, Bernadette managed to say, "I wanted her dead so many times."

Cork kept his voice gentle. "And was it finally too much?"

Bernadette's breathing came in wet little gasps. Then her eyes opened wide. "Wait a minute. I didn't kill her."

"It would certainly be understandable. She was a monster."

"I didn't kill her. And Axel didn't either. You know who you should be talking to? Aphrodite McGill."

"Why Aphrodite?"

"Axel told me she and Chastity used to fight tooth and nail."

"Did he say what they argued about?"

"Blame, for one thing."

"Blame? For what?"

"Chastity's unhappiness. How she was with men. She claimed Aphrodite had been a horrible mother. Selfish, neglectful. Abusive. That she'd tried to steal every man Chastity was ever interested in."

"What did that mean?"

"Axel told me Aphrodite was nothing short of a nymphomaniac. Anyone who walked through the door at Shangri-La was fair game. That was Chastity's take on her mother, anyway. Axel told me Chastity swore she'd never set foot in Shangri-La again and wouldn't let her kids visit Aphrodite there. If she wanted to see her grandchildren, Aphrodite had to come to the cabin."

"What did you mean about how Chastity was with men?"

"She had a reputation in high school. Maybe it was exaggerated because she was gorgeous and attracted boys like flies to honey. But Axel was sure she was seeing someone behind his back."

"He didn't care?"

"He didn't love her. She didn't love him. From what Axel told me, except for her kids, she was incapable of true affection."

"But she wouldn't divorce him."

"She had two children to feed and clothe. He had a job, a regular paycheck."

"Aphrodite McGill is quite well off. Didn't she help?"

"Chastity didn't want anything from her mother. That's what Axel told me, anyway."

"Why did you leave the library early today?"

"I didn't feel well. And your guys rummaging all through my place hasn't helped any. What were they looking for? Proof that I killed Chastity? They didn't find anything because I didn't kill her. And neither did Axel."

"Bernadette, Axel has confessed to killing Chastity."

Everything stopped. Her crying, her moving, her breathing. She sat like a woman carved of wood, her mouth agape. "No," she finally whispered.

"I took down his confession this afternoon."

"No. He's lying."

"He knew details, Bernadette."

"He couldn't have. He was so drunk when he came here that he could barely stand up."

"And he just crashed?"

"Yes. Once he lay down, he didn't move a muscle."

"If he's lying, is it possible he's covering for someone?"

"Yes, that's got to be it."

"Covering for someone he loves?" Cork eyed her steadily. "Someone who wanted him but couldn't have him?"

She sat back, looking even more devastated, if that was possible. "No, you're not tricking me. I'm not talking to you anymore."

Cork thought about pressing her to come to the department for further questioning. He was certain it was what Captain Ed Larson would have done. But assessing the woman in front of him, who seemed on the verge of collapse, he chose not to.

"You look as if you could use some help, Bernadette. Is there someone I could call?"

"No one. There's no one."

Except Axel Boshey, Cork thought. And he was likely to be out of her reach for a very long time.

CHAPTER 21

"You didn't bring her in?"

Captain Ed Larson sat at his desk, watching Cork enter the department. He was clearly surprised, maybe disappointed as well.

"She was a mess, Ed. I don't think we'd have got anything out of her. How'd the briefing go?"

"Hell Hanover practically did a jig."

"And Ben Shaver?"

"Monday's a holiday, so Boshey will be arraigned first thing Tuesday morning."

"The charge?"

"Considering the evidence, the threat over the phone, the confession, he's going for murder in the first degree."

"The confession is pretty spotty. And Axel being blind drunk, that could be problem."

"Yeah," Larson agreed. "And I still think there's more to Bernadette Polaski's part in this."

"I think we've got another angle to consider, Ed. Bernadette told me that Aphrodite and Chastity argued a lot."

"Did she say what about?"

"Apparently, Chastity blamed her mother for all her unhappiness. Sounds like it went back to her childhood at Shangri-La. According to Bernadette, Chastity wouldn't set foot in that place and wouldn't let her kids visit their grandmother there."

Bos Swain, who was going through a stack of papers at the contact desk, said, "Aphrodite's love fests at her hippie haven out there on Apostle's Cove have been grist for the gossip mill here for years."

Larson considered a moment, then said, "I suppose it could be true. But you're suggesting that we take a serious look at Aphrodite for her daughter's murder?"

"You saw how out of control she was this morning," Cork said.

"Boshey's already confessed."

"As you just said, his memory of the night is pretty spotty."

"But with enough detail there to make me believe it," Larson said.

"I'd still like to see what he has to say about this."

"Should we call Jo?"

"Probably. But let's see if Axel's willing to talk without her."

Boshey was lying on his cot, staring up at the ceiling. He turned his head when Cork and Larson stepped up to the cell door.

Cork said, "A few questions for you, Axel."

Boshey didn't reply, just turned his gaze back toward the ceiling.

"Chastity and Aphrodite argued a good deal. True?"

"Yeah."

"What about?"

"Everything. But mostly about the past, about growing up at Shangri-La."

"Any idea why?"

"Chastity was never real clear. But I always suspected it had to do with Aphrodite's approach to sex."

"Which was?"

"Anytime, anywhere, with anyone, male or female, didn't matter. Although she didn't say it, I think Aphrodite might have involved Chastity in some of what went on. Whatever it was that happened out there, it really screwed her up."

"How?"

"She wasn't a faithful wife. Not with me, not with Clyde."

"Did that make you mad?"

"I didn't marry Chastity out of love. I married her because Sunny needed a father, and, as it became obvious to everyone, Chastity was pregnant with our daughter, Moonbeam. But the truth is, Chastity treated me pretty nice, until after the ring was on her finger."

"What about Aphrodite?"

"What do you mean?"

"Did Aphrodite show an interest in you?"

"She hated me. The feeling was mutual."

"Was it always that way?"

It took Boshey a long time to respond. "Not always."

"When would that have been?"

Boshey thought some more, then sat up and swung his legs off the cot.

"Back in high school, when Clyde and me were both dating Chastity. Aphrodite used to call me and him a couple of young bucks. If we were wearing T-shirts, she'd ask us to flex our muscles so she could feel them. And not just our biceps. She had her hands all over us. She was a good-looking woman. Older, so it was a little exciting to know she was interested." He shook his head. "Since I married Chastity, I haven't had anything but grief from her. Clyde told me it was the same with him. He thought she considered us okay to fool around with but not good enough to marry her daughter."

"Considering everything you knew about her, why did you marry Chastity?"

"Mostly out of loyalty to Clyde. And for Sunny. And she was already pregnant with Moonbeam. And, I guess, because she seemed to really need me. Turned out to be the worst decision of my life."

"You killed Chastity," Larson said. "Seems to me a worse decision."

Boshey eyed him steadily. "Not a decision. Just happened. Look, if we're going to talk anymore, I want my lawyer."

"That's okay. We're done here," Cork said.

Axel lay back down and returned to staring at the ceiling.

Larson called it a day. Cork had paperwork on his desk related to the budget he would present to the commissioners at their next meeting. Before he could begin, Deputy Marsha Dross knocked at his door.

"Still here?" he said.

"Just finishing up my shift. But I'm glad I caught you. There's something I think you ought to know."

"What's that?"

She stepped in and sat down. "I was ten-seven at the Pinewood Broiler for a late lunch. I was seated at a front window, and I saw Lucy Martinelli just standing on the sidewalk, kind of frozen."

"Rocky's wife?"

"Yeah. She was just standing there in front of the Rialto Theater, staring at a poster for one of the coming attractions."

"I've seen that poster. A movie called *Child's Play*. I understand it's about a doll possessed by the spirit of a serial killer. The demon toy on that poster is scary enough to make any parent think twice before giving their little girl a doll this Christmas."

"I don't think she was really looking at the poster. She seemed to be just sort of disoriented, so I went out and asked her to join me for lunch."

"Do you know Lucy well?"

"We knew each other in high school, both of us were lifeguards on Gull Lake. Rocky was a lifeguard there, too. In those days, he was drop-dead gorgeous, a hunk. We were all interested in him, Lucy and me and pretty much every other female lifeguard, but Lucy was way more serious. There was something a little scary about him, even back then. And I could see that he was just a player. I worried about her because she seemed so fragile. Then she ended up marrying him."

"You said she looked disoriented. How so?"

"Such a faraway look in her eyes. So I asked her if everything was okay. Instead of answering she asked if I'm happy being single."

"What did you tell her?"

"That I was quite happy with my career and didn't at the moment feel the need for a husband in my life. I asked her how things were with her and Rocky and the kids."

"And?"

"She said they were in God's hands now."

"God's hands? What did she mean?"

"She claimed she experienced a miracle. She'd been purified. Made a virgin again."

"What?"

"I know. And she told me she'd been given a new name. Magdalene."

"Given by whom?"

"An angel of the Lord. I told her I didn't understand. She said it didn't matter. She and Rocky go to St. Agnes, don't they?"

"She's a regular and brings the kids," Cork said. "But I haven't seen Rocky there in forever."

"What she was saying, it all sounded very biblical. But before I could press her any further, her father comes storming in. Wild Bill grabs her, tells her he's been looking for her everywhere. I said we were just having a quiet lunch together, and I asked him if Lucy was okay. He tells me to mind my own business and hustles her out of there. Look, I just thought maybe you'd want to know and maybe because she goes to your church, you might want to follow up with your priest. And maybe you could talk to Rocky, too. I just want to be sure Lucy and the kids are okay."

"Thanks, Marsha. I'll take it from here."

"If you talk to Rocky, I'd rather you didn't tell him it came from me. We've never been very . . ." She looked for the right word and settled on, ". . . collegial."

"You're not alone in that," Cork said.

He called home and told Rose he would be late and not to wait dinner on him. Then he went to the home of Rocky Martinelli. When the suspended deputy opened the door, Cork heard a chaos of children's voices coming from inside. Martinelli gave him a cold look.

"Don't suppose you've come to apologize, Sheriff?"

"Is Lucy here?"

"Why?"

"Your wife was downtown today, apparently looking pretty lost. You wouldn't know anything about that, would you?"

"Like I told you before, she's staying with her father for a while. Maybe you should be talking to him."

"An associate confided in me that Lucy's claiming she experienced a miracle, Rocky. She claims to have become a virgin again."

"What the hell are you talking about? Who told you that?"

"I'd rather not say. She also claims an angel gave her a new name. Magdalene. And, Rocky, she said her children were in God's hands."

"Oh, Jesus."

"Do you know anything about this?"

"I don't. And I'd appreciate it if you didn't go spreading rumors."

One of Rocky's three children, a little boy with a snotty nose and hair falling into his face, pulled at his father's pant leg. "Joey took my sandwich."

"I'll make you another one. Now get back to the kitchen."

The boy glanced at Cork without a hint of curiosity and vanished into the distant chaos.

"Look, whatever's going on with Lucy, I'll take care of it, okay?"

"Fine."

Just before Martinelli slammed the door, Cork heard him mutter, "Shit."

"She's been . . ." Jo thought a moment. "Vacant, I guess, lately. Distracted whenever I talk to her at church."

They lay in bed. Cork had come home in time to read his daughters to sleep. He'd eaten a bit of the macaroni and cheese Rose had made for dinner and reheated for him. Then Rose had gone up to her room to settle in with one of her gothic romance novels, and he and Jo had called it a day as well. Now they lay in bed talking quietly in the dark. Cork had confided to Jo about Lucy Martinelli.

"I just figured that, like all mothers with young children, she's feeling overwhelmed," Jo went on. "I got the sense that Rocky never helps out much at home. But obviously it's more than that."

"There's a lot of anger in that man."

"Do you think he's aware of whatever's going on with Lucy?"

"He pointed me toward Wild Bill, so I don't know."

"Everything you've told me, it all sounds very biblical, just like Marsha said. Maybe you should check that out, Cork."

"With Saint Jag, you think?"

"I'd start there. If I wanted to get something off my chest, I'd go to him over Father Kelsey."

Cork lay a long time thinking about secrets, the kind that people probably confessed to the priest and the kind they held locked deep inside and confessed to no one. He considered Chastity and her mother and their arguments. He considered Rocky Martinelli and his wife's bizarre claim. He considered Wild Bill Gunderson and his affair with the commissioner's wife, and Bernadette Polaski and Axel Boshey, and he thought about all the lies involved, and, not for the first time, about how the secrets people tried to keep, especially in a place like Aurora, never stayed hidden for long.

Jo was asleep by then, but he laid his arm across her belly, across the rounding that was the baby she carried. He couldn't feel the child move yet, but he felt the warmth of the body that held it. Then he moved his hand up and felt the slow bump of Jo's heart, a heart as true as any he'd ever known. He trusted that no dark secrets were hidden there, and he thought to himself that he was a lucky man. No, not just lucky. Blessed.

CHAPTER 22

Saturdays always felt special in the O'Connor house, but when the children came bouncing onto their parents' bed that morning shouting, "Ghosts and goblins and witches, Daddy!" Cork remembered that this Saturday would be more special than most.

He put a pillow over his head and said, "I can't hear you."

"You promised!" Jenny sang, and Annie echoed, "You promised!"

Cork uncovered his head. "Promised what? I don't remember any promises."

"Halloween, Daddy!" Jenny said. "We're going to decorate for Halloween."

"Halloween? Never heard of it. But if it's goblins you're interested in, here's one." He made an awful face and let out a howl.

"Daddy!" Annie cried, falling back, but laughing.

"All right, all right," Cork said. "We decorate today, but after lunch. I have something to do first thing this morning. Where's your mother?"

"Her and Aunt Rose are fixing breakfast," Annie said.

"Your mother's cooking?"

"Not really," Jenny said. "Mostly she's just drinking coffee and talking. Get up, Daddy! It's late."

He found Jo in the kitchen, still in her bathrobe sitting at the table, a half-empty mug of coffee in front of her. Rose stood at the stove, where bacon was sizzling and popping in a frying pan.

"Did you sic the kids on me, Jo?" Cork asked.

"I did encourage them to wake the lazybones, if that's what you mean."

"It's Saturday. I get to sleep late on Saturdays."

"Not when the kids are crazy to put up scarecrows and witches."

"And carve jack-o'-lanterns," Rose said, turning from the stove with a pair of tongs in her hand. "We picked out pumpkins yesterday at the IGA."

Jo said, "Jenny told me Halloween is her favorite holiday after Christmas."

Cork poured himself a mug of coffee from the pot sitting on the coffeemaker. "Not a holiday."

"I'll let you explain that to her. In the meantime, you're committed."

Cork sat at the table. He could smell the bacon and realized he was hungry. "Got a couple of things to take care of first."

"Like what?" Jo asked.

"Carole Anderson at the hospital lab said she'd have the toxicology results for Chastity Boshey ready for me this morning. I'll pick those up."

"Any chance you'd let me in on the result?"

"You know better than that, Counselor. Then I'm heading over to St. Agnes. I want to talk to Saint Jag about Lucy Martinelli."

"Lucy?" Rose said. She'd been lifting the bacon from the frying pan and setting the pieces on a paper towel, but now she turned. "What about Lucy?"

Although Rose was a good-hearted person, Cork knew that

she was also a lover of gossip. In a small town, who wasn't? But he knew, too, that if he swore his sister-in-law to secrecy, it was a pledge she would keep.

"I don't want this going any farther than this kitchen, Rose. Okay?"

"You have my word."

He explained to her what Marsha Dross had told him.

"Married to a man like Rocky Martinelli, it's bound to drive any woman over the edge. But what about the children? Are they in any . . ." Rose thought about her choice of words and finally settled on "Should we be concerned about their safety?"

"At the moment, I don't think so. But I'd like to talk to Father Jude, get his take on it, if he has one."

"We'll do our best to hold Jenny and Annie at bay until you get back. But," Rose said, aiming the hot tongs at him, "you have promises to keep."

"And miles to go before I sleep," Cork said, lifting his coffee for a sip.

The priest's red Jaguar was parked in the church lot. Cork found Saint Jag in his office, working on a computer. The office in many ways reflected the complexities of Father Jude Monroe. There were photographs on the wall: Monroe in his football uniform, poised to throw a long bomb; Monroe in rappelling gear on the lip of a sheer cliff; Monroe posing with the Pope. In all of them, he was handsome in a way that Jo and Rose had confided many women of St. Agnes found uncomfortably attractive.

"Morning, Cork." The priest offered him a golden boy smile.

"At work on Sunday's homily, Jude?"

"Father Kelsey will be in the pulpit tomorrow. Just catching up on paperwork. Not here for confession, are you?"

"A couple of questions about one of your parishioners."

The priest lost his smile. "Not Bernadette Polaski."

"No. Lucy Martinelli."

The priest turned from his computer and held his hand out toward an empty chair. Cork sat down and said, "What can you tell me about Lucy?"

"Why do you ask?"

"For one thing, she was looking pretty disoriented yesterday. She's claiming to have experienced a miracle."

"What kind of miracle?"

"She says that she's been made a virgin, and an angel has given her a new name. Magdalene. I'm wondering if she might have talked to you about this. Or anything else that might shed some light on her situation."

Saint Jag frowned, then spent a few moments considering his next words. "Her father's Bill Gunderson. What do you think of him?"

"Wild Bill? He's always been a self-absorbed son of a bitch. What has that got to do with anything?"

"His wife drowned when Lucy was quite young and he raised his daughter alone. What kind of husband and father do you imagine a man like that might be?"

"No Mister Rogers, I'm sure."

"Father Kelsey told me that Gunderson used to attend St. Agnes. Since I arrived here, I haven't seen him in church once."

"He was never a regular," Cork said. "After the scandal, he stopped coming altogether. You know about that, yes?"

"Bedding the wife of a commissioner, I understand."

"That's right. But even though her father wasn't especially devout, Lucy was always here. Baptized, confirmed, married in this church."

"Lucy has come to me several times for counseling. We've

talked a lot about her childhood. I can't go into detail, but she's struggled with issues from her past. I've encouraged her to seek professional help, therapy, but she's been resistant. Afraid of the stigma. You know how a small town can be. But she's also afraid of her father."

"Rocky told me she's staying with Wild Bill right now."

The priest seemed to puzzle this. "I may have to make a visit."

"What about her husband? Has she talked to you about him?"

"I can't go there, Cork. Too many privileged conversations in that regard."

"Rocky didn't seem to know about his wife's fantasies."

"Like his father-in-law, he's more Catholic in name than in practice. He almost never comes to mass. So I don't know if he's aware of his wife's state of mind. He's one of your deputies. Is this something you might talk to him about?"

"I have. He seemed ignorant. There are no real legal grounds at the moment for me to pursue it any further. But let me ask you this. Do you think she presents a danger to herself or her children? I'm asking as an officer of the law now."

"There's nothing I know that would lead me to believe she's a threat in that way. She's just very confused sometimes. As soon as I can, I'll head out to her father's place and talk to them both."

Cork stood up and thanked the priest.

"See you in church tomorrow?" Saint Jag asked.

"I'm ushering."

That golden boy smile returned. "Place in heaven for you, Cork."

Shangri-La. That's what Aphrodite McGill called her home on Apostle's Cove. It was an odd-looking structure, built in the late 1960s by a wealthy architect who'd spent a good deal of time in

Asia and who, everyone in Tamarack County speculated, was tripping on LSD the whole time he was at work on the place. The result was a bizarre mixture of Prairie School design and pagodas. He'd been a kind of guru as well, attracting a gaggle of misfits and malcontents searching for a place that might reconnect them with nature instead of a modern world, a place where they might finally fit in. Shangri-La, most of them came to realize, was not that place, and gradually they drifted off in search of other elusive Edens. But one disciple stayed, a free spirit who called herself Aphrodite and who, while in residence at Shangri-La, had given birth to a daughter. There was no father listed on the birth certificate, but she'd married the crazy architect, so most folks in Aurora assumed it must have been him. When he died of a barbiturate overdose, he left Shangri-La to Aphrodite, along with his substantial financial holdings. Aphrodite and her daughter were set for life.

Apostle's Cove is a small inlet on Iron Lake a couple of miles south of Aurora. It was so named because an early missionary, who'd come to the wilderness to convert the heathens, had briefly established himself there. The rigors of life in that far north wilderness, so the story went, led to madness, and he ended up claiming to be one of the twelve Apostles, St. Peter to be exact. In the end he was hauled back to wherever it was he came from. But the cove retained the name that hinted at his unsettled state of mind.

Shangri-La had been built on a point of the cove. From the vast back terrace of the estate, the distant lights of Aurora were visible, as Aphrodite was fond of saying, "like the sparkle of fairy dust." The front of the grounds opened onto the county highway, and passing vehicles were treated not only to the view of the flat roofs and jutting pagodas but very often to the sight of Aphrodite's pink, flower-decorated VW bug, which she parked conspicuously in front of her home. She'd had several Beetles over the years, all of them pink and all of them named Tinker Bell.

When Cork pulled into the circular drive, he saw that a shiny black pickup sat behind the current iteration of Tinkerbell. In a county like Tamarack, black pickup trucks were a dime a dozen. He parked, rang the front doorbell, and from inside heard the melodious notes of three little gongs. It took a while for Aphrodite to open the door. When she did, she wore only a silk kimono, her feet were bare, her toenails painted cinnamon red. Her raven hair was swept up in a bun, held in place by an ornate Japanese pin. Loose tresses trailed down the nape of her neck like little black snakes. Her eyes were a bit unfocused. But she didn't look at all like the crazy woman who'd attacked Cork in the sheriff's department the day before. She wore lipstick and eye shadow and face powder and a rather pleasant perfume.

"What?" she said abruptly.

"May I come in, Aphrodite?"

"What for?"

"Some things we need to talk about."

"We can talk here."

From inside came a man's voice: "Who is it?"

Cork recognized that voice only too well. "It's Cork O'Connor, Bill," he said, speaking loud enough to be easily heard.

A moment later, Wild Bill Gunderson stepped up behind Aphrodite. He wore an undershirt and khakis. His feet were bare. His thick mane of hair was mussed a bit, as if someone had been running their hands through those silver locks.

"What do you want, O'Connor?" Gunderson demanded.

Cork was sorely tempted to ask if the ex-sheriff was there to console the grieving mother, but he diplomatically held his tongue. Instead, he said, "I understand Lucy's left Rocky and is staying with you at the moment, Bill. She was in town yesterday, looking pretty disoriented. Any idea what's going on with her?"

"She's always been a little crazy. But what the hell are you doing here?"

"A couple of important pieces of information to offer Aphrodite, and a couple of questions as well. We can do this here, or I can take Aphrodite down to the department and we can have our discussion there."

"You can't just haul her off," Gunderson said.

"She made quite a scene there yesterday morning. I still might be tempted to charge her with assaulting an officer. Plenty of witnesses. And I got the tox report from the urine sample she gave yesterday. Cocaine, Adderall, and alcohol. Quite a cocktail, some of the ingredients illegal."

"Oh, let's get this over with," Aphrodite said. "Come in."

Inside, Shangri-La was an eclectic museum of Asian influences. An extensive oriental rug covered most of the polished wood floor. Huge vases with ornate designs stood in the corners, some empty, some containing tall dried reeds with brushy ends. A delicate screen painted with cranes separated the vast living room from the equally vast dining room.

Aphrodite sat on the sofa, which had a heavy-looking frame made of some dark red wood. Gunderson sat beside her. She nodded for Cork to sit in a chair that looked a bit like a torture device.

Aphrodite picked up a gold case from the coffee table, lifted a cigarette from it, and lit the tip with a big ceramic lighter shaped like an egg. She blew smoke toward the ceiling and said, "So what is it you want to talk to me about?"

"I came to tell you that I'm releasing Chastity's body today."

"It's about time."

"I apologize for the delay, but I needed to get something checked first."

"Oh? And what was that?"

"I asked the folks at the hospital lab to run a toxicology screen of her blood. The night she died, in addition to alcohol, she'd been using cocaine."

Aphrodite tapped the ash from her cigarette onto a small ceramic tray adorned with an image of Mount Fuji. She said nothing, but her eyes seemed to focus a bit more sharply.

"Any idea where she might have got the drug?" Cork asked.

"Not from me, if that's what you're suggesting."

"I wasn't suggesting anything. Just asking."

"Maybe you should be asking Axel Boshey that question," Gunderson said. "God only knows what that man was into before he committed murder."

Cork ignored his former boss. "Aphrodite, you told me that after Chastity called you about the fight she had with Axel, you didn't go over to her place. Is that right?"

"That's right."

"Where did you go?"

"What?"

"Where did you go that night?"

"What makes you think I went anywhere?"

"One of my deputies saw you driving Tinkerbell, heading back toward Aurora around eleven."

She looked away and brushed at her kimono as if a bit of cigarette ash had fallen there, though Cork had seen nothing of the kind. "I might have been out for a drive to clear my head. I do that sometimes. I don't remember."

"Are you insinuating she had something to do with Chastity's murder?" Gunderson bellowed.

"Insinuating nothing, Bill. Like I said, just asking questions."

"I think you've asked all you're going to," Gunderson said.

"There's another reason I'm here." Cork braced himself for

what he had to say next. "Aphrodite, there's something I haven't told you about Chastity."

"What is it?"

"It's not going to be easy to hear."

Aphrodite set her cigarette in the ashtray and glared at Cork. "What is it?"

"When she died, Chastity was pregnant."

The woman's face went white, her eyes went wide, and a moment later, she fainted, toppling right into Wild Bill Gunderson's lap.

CHAPTER 23

"Fainted?" Ed Larson put down his leaf rake and took off his work gloves.

"Fell right over."

"Shock?"

"Probably combined with some medication she'd taken."

Cork had gone directly from Shangri-La to the home of his deputy, where he found Larson raking leaves in the front yard. The sky was blue and cloudless, the day unseasonably warm for late October. Under the brim of his ball cap, sweat dripped down Larson's brow. Cork had shared with him the results of the toxicology screening and then his conversation with Aphrodite McGill.

"Medication?"

"That's what she called it when she came around a minute later. She didn't get more specific."

"Got a speculation?"

"Who knows? What I do know is that she was vague about where she'd been the night Chastity was killed, probably lying to me."

"And the fainting?"

"That was real enough."

"You don't actually believe she had anything to do with her daughter's death, do you?"

"I think that despite Axel's confession, we still don't know the truth of what happened that night. Axel's scheduled to be arraigned first thing Tuesday morning. Maybe there's time to figure this out yet."

"Cork, we have a signed confession with details. Bottom line is that whatever else might have been going on that night, Axel Boshey killed his wife."

"Then why all the lies?"

"What lies?"

"Aphrodite's, Bernadette's, Axel's."

"Axel's?"

"First he tells us he doesn't remember. Then he tells us he sort of remembers. Then he fills in a few details."

"Questioning does that, sparks memories."

"I don't know, Ed. It just doesn't feel right."

"What else can we do? What rocks haven't we turned over?"

"Chastity was seeing someone, I'm sure. We don't know who that was, but we should find out."

"How?"

At the moment, Cork had no answer. "I'll let you know if anything occurs to me. But you keep puzzling it, too, okay?"

"You're the sheriff," Larson said. He watched Cork head back to the Bronco, then returned to raking his leaves.

When Cork arrived home for lunch, his children assaulted him.

"You promised we'd put up Halloween decorations today," Jenny reminded him.

"Ghosts and witches," Annie said, practically dancing.

Rose, who was setting pumpkins on the kitchen table, said, "They've been after me all morning, but I told them not until you were here."

"Where's Jo?"

"At her office. She said she had some work to catch up on."

"Daddy!" Jenny insisted. "When can we start putting everything up?"

"How long before lunch, Rose?"

"We've already eaten. But I can make you a peanut butter and jelly sandwich. Or there's some Spam I can fry up."

"A Spam sandwich sounds good."

"Halloween decorations first, Daddy," Jenny pleaded.

Rose said, "If you see to the decorations, I'll fry up some Spam. Deal?"

"Deal," Cork said. "Okay, you two, help me with the boxes. They're in the basement."

There were gravestones to be planted in the front yard, a witch on a broomstick to be hung from a low branch of the maple tree, a scarecrow to be posted beside the porch steps, two ghosts to be dangled from fishing lines one on either side of the front door, cutouts of bats and spiders to be taped to the windows. And last of all, jack-o'-lanterns to be carved and mounted on the porch steps.

Cork loved helping his daughters as they went about the decorating, though in truth, Halloween was always a bittersweet time for him. When he was thirteen, just days away from that celebration of the macabre, while Cork was raking leaves in the front yard, Cy Borkman had roared up to the house in his cruiser and delivered the devastating news that Liam O'Connor had been shot and mortally wounded. As he watched his children hang spider webbing between the uprights on the front porch, Cork considered the dark human happenings of late and thought that all the scary stories of the season didn't hold a candle to the real horrors of life.

Rose came out and said, "I have a Spam sandwich and some chips for you, Cork. And those jack-o'-lanterns are begging to be carved. I've got everything set up in the kitchen."

Cork ate his sandwich while Rose helped clean the pumpkins. Then he and his sister-in-law did some judicious guiding of hands as faces were created with special carving knives guaranteed not to cause injury. When they were finished, Rose said, "Go wash your hands, girls, while your dad and I clean up the mess."

Rose had covered the kitchen table with newspaper. Cork lifted the two pumpkins and Rose gathered the paper, which was soggy with the stringy pumpkin innards.

"You must be really good at compartmentalizing, Cork," she said.

"What's that mean?"

"You go out and investigate a horrible killing, then come home and act as if nothing's happened? Me, I can't get any of this out of my mind. I think about those poor children and about Patsy Boshey and I wonder about Axel and how someone I've sat with in a church pew could do something so gruesome. I find it all incomprehensible, and frankly, quite frightening."

"Confidentially, so do I, Rose."

"I want to believe that we're made in the image of God and that He's always with us. But where was God when Axel did what he did to Chastity?"

"That's a question for Father Jude. But, Rose, between you and me, I'm not a hundred percent sure that Axel is guilty."

"He confessed, didn't he?"

"Sort of."

"Then why are you doubting?"

"Just a feeling."

"That doesn't sound very forensic."

Cork said, "A wise man advised me that in all my considerations, there's room for feelings."

"Let me guess. Henry?"

The girls returned, Rose handed them their pumpkins, and they all trooped out to the front porch, where the jack-o'-lanterns were given prominent places on the steps. As they stood on the sidewalk to admire their work, Jo returned. She parked the car and joined them.

"Best Halloween decorations on the block," she declared.

"I love Halloween," Jenny said.

"And then we get to decorate for Christmas!" Annie cried.

"One holiday at a time," Rose said.

She and the girls headed back inside. Cork and Jo lingered.

"You look tired," Cork said. He put a hand gently on her rounded belly. "You both okay?"

"I could use a nap."

"After that, a favor."

"What favor?"

"I want to talk to your client again."

"Today?"

"Honestly, Jo, I'm not convinced that he's guilty. I think there are still questions I need to find answers to."

"You don't have a lot of time."

"I know. So," he said. "Today?"

That night as he lay in bed, Cork went over in his mind what Axel Boshey had told him that afternoon.

Chastity was doing coke before we argued. It was one of the reasons we argued. I told her she needed to stop that shit. He'd given his head a sad little shake. *This coming from a drunk.*

Cork had asked where she got the cocaine. Axel didn't know. Cork had asked if it might have come from Aphrodite.

Axel had given a nod. *That woman is a walking drugstore.*

Now, in the dark of the bedroom, Cork thought about it. Two women, one of them certainly high on cocaine, the other maybe high on that or some other mind-altering substance, both of them prone to arguing. Maybe an argument got out of hand? But an argument over what or whom? If Aphrodite were guilty of murder, why return to the scene of the crime and then call it in? Could it be that, like Axel claimed for himself, once the drug had worn off, she had no real memory of a crime she'd committed?

He wasn't sure he believed this any more than he completely believed in Axel's guilt.

He went on rolling things over in his mind.

Although Cork always tried to keep an open mind about gender when it came to crime, he couldn't help thinking that the brutality involved in Chastity's murder was far too violent for a woman to have done it. Axel believed Chastity was seeing someone. When Cork had pressed him, Axel had maintained he didn't have a clue. But he did say that he and Chastity hadn't had sex in months, so the baby she was carrying when she died wasn't his. Then whose?

"Sleep," Jo said from beside him.

"Sorry. Didn't mean to wake you."

"You can't think straight if you don't sleep. And if you don't sleep, I don't sleep."

"Do you think he's guilty, Jo?"

"He thinks he's guilty."

"What he remembers about that night is so fragmented."

"I understand, sweetheart. But I can't think straight when

I'm tired. So please go to sleep. Tomorrow we'll think about these things."

Cork gave a nod, which Jo couldn't see in the dark. For another minute, he stared at the ceiling in silence, then he said, "Tomorrow, first thing, there's something I need to do."

Jo didn't ask what that was. She was already sleeping.

CHAPTER 24

"Not going to church?" Rose said, as if Cork were committing a mortal sin.

"Duty calls," Cork replied as he headed toward the back door.

"I thought you were ushering."

"Called Bill Ambrose, asked if he'd step in for me."

"At least have some coffee." Rose held up the pot of Folgers she'd made. She was still in her robe, and the rest of the house was still sleeping. "And I'd be happy to make some toast."

"I'll get something later, thanks, Rose."

It was early, the streets of Aurora empty. Halloween decorations had gone up at many houses, and lots of lawns were planted with election signs urging a vote for George Bush or Michael Dukakis or one of the many candidates for state and local offices. He drove with his windows down, letting in the cool air that smelled of fallen autumn leaves and dewy grass. The morning was quiet. He was alone. A perfect time for deep contemplation.

It was actually a continuation of contemplation. He'd lain awake a good deal of the night thinking about both Aphrodite McGill and her daughter and what might have gone on at

Shangri-La. Aphrodite had always characterized her legendary love fests as celebrations of the free spirit. Although it had been a few years since she'd organized the last one, they'd been held on the summer solstice. On that day when golden sunlight lingered longest, writers, artists, and creative souls of every kind descended on Tamarack County and gathered on the grounds of Shangri-La. Unlike Las Vegas, what happened at Shangri-La didn't always stay there. Although the tales that spread afterward were undoubtedly exaggerated, at the heart of them all was the unabashed expression of free love that spilled over everywhere on Apostle's Cove throughout that long summer night. Despite the fact that the smell of burning marijuana drifted heavily on the air and there were, most likely, lots of other illicit substances involved, law enforcement had never intruded on Aphrodite's yearly celebration. Her relationship with Wild Bill Gunderson probably went a long way in explaining this.

But Aphrodite's reputation didn't rest on those once-a-year love fests alone. Many a married woman in Tamarack County had reason to suspect that Aphrodite's roving eye had, at one time or another, lit upon a restless husband.

Was it any wonder, Cork thought, that a daughter who'd grown up at Shangri-La with a role model like Aphrodite might not end up as the most faithful of wives?

It was early yet, the day windless, Iron Lake a mirror of the azure sky and the saffron morning sun as he pulled up and parked in front of the Boshey cabin on Timber Lodge Road. Yellow crime scene tape still crossed the door. Inside, nothing had been changed since the brutal murder occurred. Murders, Cork reminded himself. A lake of blood, dried now to the color of ancient rust, still lay on the floor, with Aphrodite's bloodied footprints leading to the phone on the wall.

Standing in that room where the crime had occurred, he suddenly realized something that, since he'd been focused on all the evidence of violence, he'd missed before. There were lots of framed photographs hanging on the walls and on the mantel and unframed photos attached to the refrigerator door with magnets. All of them were of the children, Sunny and Moonbeam, or of Chastity with her children. Neither Axel nor Clyde Greensky nor any other adult had a place in those photographs. Cork understood that whatever demons she might have struggled with, Chastity Boshey cared deeply about her children. In so much of his thinking, he'd been hard on the young woman. But now he felt his heart soften a little.

He went outside and walked to the woodshed where Axel's bloodstained clothing had been found. Then he sat next to the gas pump at the end of the resort's dock, staring at the lake, trying to put it all together, trying to see if they'd missed something important, trying to make firm in his conscience that Axel's confession was a statement of truth.

Did it really make sense that Axel, drunk out of his mind and crazy with anger, plunged that fireplace poker again and again into the body of a pregnant woman? Was there plausibility in the idea of a mother-daughter confrontation, fueled by drugs, gone horribly awry? Could something entirely different, something he hadn't thought of yet, be the real heart of that terrible crime?

He considered the probability that Chastity was involved with another man. Who might that have been, and could he have had something to do with Chastity's murder?

Round and round, like a crazy carousel, Cork's mind went over everything. He was still deep in thought, without a clear awareness of time, when he heard a vehicle approaching on Timber Lodge Road. He turned from the lake and watched an old station wagon roll slowly toward Boshey's cabin and stop at the mailbox.

He knew the wagon and the driver, and he walked over to meet this arrival.

For a good long while, Dave Briddon had been the rural mail carrier for Tamarack County. He had more than a decade on Cork, being somewhere in his late forties. He was English, had come to Aurora in the days when Shangri-La still lured a lot of free spirits to the North Country. Like most of the early apostles of the hedonistic lifestyle at the estate, he'd grown disillusioned and left. From there, he'd traveled the world—India, New Guinea, the Orient. He'd met his wife, Lorraine, while on a birding expedition in the Biebrza Marshes on the border of Poland and Belarus. They'd married on a camel safari in Kenya. But Cork had always believed that once the beauty of the great Northwoods set its hook in your heart, it pulled you back. Although Briddon had abandoned Shangri-La, his love of the beautiful Northwoods stayed with him, and he returned to Tamarack County with his bride. In his days at Shangri-La, Briddon's hair had hung down to his shoulders and he'd dressed in typical flower child garb. Now, only a fringe of short graying hair was left on his scalp, and he was more prone to wear flannel than flowered shirts and love beads.

"Morning, Dave," Cork greeted him. "You deliver mail on Sundays now?"

"Not usually, Cork. Especially not out this way. Since Edna and Jake closed up their resort, the caretaker's cabin is the only stop on Timber Lodge Road. But I got an official-looking letter here addressed to Axel." Briddon held up an envelope. "I could have brought it out yesterday, but I wasn't certain I should. I mean, nobody's there now. What do you think?"

"I'll be happy to take it to Axel. But probably you should redirect his mail to his mother's place in Allouette."

"Will do."

Briddon handed Cork the envelope. The return address was the V.A. hospital in Brainerd.

"Say, Dave, you were in residence at Shangri-La back in the early days. Ever visit there now?"

"Hell, no. Except to deliver mail. If Lorraine thought I'd been out to see Aphrodite, she'd skin me alive. But," he added, looking a little wistful, "I sure have lots of interesting memories of that place."

"What was it like back in the day?"

"Well, everybody knows about what she called her love fests. But Aphrodite didn't have to wait for the solstice to have her fun, I'm here to tell you."

"Fun with you?"

"Me and Aphrodite, sure. Aphrodite and you name him, she's had him. Or at least, that's how it was in the old days."

"Were you jealous?"

"Hell, no. It was never serious with Aphrodite. At least with me. Maybe other guys were different, I don't know."

"Anyone else a regular at Shangri-La?"

"You mean since the gatherings stopped?"

"Or back then even."

"Maybe you should be asking Aphrodite."

"Think she'd tell me?"

"Discretion was never her forte."

Briddon craned his neck out the window of his station wagon, which had been modified with the steering wheel and pedals on the passenger side for easy access to rural mailboxes. He eyed the Boshey mailbox.

"You take something out of there, Cork?"

"No. Why?"

"The flag's up, signal that there's something in there for me to pick up. But the box is empty."

"When was the last time you were out here?"

Briddon thought a moment. "Few days ago, I guess. The day Chastity . . . Well, you know." He looked aggrieved for a moment, then brightened, said, "TTFN," gave Cork a final nod, and drove away.

As he headed back to Aurora, Cork tried in vain to remember the status of the mailbox on the morning he'd found Aphrodite sitting in the pool of her daughter's blood. Although it was a small detail and probably had a perfectly logical explanation, Cork, in the manner of a cop, filed that oddity away for future scrutiny.

Axel Boshey looked up from reading the letter Cork had given him. "Neurotoxicity."

Cork stood leaning against the bars of the cell. "What's that?"

"I was discharged from the army because of illness. Been seeing doctors at the V.A. hospital in Brainerd. They finally gave what I got a name. Neurotoxicity."

"What is it?"

"I guess it's different depending on who you ask. Me, I hurt everywhere. I get these skin rashes. Sometimes I don't remember things too well."

"Blackouts?"

"Kinda. In the service, I was part of a group responsible for disposal of used chemicals. Never told what those chemicals were. Mostly, we just burned them. They gave us masks to wear, but they didn't really help much."

Cork wondered if Axel was setting up some kind of mitigating circumstance to present to Judge Parrant at his arraignment or sentencing but dismissed the thought almost immediately. It had been obvious that since Boshey returned from his military service, he'd been a man in pain. Cork had thought it was mental. But maybe it was more than that.

"Anything they can do for you?"

"They're still trying to figure that one out."

"Sorry, Axel."

"Brainerd's a long way to go for treatment, Sheriff. Maybe prison'll be easier."

Boshey offered a smile that held no humor.

CHAPTER 25

"Neurotoxicity?" Jo said.

She was changing out of what she'd worn to church that morning, a ruby-colored dress she'd recently bought. Although it was a maternity item that would accommodate the growing swell of her body, Cork nonetheless found it enticing.

"I never heard of it either," he said. "You might want to do some research."

She hung the dress in the closet and turned to him, now wearing only a black bra and black maternity briefs. "Are you helping the defense? Our county attorney might have something to say about that."

Cork went to her, took her in his arms, and delivered a passionate kiss. "What do you think he'd say about me truly consorting with the enemy?"

She smiled but gently pushed him away. "Easy, Sheriff. We have a house full of children and a Sunday dinner to prepare." He stepped back, and she took a blouse and slacks from the closet. "I wonder if Patsy knows about this."

"She hasn't said anything to you?"

"She's been worried about him for a long time, about his erratic behavior, but she's never mentioned him visiting doctors at the V.A."

"I think a trip to Allouette may be in order," Cork said.

As she buttoned her blouse, Jo said, "By the way, in his prayers for the people today, Father Jude included the Martinellis."

"What for?"

"He wasn't specific. But I asked him about it after church, and he gave me some information to pass along to you."

"What's that?"

"Bill Gunderson has put his daughter in a sanitarium near the Twin Cities."

"Lucy Martinelli? What for?"

"Psychiatric evaluation, apparently."

"Wild Bill took her there? Not Rocky?"

"I suppose someone had to stay with the kids."

"I'm sorry to hear it's come to that. Rocky's suspended, but I'll probably change that to leave time until he gets the situation resolved."

"Rose said she's going to put together some meal items to take to the Martinellis to help out. As I understand it, Rocky's not much of a cook."

"Only Rose doing meals for them?"

"Don't look at me. I'm not much of a cook either. But Rose said she'd get some of the other church women to help."

After a Sunday dinner of roasted chicken, mashed potatoes, green beans, and apple pie for dessert, they left the girls playing with Barbie dolls and Rose nestled in an easy chair, reading a Gothic romance titled *Dark Desires*. Cork noted that the woman on the cover, who was in the embrace of a young, swarthy adonis, wore a dress the same enticing red as the one Jo had been wearing that morning.

They tried Patsy Boshey's house first but got no answer.

"Still hiding out at the Ganschinietz place, I suspect," Cork said.

When Cork and Jo arrived at the Ganschineitz cabin, they found that Henry Meloux and Sam Winter Moon had come to visit as well. Little Sunny was sitting on the floor in front of the television eating a sandwich of fried bologna, what folks on the rez jokingly called "Indian steak." Moonbeam was nestled on Patsy's lap, clutching a teddy bear in her little arms.

"Still being hounded by the press, Patsy?" Cork asked after they'd greeted one another, were seated, and had declined an offer of coffee.

"I keep hearing from folks that Hanover's trying to track me down, though Lord knows why. I have nothing to say to him."

"I got a call from George LeDuc," Lynn said. "He told me Hanover's been pounding on doors all over the rez, asking all kinds of questions."

"No law against asking questions," Sam said. "But I'm sure no one is giving him any answers."

"I have a couple of questions for you, Patsy," Cork said.

"Wait just a minute," Lynn said. "Sunny, let's you and me and Moonbeam go play in the backyard for a while. I think I saw a fox out there this morning."

Sundown had finished his sandwich and was on his feet in an instant. "Can we catch it?"

"I think he'll be too tricky for us, but let's see."

She lifted Moonbeam from Patsy's lap, took Sunny's hand, and as she walked them out the back door, Patsy said, "*Miigwech*, Lynn." When the children had gone, Patsy said, "What do you want to ask?"

"Did you know Axel was seeing Bernadette Polaski?" Cork said.

"The librarian in town? Seeing?"

"In a relationship."

"News to me. But, with a wife like Chastity, who could blame him?"

Cork looked at Winter Moon. "Bernadette worked summers for you, Sam. When her parents were killed, you were the shoulder she leaned on. Are you still close?"

"We talk."

"Did she tell you about her and Axel?"

"Not a word. She's very good at keeping things to herself."

"Okay, next question for you, Patsy," Cork said. "Did you know that Axel is suffering from something called neurotoxicity?"

She appeared distressed at this. "What? What is that?"

"I'm not entirely sure, but Axel told me this morning that he feels a good deal of pain, gets rashes, and sometimes has issues with his memory."

"I knew about his blackouts. I thought it was the booze. He didn't share his pain with me. A lot of pain?"

"You'd need to ask him."

"Sometimes, I could tell he was hurting. When I asked, he told me it was nothing."

"Probably didn't want you worrying," Sam said.

"What about you, Henry?" Cork asked. "Did you know about this ailment?"

Meloux had been noticeably quiet. Now he said calmly, "He shared many things with me, but he asked me to keep them to myself. I made that promise."

"Keep them even from me?" Patsy said.

"The choice was your son's."

"Can you share anything now, Henry?" Cork asked.

"I have not been released from my promise."

"What does this have to do with why he's in jail?" Sam asked.

"Maybe nothing," Cork said. "But the more we know, the more we might be able to get at the truth of Chastity's death."

"Axel confessed," Sam said.

"Still a lot of unanswered questions," Cork said. "And I have one for you, Sam. Did you ever visit Shangri-La on the summer solstice?"

"I'd've been a fool not to check out what all the hullabaloo was about."

"Anything ever happen between you and Aphrodite McGill?"

His lips showed only a hint of a smile. "A gentleman never tells. But she admitted to me on more than one occasion that she had a weakness for, in her words, 'Indian warriors.' She said she liked a man with a few battle scars on his body."

"I'd like to be there when my son's in court on Tuesday," Patsy said. "Would that be all right?"

"Of course," Jo said.

"I'll take you," Sam offered.

Henry Meloux sat quietly, his face unreadable. But when Cork and Jo got up to leave, the old Mide said, "The way to the heart is not through the body. Generosity of spirit is what opens that door."

"Meaning what, Henry?" Cork asked.

Meloux gave his head a little shake. "Why is it, Corcoran O'Connor, that you always ask a question you already know the answer to?"

"Henry always gives me a damn riddle," Cork said as he and Jo drove back to Aurora. "Just once I wish he'd give me a straight answer."

"Generosity of spirit seems pretty straightforward to me."

"But in what context?"

"I suppose that's the riddle. But I found Sam's comment about Indian warriors pretty revealing."

"Of what?"

"It's got me wondering if that might have included Axel."

Cork considered this a moment, then said, "Axel told me Aphrodite was awfully handsy with him back in the day. And she named herself Aphrodite for a reason. Maybe I need to press your client a little bit more on this issue."

"Not unless I'm there."

"Of course, Counselor."

But an hour later, when he did press Axel Boshey, the man replied, as if Cork were crazy, "You gotta be kidding me."

"Serious question, Axel. Did you ever have sex with Aphrodite McGill?"

Axel hesitated a moment, glanced at Jo, then said, "Not after I married Chastity."

Cork could see the surprise on Jo's face.

"Did Chastity know about your relationship with her mother?"

"Relationship? It was just sex. And just once. After I got back from the Mideast. I bumped into her at a bar in town. One thing led to another, and we ended up at Shangri-La."

"Did Chastity know about this?"

"Yeah. Aphrodite made sure of that when she found out Chastity and I were going to get married. Caused a huge row. Chastity accused her mom of taking every man she was ever interested in."

"Did you and Chastity argue about it?"

He shook his head. "It was Aphrodite she was pissed at. When me and Chastity argued, it was mostly about domestic stuff. You know, the house, finances, the kids and what was best for them." He looked down at his hands, which were folded as if in prayer. "We also argued about her drugs. And my drinking. I'll cop to that one."

Afterward, as they drove from the jail, Jo was unusually quiet.

"What are you thinking?" Cork finally asked.

"Just wondering something."

"What?"

"Did you ever have sex with Aphrodite McGill?"

Cork laughed. "I was in high school when Shangri-La was built. Then I was patrolling the streets of South Chicago. When I returned home to Aurora, I was married to a woman who not only satisfied me in every way but would kill me if I had anything to do with Aphrodite McGill. Okay?"

"Thank you. That's exactly what I wanted to hear."

"But I may be the only man in Tamarack County who hasn't been bedded by that woman."

Jo became quiet again. After a minute, she said with a note of sadness, "I can't help wondering about Chastity Boshey and what must have happened in her childhood to create such animosity toward her mother. I'm thinking about her life at Shangri-La. Those solstice love fests and what sounds like a constant parade of paramours through that house. I'm also wondering if it's possible she was the victim of some abuse or even exploitation. Which might explain both her hatred of Shangri-La and her own sexual proclivities."

"Apostle's Cove," Cork said. "That sounds sort of New Testament, you know. Kind of hopeful. But from all the stories I've heard, it seems more like Sodom or Gomorrah."

"I love our house on Gooseberry Lane," Jo said. "And I'm thinking right now about our daughters and how glad I am for the family they're part of. You and me and Rose."

Cork reached out and touched the slight swell of her belly. "And that little munchkin, whoever he or she will be."

She put her hand over his. "I haven't had morning sickness with this one. Patsy Boshey tells me that's a sign it will be a boy."

"Maybe we should consult Henry."

Jo laughed.

"What's so funny?" Cork asked.

"You said you may be the only man in Tamarack County who hasn't been with Aphrodite McGill. What do you think about Henry?"

That was a question Cork couldn't even begin to answer.

CHAPTER 26

Axel Boshey's arraignment took place on Tuesday. Because Axel had been drunk to the point of blackout and was fuzzy on details in his confession, Jo had convinced him to enter what was called a Norgaard plea, which was allowed in situations in which a defendant acknowledged the strength of the prosecution's argument against him while also acknowledging that because of impaired memory, he had no real recollection of committing the crime. Though she gave Axel no guarantees, she hoped it might reduce the sentence that would eventually be handed down. His appearance was brief, but the courtroom was packed. Cork felt as if a circus had come to town. Aside from Axel, the only Ojibwe faces present belonged to Axel's mother, Patsy, and Sam Winter Moon, for whom Jo had made sure seats were saved behind where her client sat. Axel Boshey showed no emotion whatsoever when the charges of homicide, which included the unborn child, were read. Judge Parrant set the sentencing hearing for two weeks hence. The bailiff led Boshey from the courtroom, and a couple of Cork's deputies escorted him back to his jail cell.

Hell Hanover was among the reporters clamoring for a statement from Boshey's attorney. When Jo offered "No comment," someone in the crowd called out, "He killed a baby. Hanging's too good for him!" Jo calmly replied, "We no longer execute people in Minnesota." To which Hell Hanover, who was in the forefront of the reporters, said, "Maybe we need to start again."

It struck Cork like a scene from an old western, a lynch mob mentality. And as he sat with Jo and Ed Larson in his office afterward, he mentioned this to her.

"It was a sudden, brutal murder," Jo said. "It has people scared."

"Not so much scared, I think, as confirmed in their beliefs about Indians," Cork said. "Chastity's murder has stirred things up so that all the hate and anger that lies beneath has come to the surface. I've lived here all my life and I've seen it before. Doesn't take much to bring out the worst in people."

"He was going to plead guilty. At least I got him to agree to the Norgaard Plea, which may help at sentencing," Jo said. "But I can't help thinking that if we had more time, we might come up with the real truth of that night."

"All the evidence is against him, and we have a signed confession," Larson pointed out. "It's a slam dunk."

"The confession is troubling in many respects," Jo said. "His memory of what happened is so unclear, Ed."

Cork said, "You've done your best, Counselor. Maybe it's time you let it go."

"Is that what you're going to do?"

"A few loose ends I'd like to tie up first."

"Care to share?"

"Not at the moment. Don't you have a practice to run?"

As Cork saw his wife out, Hell Hanover walked into the department.

"Jo." The newspaperman greeted her in an overly friendly way. "Interesting proceeding."

"What do you want, Helm?" Jo said.

"Nothing from you, thanks, except maybe a statement for the record."

"I've got nothing to say."

"Just like in the courtroom representing your client."

"What do you have against Axel Boshey?" she asked.

"Only that he got away with murder once. If he'd been put away then, this wouldn't have happened."

"He got away with nothing," Cork said. "He was cleared of any wrongdoing, cleared legally."

"And then he marries the dead man's widow. Now that he's admitted to killing her and her child, maybe he'll tell the truth about what really happened to Greensky."

"I'll see you later," Jo said to Cork just before she marched out. "I've got better things to do than stand here listening to this tripe."

After she'd left, Cork said, "What do you want, Helm?"

"Actually, I'm here on behalf of Aphrodite McGill."

"Here as a newspaperman?"

"A friend. She couldn't bring herself to be at the arraignment. But she has a request. She wants to see you."

"What about?"

"She didn't say. She just asked me to make sure you came to see her."

"Asked you as a friend?"

"That's right."

Cork had a pretty good idea just what kind of friend Aphrodite had been to Hanover.

"Tell her I'll be there."

"When?"

"When I'm good and ready. Don't you have a diatribe to write for your rag?"

"I have the perfect headline. 'Justice at Last.' What do you think?"

"I think I've had enough of you for right now."

Cork spun away and headed to his office. At his back, Bos Swain said from the contact desk, "You heard the sheriff, Hell. Are you leaving, or do I have to ask an officer to escort you out?"

It was well after noon before Cork arrived at Shangri-La. He could have come earlier, but he didn't want Aphrodite getting the idea that he jumped to her beck and call the way other men seemed to. Still, he was curious to find out what she had to say.

He parked beside her pink, flower-decaled VW and rang the front doorbell. Aphrodite answered wearing a red silk dress, her hair beautifully brushed and draping over her shoulders in a spill of midnight black. She'd spent time on her makeup and had misted herself with a subtle perfume that hinted at jasmine. The woman before him was, he had to admit, a beauty. But he had a pretty good sense of what lay beneath.

"Thank you for seeing me," she said in a soft voice. "Won't you come in?"

She stood aside, but as he entered, Cork couldn't help thinking that he might be stepping into the web of a black widow spider.

"Would you like something to drink?" Aphrodite offered. "I have a nice Loire Valley Sancerre blanc chilled and perfect for a warm autumn afternoon."

"Thank you, no. I'm on duty."

"Of course you are. Shall we sit on the patio? I love the view of the lake from there."

"Lead the way," Cork said.

He followed her into the gallery of collected art that was her living room, then through French double doors onto a broad stone terrace overlooking Iron Lake. She walked to a table shaded with a blue umbrella. On the table was a silver bucket in which a bottle of wine sat nestled in ice. Aphrodite took one of the two chairs, Cork the other. The woman crossed her legs, and the slit in her red dress parted enough to show a good deal of her bare thigh. She smiled at Cork, then her gaze drifted to the lake.

"Have you ever felt that you were guided somewhere?" she asked, her voice still as soft as the silk dress she wore.

"Physically or metaphysically?"

She smiled. "You're quite intelligent for a cop."

"Most cops I know have pretty good brains."

"Most cops I know have pretty good bodies as well." She arched an eyebrow. She looked again at the lake. "I was lost before I came to Shangri-La. When I arrived here, I knew it was the place I'd been waiting to find."

"Others came to Shangri-La before you and felt that same way. They didn't stick around."

"For them it was a lark. For me, it became my life."

"What is it you wanted to talk to me about?"

"You think I might have killed my daughter."

"I believe we don't know the truth of what happened that night. You lied to me when I asked you where you were. And when I called you on that lie, you gave me the vaguest of answers."

"Out driving, I said." She smiled. "You're right. The truth is, I was visiting a friend."

"Does he have a name?"

"What makes you think it's a *he*?"

"Give me a name."

"Discretion dictates that I refrain."

"Discretion? Seriously?"

"Do you know what you are? You're just a provincial cop, and a judgmental one at that."

"Until you give me a name, I'll continue to be a provincial, judgmental cop who doesn't believe what you're trying to offer as an alibi for your whereabouts the night your daughter was killed."

A polished wood cigarette case with an ornate inlaid design sat on the table beside the ice bucket, along with a gold lighter. Aphrodite opened the case, drew out a cigarette, and lit up. She sent a stream of white smoke toward the lake, momentarily clouding over the deep blue of the water.

"I don't like being alone here," she said.

"You told me this was the place you'd been waiting to find."

"I love Shangri-La. It's the loneliness I don't like."

"A name, Aphrodite."

"You were raised Catholic, yes?"

"What does that have to do with anything?"

"Strict morals. I'm guessing that's part of why you're so judgmental. I raised Chastity to follow the instincts of her body and spirit, not a set of rules chiseled on stone tablets. Our bodies have been created with such potential for giving and receiving pleasure, and yet all most people do is deny themselves. If you believe in God, why would he create us so? Surely not to fill us with guilt for giving in to our natural desires."

"We're getting nowhere," Cork said. "And I still don't know why you wanted to talk to me."

"I want to see my grandchildren."

"That's not up to me."

"My . . . meltdown . . . the other day at the courthouse. It's cast a bit of a shadow over me when I've tried to talk to the people at the county. You might be able to do something about that. I would be grateful." She reached out and placed her hand on his knee."

"As I understand it, Chastity was dead set against her children ever setting foot here. Why would that be?"

The hand on his knee was quickly withdrawn, and the coquettish demeanor dropped away. "She could be a spiteful, willful child."

"Is that what you argued about the day she was killed? The grandchildren? Did it make you angry, the way you were angry at the courthouse during your meltdown?"

Aphrodite McGill didn't respond. She drew again on her cigarette and expelled smoke from her nose in a furious cloud.

"Do you see why I'm so interested in your alibi for the night she was killed?" Cork said. "A name, Aphrodite."

He could see the muscles of her jaw working, as if trying to prevent her from speaking. But at last she said with a kind of growl, "Eleanor Roosevelt."

CHAPTER 27

Cork found the head librarian sitting at the checkout desk. As usual, the library was quiet, the kind of quiet that Cork normally found soothing to the soul. But as he walked toward Eleanor Roosevelt, the quiet felt different, as if it carried an electric charge that was about to spark.

She looked up from the book she was reading. "*Salaam alaykum,* Cork." She smiled and said, "Arabic."

"I need to ask you a rather delicate question, Ellie." Cork spoke in the same whisper the head librarian always used, though this time it wasn't about preserving the sanctity of the place.

"I'm all ears," she said, leaning toward him in mock conspiracy.

Cork glanced around to ensure they were alone. "I need to ask you about Aphrodite McGill."

Her face barely changed, but Cork saw a slight tension around her mouth. "Yes?"

"She claims she was with you the night her daughter was killed."

Ellie hesitated, then sat up straight. "That's right."

"Quite late."

"She left around midnight, I believe."

"What was she doing there?"

Ellie's eyes were like iron. "Visiting. People do visit, you know."

"Do you ever visit her at Shangri-La?"

"I do not."

"Any reason?"

"Shangri-La has one kind of reputation. I have another."

"So, when Aphrodite visits, it's always at your place?"

"Yes."

"Does she visit often?"

"What possible help could this line of questioning be to you, Cork?"

"I'm trying to figure out the truth of a tragic death, Ellie. All I'm getting from people are lies and obfuscations."

"Axel Boshey has confessed to killing his wife."

"It may be possible that's another obfuscation. What about you and Aphrodite?"

"What about us?"

"Chastity told Axel that for her mother, when it came to sex, it could be anytime, anywhere, with anyone, male or female."

The librarian considered him for a very long time. "You are a public figure. You know that you're scrutinized closely. That everything you do is seen as a reflection on this community."

"Yes. And?"

"Do you imagine I would have been the head librarian in a town like Aurora for very long if it became broadly known that I share certain proclivities with Aphrodite McGill?"

"I understand. And I hope you understand that what we talk about goes no further."

"What else can I tell you? What we do when we're together?"

"Aphrodite is not above using the secrets shared with her as leverage. I just want to be certain that what she's told me about that night is the truth."

"She hasn't strong-armed me, if that's what you mean."

"Aphrodite has an appetite for many things, including illicit drugs."

"I don't share all her appetites, if that's what you're wondering. I drink wine when we're together."

"And Aphrodite?"

"I don't ask. But . . ." She thought for a moment. "Sometimes her state of mind concerns me."

"And that night?"

"I was concerned. I suggested she stay with me. She chose to leave."

"Thank you, Ellie."

She seemed to relax just a bit. "I still remember how excited you were when I insisted that you read the Sherlock Holmes stories. Maybe I should have suggested baseball stories instead."

"This conversation is strictly confidential, Eleanor. You'll be suggesting books to children for a long time to come, I guarantee. And then it will be Bernadette's turn."

"I think not. She called me over the weekend. She's quit."

There was no answer when Cork knocked at the door of Bernadette Polaski's apartment. He knocked at the apartment next door but didn't recognize the man who answered.

Although he was in uniform, Cork flashed his badge. "I'm wondering if you know anything about your neighbor, Bernadette Polaski."

"Moved out yesterday."

surprise me that she might have reached out to him. Or him to her, given the woman he married."

"Did she talk about having family anywhere else?"

"Not that I recall. Why this deep interest in her?"

"I'm not convinced Axel killed his wife."

"As I understand it, his confession's pretty damning."

"I'm wondering if he's covering for somebody."

"And you think that might be Bernadette?"

"I don't know, Sam. Hell, I'm just trying to make sure we get it right before we send a man off to spend the rest of his life behind bars."

Winter Moon smiled broadly. "You remind so much of your dad."

"I wonder what he'd do in my place."

"Probably exactly what you're doing. Just keep on digging."

There was a place where Cork sometimes retreated when everything felt overwhelming to him. He drove north out of Aurora, along a gravel county road to where an ancient double-trunk birch marked the beginning of the path to Crow Point.

Meloux was seated on the wooden bench outside his cabin with his yellow mutt nearby. Both Meloux and Walleye, sitting in the warm October sunlight, watched him approach across the meadow, neither of them looking particularly interested.

"Boozhoo," Cork said and offered the old man some tobacco.

Meloux took the offering and nodded toward the empty part of the bench. Walleye, who'd been sitting on his haunches, settled down on the ground at the old man's feet.

"Axel Boshey," Cork said.

"These days, Corcoran O'Connor, you are a bird with only one call."

"I'm trying to get at the truth, Henry. And I'm not getting it from Axel. Or from anyone else, for that matter. Have you heard that he's pled guilty to killing his wife and her unborn child?"

The old man shook his head but didn't seem surprised. "I could see the direction of the path he'd chosen."

"I can't say for sure, but I think he may be covering for someone. I can't get him to admit it and I don't know how to make him crack. You worked with him. How did you get him to open up to you?"

"I am Mide. People come to me ready to open themselves. I like to believe I help them find freedom from what troubles them. You are different. Freedom is not what people think of when they see that piece of metal you wear."

"Help me understand why a man who might be innocent would choose to go to jail. Is it about love? Honor? What?"

"The heart has reasons that the head may not understand. Maybe the path the man has chosen for himself, even if you do not understand it, is one you should respect."

"Put him behind bars, even if he didn't do this terrible thing? Where's the justice in that? And if he's not guilty, then there's someone out there who is and should be brought to justice."

"What is justice?"

"The law tells me what justice is."

"In my experience, Corcoran O'Connor, and in the experience of our people, the law is not always concerned about what is just."

"If I don't have the law to guide me, Henry, what do I have?"

"You are sometimes like a deaf dog. You look at me as if you are listening, but you do not hear a word I say. I have told you many times where to turn for the truth and still you ask."

And still you ask. Cork left Crow Point just as confused and frustrated as when he'd come, kicking Meloux's words around in his head, but thinking to himself, *Wasn't that what it was all about, that you just kept asking questions until you found the answer?* He knew what Meloux meant. The answer wasn't out there. Not the answer Meloux thought was important anyway. But because Cork was the one who'd been given the piece of metal, as Meloux called it, maybe he had a different idea of what was important.

"Damn, Henry," he mumbled as he walked through the wilderness back toward his Bronco.

CHAPTER 28

Axel sat slumped on the other side of the table in the interview room, looking like a plant wilting in the sun and in need of water. Jo sat beside him. Cork had asked her to be there as he tried a final time to crack the man open.

"Let me ask you a question, Axel," Cork began. "Do you love your kids?"

Axel's eyes were deep wells of longing. "You know I do."

"Do you have any idea what's going to happen to them when you go to prison?"

"I want my mother to raise them."

"Aphrodite will fight to get them, I'm sure. And she has all the money she needs to do that."

"Yeah? Well, here's something you can use to make sure that doesn't happen. Chastity caught her mother doing things with Sunny."

Cork glanced at Jo, who seemed just as surprised as he. "What kind of things?"

"Getting herself and him naked together. She fed Chastity

some kind of bullshit about just wanting Sunny to begin to appreciate the beauty of the human body."

"When was this?"

"A little over a week ago. Chastity went nuts, told Aphrodite she would never let her near the kids again."

"What did Aphrodite say to that?"

"I wasn't there, but Chastity told me the blowup between them was huge. Look, Sheriff, I'm going away for a long time, maybe for the rest of my life. There's only one thing I want and that's to know that my kids are safe. I want them brought up by my mother."

"I can't guarantee anything, Axel. That kind of decision is out of my hands."

Axel turned his face toward Jo. "You're a pretty good lawyer."

Jo said, "I can't guarantee anything either."

"If you told me the truth of what happened the night Chastity was killed, I might have a shot at getting you what you want," Cork said.

Axel stared at his hands, which were splayed on the tabletop like flattened roadkill. "I've told you the truth."

"Bernadette's left town, Axel. Just ran off."

He didn't look up.

"She loves you," Cork said. "As near as I can tell, the feeling is mutual. You wanted a divorce from your wife so that you could be with Bernadette openly. But Chastity wouldn't give you that. If I were Bernadette, that would make me pretty angry. Maybe angry enough to commit murder. Maybe she told you what she'd done and you did your best to help cover up her crime. No one could blame you for—"

Boshey didn't let him finish. "Bernadette's got nothing to do with what happened to Chastity. I killed that bitch. Me. Just me. And I'm not one bit sorry that I did."

Cork had no deep emotional connection to Axel Boshey, but he felt something heavy in his chest, a stone on his heart. He knew in a way that had nothing to do with the evidence and the law that there was something not right about this case, that the truth of Chastity's death might remain a mystery forever.

What is justice? he thought, looking at the man whose life was going to be bounded by prison bars and prison rules and a prison hierarchy in which, Cork knew, Indians were at the bottom. The path Axel Boshey had chosen was one that would probably lead to hell. There was nothing Cork could do about that. His own path was laid out by the responsibility of the badge he wore. Despite his misgivings, his duty was clear.

"All right, Axel," he said, rising. "That's that."

On Halloween, as fate would have it, a day that celebrated so much that was grotesque in the human psyche, Boshey stood in the courtroom impassively as Judge Robert Parrant passed sentence. Due to the savagery of the crimes, Axel Boshey would spend the rest of his life in prison without hope of parole.

- PART II -

NOW

CHAPTER 29

Stephen and Belle lived in the upper of a duplex in a pretty neighborhood of St. Paul called Tangletown. When Cork parked on the street in front, Rainy said, "It'll be good to find out why he's been so secretive."

"He said that I would understand when I got here."

"Just like a lawyer to make everything complicated."

Belle had a pan of lasagna in the oven and garlic bread on the table and, for a place that a young Native couple called home, it smelled oddly Italian. Stephen and Belle had been married two years. Cork couldn't have asked for a better union for his son. Belle was already a lawyer, working now for the Tribal Law and Policy Institute in West St. Paul.

Stephen took their coats and walked them into the living room, where two people sat. Cork knew one of them—Sundown Boshey. Axel's stepson was in his late twenties. Sunny was tall, a bit angular, with midnight black hair, mahogany eyes, and an easy smile. Cork had watched him grow up under the guidance of Patsy Boshey, who'd done a fine job of raising her grandson and his sister, Moonbeam. Currently, he was an assistant professor at

Metropolitan State University, teaching Native American literature, among other things. Cork still sometimes ran into him when Sunny brought his family to Tamarack County. Despite the fact that Cork had been responsible for sending his father to jail, the young man had never seemed to harbor ill feelings toward him.

The other visitor was a stranger. She was diminutive, had long dark hair with auburn highlights, smart brown eyes, and cheeks that were round like a chipmunk's. There was something about her that was vaguely familiar to Cork. When she stood up to greet him and offered her name, he understood.

"Marianne Polaski."

It took a moment for Cork to realize why she looked a bit familiar. "Are you related to Bernadette Polaski?"

"Her daughter," the woman said.

"And the daughter of Axel Boshey," Sunny added. "She's my half sister."

Cork studied them both, then eyed Stephen. "This was what you were keeping from me."

"I wanted to see the look on your face. And, Dad, it's priceless."

"Something to drink?" Belle asked. "I've got a nice chianti. Or beer, or coffee, or spring water."

"I'm fine," Cork said.

"Me, too," Rainy said.

"All right, then. Dinner in ten."

"I'd help," Rainy said, "but I want to hear this story."

"That's fine," Belle said. "I'm already up to date."

Cork and Rainy settled in, and Cork said, "From the beginning, if you don't mind."

"Growing up, I'd always been told that Clyde Greensky was my biological father, but he died when I was too young to remember,"

Sunny said. "The only vague recollections I had of a father were of Axel. My grandmother told me lots of stories about him, how much he'd loved me, but until I was sixteen, I saw only photographs of him. That was his decision. He didn't want me to see him in prison. Gram Patsy never lied to me. I knew where he was and, eventually, I knew why. But Gram Patsy sent him pictures I drew and letters I'd written to him in crayon."

"Did he respond?" Cork asked.

"Little notes at first. In prison, he discovered he had a knack for drawing, and he'd send me funny pictures, cartoon things. Later, they were accompanied by real letters."

"What happened at sixteen?"

"I put my foot down. I told Gram Patsy I wanted to see him. She brought me down here, and we visited him at Stillwater. He'd been incarcerated nearly eleven years by then. He was leading the White Bison Wellbriety program, helping other prisoners get their lives back on track. I didn't leave that day thinking of him as a man stuck behind prison walls. Even then, I saw him as someone who'd learned how to be free despite the bars he lived behind."

"Did it matter that he'd killed your mother?"

"I didn't know her. She was like someone in a fairy tale. Gram Patsy was my mother. And until I was sixteen, Sam Winter Moon and George LeDuc were fathers to me. Even Henry Meloux had a hand in raising me."

Cork knew much of this. He'd watched the boy grow, and Moonbeam, too. He'd see them sometimes in church with Patsy Boshey. Sam Winter Moon, while he was alive, and George LeDuc as well had kept him aware of the boy's progress. But Cork had never really pried into their lives, never talked to Patsy about Axel. For a long time, it was a sore spot for him. He always had a nagging sense that there were questions left hanging, answers behind a door he didn't know how to open. And he had his own life to live, his own family to worry about, his own tragedies to deal with.

Cork looked to Marianne, who'd been quietly listening as Sunny told his part of the tale. "What's your story, and how did you two manage to connect?"

"I was born in Evanston, Illinois, seven months after my mother left Aurora."

It came back to Cork then, how sick Bernadette Polaski had seemed when he was conducting his investigation of Chastity Boshey's death.

"Of course," he said, more to himself than the others. "She was pregnant. But why Evanston? Family there?"

Marianne shook her head. "Just a good friend she'd gone to college with. A librarian, like her. After I was born, she helped Mom get a job working at Northwestern University."

"Did Bernadette marry?"

"I was raised by a single mother, who did a pretty good job of it, if you ask me."

"Did she ever say anything about who your father was?"

"She had a picture she would show me sometimes, but I grew up believing he'd died before I was born. I knew something wasn't right. I had no relatives. No cousins, no aunts, no uncles. Just Mom and me. But when Mom died—"

"When was that?" Cork asked.

"A year ago. It was sudden. A pulmonary embolism. When she died, I decided to see if there might be some family out there somewhere. So I did the Ancestry.com thing." She smiled at Sunny. "And I discovered that I have a brother."

"When I told my father about Marianne, he wanted to see her, if she was willing."

"It was hard at first," the young woman said, "thinking that my father was a murderer, but Sunny assured me he was a good man. He told me about White Bison and Wellbriety, so I decided to visit. Sunny came with me. And he was right. Axel Boshey is a wonderful man. And no murderer."

"But wait a minute," Cork said, beginning to put the pieces together. "If you both share Axel's DNA, then—" He stared at Sunny. "Clyde Greensky wasn't your biological father."

"Axel Boshey is my true father," Sunny said.

Cork remembered how, at the party following the wedding of Greensky and Chastity, Axel had drunkenly proclaimed that the baby Chastity was carrying might well be his. And, son of a gun, he'd been right.

"What about your sister? What does Moonbeam think about all this?"

"That's one of the strange things," Sunny said. "Moonbeam has done Ancestry.com, too, now. We match as siblings, but Moonbeam and Marianne don't match at all."

It took Cork a moment to absorb this. Then he said with a kind of wonderment, "Axel's your father, but someone else fathered Moonbeam."

"Dinner's ready," Belle said.

CHAPTER 30

Cork barely tasted his food.

Because he'd watched Sunny and Moonbeam Boshey grow up in Tamarack County, they were constant reminders of the conviction of a man Cork had never in his heart believed was guilty of murder, and the details of Chastity's death had never faded into vague memory. In his head, he was trying now to go over the investigation he'd conducted twenty-five years earlier. What had he ignored, overlooked, failed to see as significant? Why hadn't he dug deeper for the truth?

It was Rainy who asked, "Stephen, how long have you been working on Axel Boshey's case?"

"A couple of months."

"How'd you get involved?"

"That was Sunny's doing. He contacted the Innocence Project on behalf of his father and one of our attorneys responded. When Sunny found out about me, he requested my help specifically."

"The son of the man who sent him to prison?" Cork said.

"Axel remembers you with some gratitude, Dad. You were the one who tried to get him to admit he didn't kill his wife."

"And now he wants to recant his confession?"

"Not exactly," Stephen said.

"I'm the one pressing this, not my father," Sunny said. "From what he's told me, I believe he's innocent."

Cork put down his fork, which was filled with lasagna but had been suspended between his plate and his lips for at least a minute. "So, why did he confess to a murder he didn't commit?"

"It's all about love," Sunny said.

Axel Boshey remembered almost nothing of the night his wife was murdered. One of the last things he recalled with some clarity was leaving the North Star bar after he'd called Bernadette Polaski. The next thing he remembered clearly was waking up on the sofa of her apartment with a god-awful hangover. She was gone, but she called him and told him about Chastity and that there was a lot of talk that he'd killed her. She also told him that his children had been taken to his mother's house. He'd decided it was best to lie low, but he was worried about his kids. He called his cousin and convinced Leroy to take him out to Patsy Boshey's house that night to make sure his kids were okay, and that she was, too.

"And I arrested him," Cork said.

Sunny nodded. "Things pretty much went downhill from there."

"Did he remember anything about your mother's death?"

"The argument they had that got him drinking that night. She told him she was pregnant. But they hadn't had sex in months, so he knew the child wasn't his. Dad told her he wanted a divorce. She refused and threatened that if he tried to leave her, she would see to it that he never saw his kids again. She told him he was nothing but a goddamn drunk Indian and no court in the land would side with him. He left, got drunk, and ended up at Bernadette's place."

"Did Chastity know about Bernadette?"

"Apparently not. If she did, she never said anything. Which, as I understand it, wasn't like her at all."

"You said love was the reason that your father confessed."

"There were two other things he remembered vaguely from that night," Sunny said. "When he told Bernadette that Chastity had no intention of divorcing him, she got really angry. He also thought he remembered her leaving, though he didn't know when or for how long. But when he put two and two together, his conclusion was that maybe it was Bernadette who'd killed Chastity. Then you began to question her, and that's when he decided to confess. He didn't want the woman he loved, the woman who was carrying his child, to spend her life in prison. And there was one other thing."

"What?"

"He really did see himself as nothing but a worthless drunk, and maybe this was a way to atone."

"Did Bernadette ever talk to him, tell him she was innocent?"

"After you arrested him, they never had a chance to talk. When he heard that she'd left town so suddenly, it pretty much confirmed his suspicion."

Cork looked from Sunny to Marianne. "Did they ever communicate?"

"She sent him one letter," Marianne said.

"He sent one in return telling her never to contact him," Sunny put in. "He was afraid they still might trace the murder back to her. That was it."

Cork sat back, his plate still half full. "Are you concerned, Marianne, that your mother might have been a murderer?"

"My mother's dead. And I'd like to know the truth, even if it's a terrible one. I'd hate to think of my father stuck in prison for the rest of his life for a crime he didn't commit."

"You've been visiting your father for years now, Sunny. When did he tell you about his suspicion that Bernadette might have killed your mother?"

"Not until after he learned of Bernadette's death. The truth couldn't hurt her then."

"You're pushing this, not your father," Cork said. "What does he have to say?"

"That gets tricky," Sunny replied. "Dad's been in prison much of his life. What he's done there is pretty amazing. He's helped a lot of inmates find their way. When he went in, he thought of himself as just a drunk Indian. Now he sees himself and his purpose very differently. He's not eager to leave."

"So, what is it you're hoping for?" Cork asked.

"The authorities won't look into this," Sunny said. "It's a very cold case. We're wondering if you would be willing to take it on, find the evidence to prove that my father is innocent."

A silence descended as all eyes leveled on Cork. He glanced at Rainy and could see clearly the answer she expected from him.

"I'll need to talk to Axel," he finally said.

"Already arranged," Stephen said. "You see him tomorrow."

There was no predictable pattern to life, Cork reflected that night. Chaos was in control. No direction was true. Every road turned blindly. For twenty-five years, a door had remained closed. Now it was ajar. But there was no telling what might be revealed if he yanked it wide open. And here was the oddest part—the man who stood to gain the most from an investigation might be the least willing to help.

"Why?" Cork whispered to himself.

"You like a challenge," Rainy said to him in the dark of their hotel room.

"Keeping you awake? Sorry."

"That's all right. A lot to think about, I suspect."

"A lot. I'm not sure after all this time where I would even begin."

"Do you really believe that Bernadette Polaski could have killed Chastity Boshey?"

"As I've said before, I believe anyone is capable of anything given the right circumstances."

"But in your heart?"

"You sound like Henry."

"You didn't answer my question."

"I'm going to try my best to keep an open mind. But I'm thinking I need to go back to the beginning and turn over every stone again. And that starts tomorrow when I talk to Axel."

"What if he doesn't want you poking into the past? Would you respect that?"

"You forget one thing, Rainy. If he didn't kill Chastity, and if Bernadette didn't kill Chastity, then all those years ago, I let someone get away with murder, someone who's still out there. That's what's important to me."

He felt Rainy's hand settle gently on his chest. "There," she said.

"What?"

"That's your heart speaking. Finally." She leaned to him and kissed his cheek. "Now go to sleep."

CHAPTER 31

The individual sitting across the table was so very different from the one Cork remembered. Twenty-five years earlier, Axel Boshey had been a young man broken in so many ways, and every fracture of his soul—his drunkenness, his uncertainty, his anger, his fear—could be seen in the wary look of his eyes and in the drawn features of his face. His belief in his own worthlessness ran so deep even Henry Meloux hadn't been able to help him pull those stubborn, destructive roots out completely. And maybe, Cork thought, that was part of the reason Boshey had copped to a crime he didn't commit.

The face of the man he was about to question was, in so many ways, a different face. Older, of course. Boshey was more than fifty now and the hair that had once been long and raven was grayed and cut short. His skin was etched with deep lines, around his eyes especially, as if, even in the darkness of a prison cell, he'd spent the last two decades squinting at the sun. The eyes themselves were different, resting on Cork with an almost inexplicable calm. Most obvious was the long white scar that ran from his right ear to his jawline.

"A shank attack years ago," Boshey said, as if reading Cork's eyes and the question there. "I have other scars you're not seeing." Then he said, as casually as if they'd encountered each other on the street in Aurora or Allouette, "*Boozhoo,* Cork."

"It's been a long time, Axel."

"Stephen told me about Jo. I was sorry to hear you lost her. I still have great admiration for that woman. She had a good soul."

"A lot of water under the bridge," Cork said. "For you and me both."

Boshey turned his eyes to his son. "*Miigwech,* Sunny. I appreciate where your heart is, but this is still a fool's errand."

"If I believed that, I wouldn't be here."

Boshey gave a nod, then said to Stephen, "I had forgotten your father's face, but I can see him in your face now."

"He's here to help, Axel," Stephen said.

Boshey smiled at Cork. "I'm sure you are. But you won't be getting much help from me."

"Just one question, Axel," Cork said. "Did you kill your wife?"

"What happened that night is still unclear to me. But I believe now that I didn't."

"Sunny tells me that you confessed because you thought Bernadette Polaski was responsible."

"Yes."

"Do you still believe that?"

"That's irrelevant. This is my life. How I came to be here makes no difference."

"Henry Meloux once told me that every falling leaf comes to rest where it was always meant to be. Are you telling me the same thing?"

"Make of my words what you will."

"You don't want to leave Stillwater."

"I have purpose here. Out there," Boshey said, nodding toward the window of the visiting room, "I'm not sure."

"Did she say where?"

"That woman was quiet as a mouse. Never said boo to me. Just know because I saw her loading up her station wagon."

When Cork told Ed Larson about Bernadette, Larson shrugged it off. "Her boyfriend's going to prison for murder. Two pretty grisly murders actually. Once her relationship with him becomes known, it would be awfully hard for her to keep on living here."

"What if he's covering for her, Ed?"

"Bernadette Polaski? Really, Cork? You saw how violent the attack on Chastity was. Does Bernadette strike you as the kind of person capable of that?"

"Ed, anyone is capable of anything given the right circumstances. I want to see if I can track down where she might have gone."

"I don't think she has any family here, so how do you plan on doing that?"

"There is one person she might have confided in."

"Who?"

"Sam Winter Moon. He was like the father she never had."

But when Cork questioned him at Sam's Place, Winter Moon only shook his head. "She didn't say she was leaving town, just that she was quitting her job. She didn't say why."

"She was having an affair with Axel Boshey. She never let on to you about that?"

"Nope."

"You told me that after her parents died, she looked to you for the kind of guidance a father might have offered."

"A lot of kids who've worked for me come back from time to time for advice or just to talk. Makes me feel like I've been a part of their lives they think of as good. So Bernadette talked to me sometimes. I knew she dated Axel some in high school, but I never knew it to be serious. I know she's been lonely, so it doesn't

"Out there is everyone you love, Dad," Sunny said.

"If that's true, then everyone out there should respect my wishes."

"Let me tell you where I'm coming from," Cork said. "I was never absolutely convinced of your guilt, but I still let you be put here."

"That was my decision."

"Abandoning the search for the truth was mine. And that weighs on me heavily. You didn't answer my question. Do you still believe Bernadette killed Chastity?"

"Like I said, that doesn't matter."

"Just tell me the truth."

"I have my doubts."

"Then let me ask you one more question. If you didn't kill Chastity and Bernadette didn't kill Chastity, who did?"

Boshey sat very still for a few moments, looking deep into Cork's eyes. Then he said, "When I came here, I was a man without hope. I behaved like a man who wanted to die." He ran a finger along the white line of the scar on his face. "This is because I wanted to die. But I got a visit from Henry Meloux one day. He came with Sam Winter Moon and my mother. Do you know what he said to me? He said, 'Your life does not belong to you.' I didn't understand what he meant at first. But the more I thought about it, the more I could see his meaning. My life, yours, Sunny's, Stephen's, belong to those we love. We have a responsibility to them. If I sacrifice myself because of my own weakness or for some selfish purpose, I hurt others. I steal something from them that they hold dear. Henry was telling me that I need to respect the love others have offered me. For them, if not for me, I need to value my life."

"Then why waste it locked up here, Dad?"

"It's not a waste, Sunny. When I was put here, I suffered from what they called neurotoxicity. Pain, fuzzy thinking, strange rashes. Probably from the work I did when I was in the military. What I do here, what I've come to believe about the beauty of the Creator's spirit that runs through all things, this has healed me. A gift, I believe, from the Creator. Now my days are filled with guiding others to a better place in themselves. I have a purpose that goes beyond my responsibility to my family."

"If you leave, someone else will take your place," Sunny said.

"If I leave, I lose an important part of who I am."

Cork said, "Don't you care that someone got away with murder? Don't you care that someone let you go to prison for a brutal crime they committed?"

"I have in my heart the strength to forgive that person."

"I'm after the truth, Axel. Do you have the strength in your heart to help me find it?"

Boshey considered him, his eyes still calm. "I have one request."

"What's that?"

"That if you find the truth, you'll share it with me first, and we'll decide together what do with that truth."

Cork looked to Sunny, then Stephen. They both gave him a nod. "Deal," Cork said.

Axel Boshey spent the next half hour recounting what he remembered. His argument with Chastity that led to his drinking. His phone call to Bernadette from the North Star bar. His complete lack of recall of anything thereafter, except a few dim recollections just before he crashed in her apartment.

"In your confession, you gave details of her murder."

"I got those from one of your deputies."

"Who?"

"Rocky Martinelli. He came to my cell and I thought he was going to kill me. You pulled him off me, do you remember?"

"I do."

"He told me things about Chastity's death, used them like knives trying to cut into me. Seven stab wounds with the fireplace poker. A blow across her head. Bloody clothes in the woodshed. There was such anger in that man. He really hated Indians. Or maybe he just really hated me."

Cork recalled the incident with Martinelli and his consuming hatred for Native people. It was part of the reason he eventually suspended, then fired the deputy.

"Tell me about Chastity and her mother."

"What do you want to know?"

"During my investigation, you told me that they sometimes fought like cats and dogs. In fact, shortly before she was killed, you said they'd fought about Sunny."

Sundown Boshey looked surprised. "This is something I haven't heard before. What was up with that, Dad?"

"You don't really know Aphrodite, Son. She was—maybe still is—a woman of strange appetites. A lot of wild things went on out at Apostle's Cove."

"Oh, I've heard those stories about Shangri-La. Gram Patsy never let us near that place. But what's that got to do with me?"

"Your mother accused Aphrodite of molesting you."

"I don't . . . I don't remember that."

"You were only five years old," his father reminded him.

Sunny sat back. "Jesus." He furrowed his brow, as if trying to remember. "We were never allowed to be alone with her. And we never called her Gram or Grandma. It was always Aphrodite. She was like, I don't know, distant royalty or something, not really like family. Not like any of the family we had on the rez. I guess I thought that distance was her choice."

"I wasn't there when they had that fight," Axel said. "When Chastity told me about it, she said she'd made it clear that

Aphrodite was never going to see her grandchildren ever again. She was going to tell the county people about what happened. Everyone was going to know exactly what kind of perverted woman she was."

"Do you think Aphrodite could have been responsible for Chastity's death?"

"She claimed to be all about love, but I always had a sense of deeper, darker waters," Axel replied. "I'm not sure anyone really knows the true recesses of that woman's soul. I don't know who she is now, but I believe that back then, she could have been capable of it. Especially if she was high on one of her little friends."

"Little friends?"

"Pills. She had drugs of all kinds. Called them her little friends."

Cork recalled clearly the banshee of a woman who'd made such a scene in the sheriff's department after Boshey's arrest, screaming to see her grandchildren.

"You told me back then that you thought Chastity had been seeing someone."

Boshey nodded. "We weren't a happy couple. I could sometimes see the evidence that someone else had been with her. She didn't try hard to hide it. I was seeing Bernadette, so who was I to complain?"

"Any idea who that might have been?"

"None. She always flirted with men. Could have been just about anyone."

"I understand that Moonbeam shares none of your DNA. Does she have any idea who her biological father is?"

"I don't know. Moonbeam and I don't talk."

Now that Cork thought about it, he realized that Moonbeam hadn't been involved at all in the effort to free Boshey.

"Why is that?"

"My son would have a better idea," Boshey said.

Sunny gave a little shrug. "She was always ashamed to be the daughter of someone everyone believed to be a heartless murderer. Even though Gram Patsy tried to help her see Dad in a different light, she never wanted anything to do with him. In fact, when she received the result of the Ancestry test, she said it was as if she'd been released from her own prison sentence, finally out from under that dark cloud."

"Has she ever visited you, Axel?"

"Never."

"Sunny, have you ever talked to her about her biological father?"

"We've grown apart, I'm afraid. But here's something for you to think about. She and Aphrodite have become close. Aphrodite paid for her college education. They see each other fairly regularly. In fact, I think she might be staying at Shangri-La now."

"Do you ever see Aphrodite?"

"She's never reached out to me in the same way she has to Moonbeam. I'm not sure I'd be very amenable even if she did."

Axel Boshey studied Cork. "A lot to digest, eh? No rush. I'm going nowhere."

CHAPTER 32

"He doesn't blame me for anything. I don't think he blames anybody," Cork told Rainy. "He's a man quite content with where he is in life."

"In prison?"

"I don't think he sees it as a prison. He's more like Henry Meloux than anyone I've ever met. Life has shaped him in a remarkable way."

"If he's being honest with you. And with himself."

"What do you mean?"

"I'm not just a nurse. I'm Mide. People who come to me for healing often speak their minds but not their hearts. To reveal themselves truly is to become fully vulnerable. Imagine what that must mean in a place like Stillwater prison."

They were on their way back to Aurora, talking in the car, passing through a mixed landscape of hardwood and evergreen and occasional small cultivated fields of alfalfa or corn that were empty now, long ago harvested. They were in that area of Minnesota that was transitional, easing from the agrarian, Midwest beauty of the south to the boreal beauty of the North Country.

They drove under a sky whose face was hidden behind a mask of dark clouds, which fit Cork's mood perfectly.

"Maybe you're right. But Stephen and Sunny expect me to crack open a case that's more than twenty-five years old. I have no idea where to begin."

"If you were still a cop, where would you start?"

"I'd interview everyone again. But God only knows what they remember after all this time. And if they were lying then, they'll probably lie again."

"I didn't know you when you wore a badge, but I've seen how you work. I'm sure you'll figure this one out. And what happens if you don't get to the bottom of this? Axel stays in prison, which seems pretty much what he wants anyway. So, no pressure, right?"

"It's not all about Axel. It's also about what I didn't see back then that I should have. It's about what I let happen because I was willing to say the hell with due diligence."

"All right, where do you start? What does due diligence dictate now?"

Cork thought about that one for a while as the dark sky grew even darker. Then there were flakes of white drifting past his window and making little wet splotches on the windshield of his Expedition.

"Great," he said dourly. "Snow. Not a good sign."

"Snow covers the land, gives it a fresh new face. Maybe you should look at this as the Great Mystery offering you advice."

"I know who I need advice from."

She looked at him and smiled, understanding exactly who he meant.

Cork parked at the side of the gravel county road near the double-trunk birch that marked the path to Crow Point. Snow still fell, but gently, covering the ground in a thin layer that Cork thought of as a hunter's snow. The woods, as he and Rainy walked, were silent. The air was crisp and smelled of the wet, fallen leaves that lay beneath the white blanket. Cork felt the stillness as a kind of waiting, a holding of the breath of all the spirits, the *manidoog*, of the forest, as if they, too, were puzzled and seeking answers.

When they broke from the trees, the meadow on Crow Point was a long stretch of alabaster under a gunmetal gray sky. Smoke rose from the stovepipes on each of the two cabins in the distance. Because of the overcast, the dark of evening was descending early, and lantern light shone through the cabin windows. As they approached the first cabin, the door opened, and a man stepped out. He was tall, powerful, and although Cork knew he could be a menacing figure when need be, there was nothing but welcome in his demeanor.

"*Boozhoo*, Prophet," Cork said.

"*Boozhoo*, Cork. *Boozhoo*, Rainy. Henry said you'd be dropping by." Prophet waved them toward the old man's cabin. "Go on. He's just listening to WGZS." Which was a Native American radio station broadcasting out of Fond Du Lac. "I'll be there in a minute with coffee and something to eat."

Cork heard music and singing coming from the cabin. He knocked but received no answer. When he opened the door, he found Meloux sitting at his table with a battery-powered radio in front of him. Bluegrass poured forth, lively fiddles and nasal voices. Cork didn't recognize the tune, but Meloux was grinning ear to ear and tapping his hand on the tabletop along with the music. The old man held up a finger, cautioning Cork to be patient. A few moments later, the music ended and Meloux switched off his radio.

"I have always wished I had learned to play the fiddle. It is the voice of joy," the old man said. "Maybe in the next life."

From his jacket pocket, Cork drew out a small pouch of tobacco and set it beside the radio on the table. "Sorry to interrupt."

"It is good to see you, Corcoran O'Connor. And you, Niece. Sit," Meloux said, indicating the other chairs at the table.

The cabin smelled of something savory and delicious.

"Wild rice soup, Uncle?" Rainy asked.

"It was delicious. A specialty of Prophet. He is good at finding tasty mushrooms." Meloux cocked his head. Long hair as white as the snow outside fell over his shoulder. His eyes, the color of dark almonds and set in a face with more lines than a road map of the world, settled on Cork. "What is it that has brought you this time?"

"Axel Boshey."

"A name I have not heard in a very long time."

"I spoke with him today. After all these years, he's saying now that he didn't kill his wife."

This news seemed to have no impact on Meloux. He waited patiently, as if for Cork to continue.

"He's not particularly eager to leave prison, Henry. He told me you helped him accept where he is."

"I saw him once," the old man said. "Many years ago."

"Only once?"

Meloux gave Cork a searing look. "Unlike some who seek my advice, he understood my meaning pretty quick."

"Sunny has asked me to reinvestigate that old crime," Cork told him. "He wants to free his father."

"But, as you have said, his father does not necessarily want this. Should a son not respect the wishes of his father?"

"If Axel is innocent, isn't setting him free the right thing to do?"

The door opened and Prophet stepped in holding a coffeepot in one hand and a plate of muffins in the other.

"Pumpkin," he said setting the plate on the table. "And coffee for anyone who wants some."

For more than two years, Prophet had been Meloux's companion. He'd first come to Crow Point as a mercenary, hired to kill the old man if necessary. Instead, Meloux had turned the man's heart, shown him a different path, helped him discover his true nature and name.

Prophet took tin cups from a shelf, poured coffee for Cork and Rainy and himself, and took the final chair at the table.

"Tell Prophet your story," Meloux said.

And Cork did, laying out all the old details and the new situation.

Prophet looked to Rainy. "What do you think?"

"I think that getting to the truth is more important for Cork than for Axel Boshey." She put her hand over her husband's on the table. "And I think that if he finds the truth, the question becomes, What will he do with it? And perhaps that's where a consideration of what Axel Boshey wants becomes important."

"So," Prophet said to Cork, "if you're so intent on finding the truth, what are you doing here?"

Instead of answering Prophet, Cork picked up a muffin and took a bite. "Delicious," he said. Then he said, "I always believed back then that Henry had a better idea of what happened than he let on." He eyed Meloux. "Was I right?"

CHAPTER 33

Cork had never known a man more comfortable with silence than Henry Meloux. Prophet was right up there with him now, the influence of his time with the old Mide, Cork suspected. And Rainy, who was herself full-blood Anishinaabe, seemed just fine with it as well. In the long quiet that followed Cork's question, the only sound in the little cabin was Prophet sipping coffee from his tin cup.

Cork gave in first. "Henry, I don't believe you've ever lied to me, but you've often held back the truth."

"Sometimes you and me, we look at a thing and see in it a different truth. Is yours any less valid than mine? Should I try to argue you into seeing the way I see? Better sometimes to hold to silence."

"The innocence or guilt of a man, isn't that worth arguing over?"

"That was not the argument back then. The argument was whether a man should be allowed to follow the path he has chosen for himself. This still seems to me to be the issue. From what you say, Axel Boshey is content with the path he has chosen."

"It's not just about Axel, Henry. It's about a murderer who

may still be wandering around out there free as a bird. I want to catch that bird."

"So, this is not so much about Axel Boshey as it is Corcoran O'Connor."

"It's not about me. It's about justice."

The old man gave his head a little shake. "How many times have we looked at that through different eyes?"

"When I first investigated Chastity's death, you held something back from me, didn't you?"

"You sound like a demanding child now."

"You're not answering my question. And so often I've found that it's what you're not telling me that's important. What aren't you telling me?"

The old man reached up and scratched the side of his nose, the whole time keeping his dark eyes on Cork. There was another long silence, then Meloux said, "You want me to tell you something, then I will. At the center of every web, there is a spider. If I were you, I would look for that spider."

Cork, in his fervor for the truth, had leaned more and more across the table toward Meloux in a challenging way. Now he sat back. He felt the tension that had been like a fist in him since he'd left Stillwater prison ease. He gave the old Mide a single grateful nod and said, "*Miigwech,* Henry. *Chi miigwech.*"

"I don't understand," Rainy said as they walked along the path to Cork's parked Expedition.

The cloud cover had broken a bit and hard dark hadn't yet come. There was enough evening light reflecting off the snowy ground that Cork and Rainy could see their way without difficulty.

"Uncle Henry still didn't give you a straight answer."

"Sometimes, the meaning behind Henry's words escapes me. But not this time. I think I know exactly what he meant."

"You know the spider?"

"I believe I do. I think I did twenty-five years ago. I just . . . I just gave up."

"Who's the spider?"

"Who do you think?"

"This is your mystery, not mine."

"I've told you the whole story. Think about it for a bit."

Rainy was quiet. As they walked, Cork couldn't help recalling how, for so many years, he'd walked this path with his first wife, Jo. She would listen as he ran ideas past her, what he thought Henry had meant with one riddle or another, then she would offer her own take. He still missed her. But the Creator had been generous and brought Rainy into his life. And for that, he would be eternally grateful.

"The only person in all this saga that strikes me as someone with the personality of a spider is Aphrodite McGill," Rainy finally said.

In the dim moonlight, Cork gave her a smile. "Bingo."

"How does she fit in? Or rather, how do you find out how she fits in?"

"It's been a long time, so I'd like to take a look at the files from that case, then figure out how best to proceed. People have scattered. I'll have to track them down, I suppose. There are so many pieces of this puzzle to put together."

"Does that mean you'll be tossing and turning all night?"

"Maybe."

Rainy took a few steps, then said, "I'll make the coffee."

* * *

The house on Gooseberry Lane was dark but for a single light in the kitchen. Cork and Rainy entered through the mudroom and found Jenny sitting alone at the table. It was too early for anyone, even young Waaboo, to be in bed. Jenny was hunched over a laptop. When Cork and Rainy came in, she looked up suddenly, clearly surprised.

"Sorry," Cork said. "I thought you heard us coming."

Jenny let out a deep sigh. "Working on a chapter that's just not coming together."

In addition to raising her son and sometimes managing Sam's Place, Jenny O'Connor was a novelist. She'd published two books, both of them fiction, thinly veiled accounts of cases she had been involved in along with her father. The books had been well received, sold nicely, and Jenny was under contract for a third. With this one, things didn't seem to be going so well.

"Let me guess," he said. "Daniel took Waaboo somewhere to give you peace and quiet."

"They went to the Halloween party at the Y. Daniel made Waaboo up as a werewolf. He loved it."

"And Daniel?"

"Took his accordion. He went as a geek." She pushed her laptop aside. "How'd it go in the Cities?"

"We haven't eaten yet," Rainy said. "Anything in the fridge?"

"Leftover split pea soup," Jenny said.

"Sounds wonderful. I'll heat up a couple of bowls. And I'll make some coffee."

"Coffee? This late?" Jenny said. "Oh, I want to hear everything."

Over soup and coffee, Cork filled his daughter in on all that had occurred since he and Rainy had left the day before.

"You've got your work cut out for you," Jenny said when he'd finished. "Aphrodite McGill. Cracking her will take a sledgehammer. She's always reminded me of the scary woman in that old Disney movie *A Thousand and One Dalmatians*."

"It was only a hundred and one," Cork said. "But I get your point."

Jenny closed her laptop. "Shangri-La. That place has quite a reputation. I wouldn't mind dropping in there with you when you question her, if you'd let me."

"A sudden interest in justice?"

"Call it research. She might be an interesting woman to write about someday."

"We'll see," Cork said. "No promises."

They heard the front door open, and a moment later Daniel English, Jenny's husband, stepped into the kitchen with their son, Waaboo. Waaboo, whose real name was Aaron Smalldog O'Connor, was seven years old. He was of mixed-blood heritage, adopted by Jenny, who'd literally found him under a rock when he was a baby. His face now was a profusion of brown fur, his nose black. Fur covered the tops of both hands. When he growled at them, his teeth were fangs.

"Oh, my!" Rainy said and threw her hands up as if scared to death. "Don't eat me!"

"Bet you won best costume," Cork said.

"Thecond plath," Waaboo said. He took out the fangs. "Second place. Katie Miller got first. She was the Wicked Witch from *Wizard of Oz*, all green."

"She had a pretty nifty costume as well," Daniel said. "And of course, a broomstick." He set the accordion he'd been holding on the kitchen floor and nodded toward Cork. "When you have a moment, I want to hear all about what went on in Stillwater."

Jenny's husband was Lac Courte Oreilles Anishinaabe and an officer with the Iron Lake Ojibwe Tribal Police. After Stephen's initial call, Cork had filled him in on the Boshey case.

"Later," Jenny said. "It's almost bedtime for Waaboo. And you've got to get all that fur off him."

"Come on, Wolfie," Daniel said. "Say good night, then upstairs."

When they'd gone, Cork began to gather up the soup bowls and silverware. Rainy said, "I'll take care of that. I bet you've got some investigating to do."

Just as Rainy had predicted, Cork was up late into the night, hunched over a computer in the room that had once been Jo O'Connor's home law office. For a long time after her death, it had gone unused. Cork couldn't bring himself to sift through everything that reminded him of his beloved wife. But time, as they have always said, heals all wounds, and the great wounding that was Jo's loss had become less and less painful, and eventually the room became just an office, the law books stored until Stephen might need them, the random reminders of Jo boxed up, a new computer installed every few years. Jo had decorated the office with family photographs, all still hanging on the wall, shots of camping outings and birthdays and vacation spots, and in the center, a family portrait, posed at the studio of Larkin Photography. It was the last photograph of the whole family together, taken nine years earlier, in the summer just before the chartered plane in which Jo was a passenger vanished in the mountains of Wyoming. Jo wasn't the only one in the photograph who was no longer among the living. Brain cancer had taken Cork's younger daughter, Annie, two years earlier.

Looking at those photos, he found himself thinking darkly about the past, about all those he'd lost over the years in such tragic ways—his father, a wife, a child. Still, he'd been luckier than some. He'd had many years of happiness with those he loved, been given so many blessed moments that were stored in the vault of his heart. He thought about the long scar on Axel Boshey's face and wondered about the kinds of memories more than two decades in prison had left in that man's heart. The dark weight of his own guilt in that tragic circumstance settled on his shoulders.

There was a soft knocking, and he found Jenny standing in the open doorway.

"Okay if I interrupt?" she asked.

"Can't sleep?" he said.

"Still trying to hammer out something for this new manuscript. I keep going round and round."

"You haven't told me what this new one is about."

"Hemingway warned that if you say too much about a work in progress, you can talk out all the energy of the story." She came and sat in the empty chair on the other side of the desk. "I've been trying to write about what's happened in the last couple of years. The murdered girls, Waaboo threatened, Annie dying. It's not going well."

"Any idea why?"

"I'm thinking it's too soon. My vision's clouded by all the hurt."

"Maybe you need to write about something not so recent."

She leaned on the desk and eyed him meaningfully. "That's exactly what I've been thinking. What I might try instead is a story based on Chastity Boshey's murder."

"There's still so much unknown about that."

"I write fiction. I can make stuff up. But it would be good to have a true framework to hang all my imaginings on. It's pretty intriguing. A brutal murder. The man who confessed, now unconfessing. A detective asked to find the truth after all these years. And who knows? Maybe you'll find that truth while I'm at work on the story."

"I get the feeling there's more to this."

"Okay, I'm thinking that if I did choose to write about Chastity and Axel and all of it, disguised as fiction, of course, it might be helpful if I shadowed you."

"Ah." Cork sat back. "Taking notes?"

"Maybe. Mentally at the very least. Maybe I could even offer some insights. You know, someone not so emotionally involved. A disinterested observer."

"In my experience, it's tough enough to get answers from people when it's just me asking. Bring along a disinterested observer and I might get nothing."

"Or you might get someone who finds it easier talking to a young, sympathetic woman rather than an old former cop."

"You said observer."

"I'll just watch, then, and smile pleasantly. You could think of me as Watson to your Holmes."

"What if I don't find the truth?"

"Something tells me you're not going to let that happen this time around. So what do you say?"

Cork thought on it a few moments more, then smiled and said, "All right, Watson. I guess the game's afoot."

CHAPTER 34

Sheriff Marsha Dross said, "Of course I remember the Boshey case. The first homicide investigation I ever worked. So, I heard by way of the grapevine that you visited Boshey in Stillwater yesterday, that he claims he was innocent. True?"

Cork and Jenny sat in Dross's office. Through the window, the morning sky above Aurora was a deep azure. It was early still, the streets of town only just beginning to come alive with folks on their way to open shops or wait tables or meet for breakfast at a place like Johnny's Pinewood Broiler. These wouldn't be tourists. The leaf-peeping season was over. Although there'd been a snowfall already, the layer was too thin to be of use to snowmobilers or cross-country skiers. It would still be weeks before the ice on Iron Lake was thick enough to support shanties for fishing. This was a time that everyone in the tourist business called "shoulder season."

"Not exactly," Cork said. "He's recanting his confession, but he's still not one hundred percent sure what happened that night. I think he continues to harbor some concern that he might have been somehow responsible."

"And he's asked you to take another look at things?"

"Not him. If I can believe him, and I do, he's quite content with his life in Stillwater. It's Sunny Boshey who's pushing this. And Stephen."

"So what do you need from me?"

"I want to take a look at everything we collected back then. Statements from everyone we interviewed, officers' notes, evidence, anything we might still have on the case."

"If you want to go through the Property Room, I'll have Foster, he's our evidence custodian now, give you full access. Do you have any idea where this might lead you?"

"To a spider, I hope," Cork said.

He and Jenny spent the morning going over the files on the Boshey case, reviewing the statements taken from everyone involved, scanning the notes Ed Larson and Cork himself had made. As lunchtime neared, Marsha Dross came into the Property Room.

"I'm popping over to the Broiler. Care to join me?"

Cork arched his back and rubbed the muscles of his neck. "I could use a break."

"Me, too," Jenny said.

Johnny's Pinewood Broiler, an institution in Aurora for decades, smelled of all things fried that afternoon. Johnny Papp, who owned the establishment, greeted them as they came in. "I heard you closed up Sam's Place early this year, Cork. Business is slow here, too."

"Wasn't that, Johnny. Personal matters to attend to. Could you give us a booth in a corner?"

Papp grinned at the group. "Cops. You always want to sit somewhere you can see the whole room."

After they'd been seated and had ordered, Dross asked Cork, "What did you mean when you said your investigation might lead to a spider?"

"If I eliminate Bernadette Polaski as a suspect and look at everything and everyone involved back then, the common thread that connects them all is Aphrodite McGill. The spider at the center of the web. There's Aphrodite and Chastity. Aphrodite and Axel. Aphrodite and Wild Bill. Aphrodite and half the men in Tamarack County."

"That has to be an exaggeration, Dad," Jenny said.

"Only slightly," Cork said. "So here's what I'm thinking. Chastity and her mother argued about many things. In my notes from the investigation, I jotted down something Axel said. He told me that one of the accusations Chastity threw at her mother was that Aphrodite tried to steal all her boyfriends. Axel admitted to having sex with Aphrodite before he married Chastity. Axel also said that he believed Chastity was seeing someone. So maybe that someone was also seeing Aphrodite."

"They were sharing a lover?"

"Sharing implies consent. As I said, according to Axel, it was a point of contention. If it happened, I don't think Chastity was on board with it at all."

"And?" Jenny said.

"When he did the autopsy, Sigurd Nelson found evidence of recent sexual activity. Axel denied it was him. He maintained that they hadn't had sex in quite some time. We asked Sigurd to take a DNA swab. Because Axel confessed, we never had it analyzed."

"We could do that now," Dross said.

"That's what I was hoping for. And here's something else. The phone records showed no phone calls to or from the Boshey cabin after Axel claimed to have left. So, if Chastity had a tryst that night with her lover, how did he know Axel was gone? It wasn't through a phone call."

Dross thought a moment. "A signal of some kind?"

"We had a signal in college when the dorm room was available for action," Jenny said. "A candle in the window."

Cork arched an eyebrow. "Action in your dorm room?"

"Girls just wanna have fun," Jenny said with a little shrug.

"Okay, so here's a thought," Cork went on. "When I was going through my notes this morning, I came across one I made about the mailbox at the resort. After Chastity was murdered, I found the flag raised. According to Dave Briddon, who was the rural mail carrier back then, that should have signaled there was something to be picked up. But the mailbox was empty."

"Someone took something from it?" Dross said.

"That was what I thought back then. But I have a different idea about that now. What if it was the signal that Chastity used. Whoever the lover was would see the flag raised, the mailbox empty, and know that the coast was clear."

Dross looked unconvinced. "That's a lot of speculation."

"I think a lot of speculation is going to be required."

Their food came. As they ate, Dross asked, "More work in the Property Room after this?"

"It's time to take the bull by the horns. Jenny and I are heading to Shangri-La."

"Stepping into the middle of the web, Dad?"

"We're going to start shaking it a bit."

"Be careful, Cork," Dross advised. "We all know Aphrodite. She's one spider that can bite."

Years earlier, Aphrodite McGill had given up driving her pink Volkswagen covered in flower decals. The house and grounds of Shangri-La were not so carefully maintained as they once had been. But Aphrodite continued those activities that had made her such an object of lascivious speculation. She was still the subject of rumors regarding dalliances with various locals. She still held gatherings on the summer solstice, though they weren't as well attended or as riotous as in the old days. Every Halloween, she hosted a grand costume ball to which no children were ever invited. She'd become overly fond of saying that what happened at Shangri-La stayed at Shangri-La. In a place like Aurora, Minnesota, where Thanksgiving dinners were straight out of a Norman Rockwell painting, summers were filled with Little League games, teenage girls still dreamed of prom dresses, and more people than not attended church every Sunday, Aphrodite McGill stood out like a cockroach on a wedding cake.

One change was that Aphrodite drove an Escalade now, with no adornments, so there was no reason to leave it out on display, as she'd done with her pink bug in the old days. Cork pulled into the empty circular drive and parked. The front of the house had been extensively decorated for Halloween—ghouls and witches and jack-o'-lanterns and a skeleton that stood twenty feet tall. In the bright October sunlight, that giant construction of bones cast a dark shadow across the grand house. When Cork knocked on the door, it was opened by a devil, replete with a pitchfork and long tail. She reminded him of Hot Stuff, the little devil in comic books.

"Yes?" the devil said.

Although it had been a very long time since Cork had seen her, he knew the young woman in the costume. Her face was so very like her mother's.

"Moonbeam," he said.

The devil looked at him blankly.

"Cork O'Connor. I'm a friend of your grandmother, Patsy Boshey."

"Gram Patsy and I don't talk these days."

"I'm sorry to hear that. Any reason?"

"I'm certainly not going to share that with a stranger."

Cork could hear music playing inside the house. Opera. Some kind of grand aria. Or something. Cork didn't know opera. Then over the music a familiar voice sang out, "Who is it, darling?"

"Just people," Moonbeam called over her shoulder.

"Well, invite them in."

With clear reluctance, the devil stepped aside.

They stood in the foyer of the grand house. From there, Cork could see that much of the rest of the house had been, like the outside, decorated for the season. Aphrodite McGill swept into view. She was dressed as Cleopatra—a gold, tight-fitting dress, a tiara with an asp at the crown, eyelids darkened with kohl, gold slippers on her feet.

Although she'd edged into her early sixties, she had, through the magic of much costly cosmetic surgery, Cork surmised, managed to keep her face looking far more youthful than her age. She was smiling broadly. Then she saw Cork and her whole demeanor changed.

"Oh," she said. "You. What do you want?"

"A little early for costumes, isn't it, Aphrodite?"

"Just trying out possibilities," she said. "For my Halloween extravaganza."

"I'm not sure that you've met my daughter Jenny."

Aphrodite gave her a slight nod, which seemed to Cork much like the deigning gesture of an Egyptian queen.

"And I'm not sure if you've heard," Cork went on. "Axel Boshey has recanted his confession in the killing of your daughter." He looked at Moonbeam. "Your mother."

"Axel was always a liar," Aphrodite said. "And what difference does it make anyway?"

"Sunny"—again he eyed Moonbeam—"your brother, has

asked me to take another look at the case, in light of what Axel is saying now."

"Sunny's always been too soft on that man," Moonbeam said.

Cork caught sight of a figure—a man, he guessed from the bulk and build—lurking far behind Aphrodite. Although the figure wore no costume, he did wear a mask, the face of a fleshless skull.

"That monster butchered my little girl," Aphrodite said. "He should have been hung."

"We don't do that in Minnesota, especially if a man is innocent."

"You'll get no help from me, if that's why you're here. I have nothing to say to you."

"Just let me point out the same thing I pointed out to Axel. If he didn't kill Chastity, then whoever did is still out there. Don't you want to know who that might be?"

"I know who killed my daughter. I've always known. Now, I'd appreciate it if you'd just leave me alone."

Cork looked at Moonbeam. "Wouldn't you like to know the truth of your mother's death?"

The eyes of the face in the devil costume simply stared at him.

Then Cork said, "And don't you want to know who your real father might be?"

"Get out!" Aphrodite said.

"We're going," Cork replied.

Cork took one last good measure of the figure lurking in the background. Whoever was behind that skull mask realized he was being scrutinized and slipped out of sight. Then Cork turned and, with his daughter, stepped outside. The door was closed firmly at their backs.

"How old is Aphrodite, Dad?"

"A couple years older than me."

"I'll say one thing for her. She still looks good."

"She can afford to. I've heard she uses the best plastic surgeon in the Twin Cities. Get this. I've been told his name is Dr. Butcher. Swear to God."

Jenny laughed, then said seriously, "Did you see the look on Moonbeam's face when you asked that final question?"

"I did," Cork replied.

Jenny said, "She wants to know."

CHAPTER 35

It was nearing the end of the school day, and Jenny wanted to be home to greet Waaboo. Cork dropped her off at the house on Gooseberry Lane, then headed to the rez. By the time he arrived at Sweetgrass Assisted Living in Allouette, the thin layer of snow that had been a taste of winter had completely melted away under the late October sun. Sweetgrass, like so many other establishments in Tamarack County, had been decorated for the Halloween season. When Cork entered the reception area, he was greeted with a display of jack-o'-lanterns. Although there were the usual faces, both sinister and goofy, many were of intricate design.

"A pumpkin carving contest," the young woman at the reception desk explained as he signed in on the visitors' log. "The winner gets a gift certificate for Sunday brunch at the Four Seasons."

He found Patsy Boshey sitting in a large common room with half a dozen other women elders, all of them knitting while they chatted. The windows of the big room looked out toward Iron Lake and the marina, which the tribe had built only a few years earlier. Under the bright sun, the surface of the lake shone like a sheet of newly forged steel.

"*Boozhoo,* Aunties," Cork said. "Knitting Christmas sweaters?"

"Baby blankets, Corkie," Lynn Ganschinietz said. After her husband, William, had passed away, she and her lifelong best friend, Patsy, had moved into Sweetgrass together. "The folks over at IHS distribute them where needed."

"It's supposed to keep us out of trouble," Patsy said, then laughed as if that were a ridiculous hope.

"Patsy, I'm wondering if I could talk to you. Somewhere private?"

"Girls," Patsy Boshey said, rising. "I got a date."

They talked in her room, which was a neat furnished studio. She had photographs of Sunny and his wife and their children framed and prominently displayed on the bureau. There was also a photograph of Moonbeam, somewhere in her teens, wearing a jingle dress, her hair in two dark braids, beaded earrings dangling. Taped to the refrigerator were crayon drawings on manila paper, childish but remarkably good.

When she saw Cork eyeing them, Patsy said, "I have a granddaughter in St. Paul who'll be a famous artist someday. Would you like some tea? All I have is herbal."

"No, thank you, Patsy."

"Have a seat." She held out a hand toward an easy chair. She took the love seat. "I'm guessing you want to talk about Axel. Sunny told me what he was up to with his father."

"I spoke with Axel at Stillwater yesterday. Sunny was there. So was Axel's daughter, Marianne."

"Ah." Patsy nodded.

She was nearing eighty now. Although she'd raised Axel, then raised Sunny and Moonbeam, her face held none of the deep lines that so often came with the worries of parenting and grandparenting. The look in her eyes was still smart and alert. Cork had watched her knit while she was with the women in the common room, and her hands had been remarkably steady. Although like all Native people she'd dealt with more than her share of challenges, Patsy Boshey seemed to have come through life in pretty good shape.

"What a lovely surprise she is," Patsy said.

"Yes, but it's Moonbeam I want to talk to you about. I just came from Shangri-La."

"Oh?" Her face changed, became troubled. "Did you also talk to that woman?"

"Aphrodite? Yes."

"Bane of my existence."

"Moonbeam seems quite close to her."

"She bought my granddaughter."

Cork gave her a quizzical look.

"Right from the get-go, she lavished her with gifts."

"What about Sunny?"

"I made sure she stayed away from Sunny. I knew what she'd tried to do with that boy. I did my best to protect Moonbeam, too. But that witch had her ways of getting around me."

"Moonbeam told me that you two aren't in touch at the moment."

"Her choice. When she decided to move into that place, I told her exactly what I thought of her decision. She hasn't spoken to me since." Patsy looked out the window and stared at the shiny surface of Iron Lake. "I think I may have lost her."

"You know that Axel isn't her father."

She nodded. "Chastity was sneaking around behind Axel's back the whole time they were married. When Sunny told me about the DNA test and Moonbeam, I wasn't surprised."

"Do you have any idea who she might have been seeing?"

"Axel would be a better one to ask."

"He's not being particularly helpful."

"Try asking that witch of a woman who birthed Chastity. But what difference would it make knowing who the father was?"

"Chastity was with someone the night she was murdered. Whoever that was, he may have been responsible."

Patsy closed her eyes a moment, then said, "I know this will sound bad, but I'm glad Chastity didn't raise Sunny and Moonbeam. I can't help thinking whoever killed her probably had good reason."

It was late afternoon by the time Cork pulled into the driveway of Ed Larson's home. Larson was one of the Old Martyrs, and he and Cork still played basketball together regularly. Larson had long ago retired from the sheriff's department and now drove a school bus, but not because he needed the money particularly. His wife, Verna, had passed away not long after Ed retired. Their only child, Tamara, lived in Chicago with her family. Driving the school bus kept him busy, and because his grandchildren were so far away, it kept him connected with the energy of children, which he said he missed.

Larson cracked open a couple of Leinie's. Although the air was cool, the two men sat on a bench on the front porch. Larson had raked his leaves into big orange bags made to look like jack-o'-lanterns. He'd put out a scarecrow and hung a couple of ghosts from the limbs of his maple tree. He still wore wire-rimmed glasses that made him look bookish. And he still dressed like a college professor, even when driving his school bus.

"I heard that Axel Boshey's claiming he wasn't guilty," he said.

"I talked to him yesterday down in Stillwater. He's not actually saying he was innocent. He's just recanting the confession."

"There's a difference?"

"He's still fuzzy on what actually happened that night."

"He knew so many details."

"He got them from Rocky, when Rocky attacked him in the jail cell."

"Oh, yeah, I remember that. Got Rocky suspended. Then you fired him."

"Martinelli hated Native people. Way too many complaints. The man was a lawsuit waiting to happen."

"What else did you learn from Boshey?"

"Bernadette Polaski is dead. Turns out the reason Axel confessed was that he thought Bernadette may have killed Chastity. Bernadette was pregnant with Axel's child, and Axel didn't want her going to prison."

Larson sipped his beer while digesting this piece of information. "Did Bernadette kill her?"

"I don't think so. And neither does her daughter, the child Axel fathered."

"You met her?"

Cork recounted everything that had transpired during his visit to the Twin Cities.

"So, if Bernadette didn't kill Chastity, why did she run?"

"Shame, I'm guessing. Imagine sticking around Tamarack County when everyone knows you're carrying a confessed murderer's bastard child."

"Yeah," Larson said. "I get that. Still, she had plenty of motive for killing Chastity. I think it would be a mistake to write her off completely now that Axel's pulling the plug on his confession."

"We'll keep her on the back burner."

"We?" Larson shook his head. "I drive a school bus now. Happy doing just that."

"That's fine. I've got a new partner. Jenny's giving me a hand with this investigation."

"Ha!" Larson slapped Cork on the back. "She's helping you and getting material for another novel. Am I right?"

"That's her plan."

"You're lucky," Larson said. "You have a child and a grandson still here. Must never get lonely around your place."

"Hectic," Cork said. "Never lonely. But here's something else I've been thinking about, Ed. I went over the notes on the interview I did with Aphrodite the morning I found her sitting in a pool of her daughter's blood. She claimed that she and Chastity were close and talked on the phone all the time. Axel told me that wasn't true at all. Chastity hated her mother, wanted nothing to do with her. According to my notes, Aphrodite claimed that the night Chastity was killed, she and her daughter had talked on the phone about Axel and his drinking. The next morning, when Aphrodite tried calling, Chastity didn't answer, and that's why she came to the cabin. When I took a look at the phone records we pulled for the Boshey cabin during the investigation, there was no phone call made to Shangri-La or from Shangri-La the night Chastity was killed. When Axel confessed, we didn't follow up on that detail. But now I wonder why Aphrodite lied."

"Did you ask her that today?"

"I didn't have a chance to ask much of anything."

Larson sipped his beer and ruminated a bit. "So, you're thinking Aphrodite might have had something to do with her daughter's death? But if I recall correctly, she seemed pretty upset by the whole thing."

"That could have been an act. And you weren't there the morning Aphrodite stormed into the department, high as a kite, demanding to see her grandchildren. That woman was a banshee. I had to lock her up."

"A lot to think about, Cork. But after twenty-five years, how do you prove anything?"

That was a question for which Cork had no answer.

CHAPTER 36

It was dusk when Cork left Larson and got into his Expedition. He spent a moment punching in the number for the landline at the house on Gooseberry Lane. Rainy answered.

"I won't be home for dinner. A couple of things I need to take care of."

"We'll keep something warm for you," Rainy promised.

Cork heard Jenny in the background. "Is that Dad? Can I talk to him?"

"Here's your daughter," Rainy said.

"What's up, Dad? Can I help?" Jenny asked.

"I'm just going to drop by Sam's Place. A couple of things in my files there I want to check."

"When you get home, you'll bring me up to date?"

"That I will." Then he added, "Watson."

He drove through Aurora, a town he'd known from birth, along streets he'd walked and biked as a kid, past houses he'd delivered newspapers to and in which, across the course of his life, he'd attended birthday parties and anniversary celebrations and memorial gatherings. The day was sliding into dark, sidewalks emptying, lights winking on through windows in which curtains were being drawn.

He pulled into the gravel lot of Sam's Place and stood for a moment looking past the old Quonset hut at Iron Lake, whose surface, in its reflection of the deep purple sky, resembled a great bruise. He quietly blessed Sam Winter Moon, who'd willed him the little business. Serving burgers, fries, and shakes alongside his children and the children of so many others through the years had given him great pleasure. He had no idea who would take over the business when he finally chose to step away. Annie was gone. Stephen was going to be a lawyer. Jenny was making a mark as a writer. Maybe Waaboo would be old enough by then and willing. Only time would tell. He took a deep breath. He had other things to think about now.

Inside Sam's Place he turned on the bulb in his office area and began going through file drawers looking for a folder that he only dimly remembered. Very early on in his capacity as a private investigator he'd been asked by a fellow parishioner, a single mother, to look into a fight in which her teenage son had been involved. Roger Sakala had worked two seasons at Sam's Place. Cork liked the kid, had occasionally offered the kind of advice a father might have. But that summer, Roger had worked for Aphrodite McGill instead, taking care of the large grounds of Shangri-La, the mowing, weeding, planting, raking. Roger was a big, athletic kid with a good build on him. Aphrodite, Cork found out in his investigation, usually asked him to work without a shirt on.

The fight had involved a man named Buster Gaines, who ran a garage where Aphrodite had some work done on her car. Aphrodite claimed the man had stolen a bracelet she'd left in the glovebox. The man denied it. There was not enough evidence for the sheriff's people to become involved. A few days after Aphrodite's accusation, Roger Sakala confronted Gaines, demanding the return of the bracelet. Gaines told him to get lost. A fight ensued. Both parties were pretty well damaged, but neither wanted to press charges. Roger refused to talk to his mother about it. That's when she asked Cork to intervene.

It took some doing, but Cork finally got the truth out of Roger. The kid claimed that Aphrodite McGill had promised certain favors if the kid was able to secure the bracelet, or at the very least, make Gaines pay heavily for the theft. When Cork pressed him, Roger confessed that Aphrodite had been as good as her word.

Cork scanned the file he'd created on the incident. It was pretty thin, but it contained notes on an interview he'd conducted with Aphrodite at the time. She'd denied everything Roger Sakala said, but also pointed out that the kid was seventeen, beyond the age of consent. So the hell with Cork, the kid, and Mrs. Sakala. Roger was subsequently dismissed from her employment.

Night had come as Cork sat in the harsh light of the bulb above the table where the open file lay. He found himself wondering if it were possible that Aphrodite might have wielded enough of the same allure and control over someone twenty-five years ago, someone who could have been seduced into killing Chastity Boshey. It was a stretch, but Cork couldn't help envisioning that woman, eight-legged and many-eyed, at the center of a spider's web.

He'd been listening to the radio as he worked, and now a song came on, one that had been released that summer and he couldn't help liking, "Don't Worry Be Happy" by Bobby McFerrin. The tune and lyrics were delightfully simple and impossibly upbeat. No matter what happens, McFerrin advised, don't worry. Just be happy because everything will work out. Although that hadn't been Cork's general experience in life, the song always made him smile.

Just as the tune ended, a metallic scraping came from the wall on the outside of the Quonset hut. It was like the scratch of a branch shifting against the hut in a wind. But there'd been no wind when Cork entered Sam's Place. He turned off the radio, rose, and looked through the window to the dark outside. The scraping stopped. He turned and started back to the table. The metallic scraping came again.

Cork went to the door and stepped outside. The air was calm, the night quiet. The scraping came once more, this time from just around the corner of the hut. As Cork walked that way, the noise ceased and the only sound was the crunch of the soles of his shoes on gravel. He turned the corner. And the night exploded.

The first blow was to his face. It knocked him back and he went down. The next blow was a kick to his ribs. The final blow was once again to his face, but this one delivered by a steel-toed boot.

The darkness that slowly descended had nothing to do with the night. As Cork yielded to that black, a voice whispered harshly into his ear.

"Axel Boshey is a liar and a murderer. You stay away from Aphrodite, or the next time I won't be so gentle."

Cork had no idea how long he'd been out. When he woke, a half-moon had risen, shedding a ghostly light all around him. He tried to sit up. The world spun. He leaned over and puked, a retching that made his ribs feel as if they were being kicked again. He took a few minutes to gather himself, then slowly stood, using the side of the Quonset hut for support. He made his way toward the door, which was still open. As he passed his parked Expedition, he saw that the tires had been slashed.

Inside, he picked up the cell phone he'd left on the table. He punched in Jenny's number. When she answered he said, "Watson, I need a ride."

CHAPTER 37

"Nothing?" Sheriff Marsha Dross said.

"Dark night. And whoever it was, they hit me before I had a chance to see anything."

It was nearing one a.m. Cork sat on the examination table of an ER room at Aurora Community Hospital. Jenny was there, and Rainy, who'd called the sheriff's department. Daniel English wanted to be there as well, but somebody needed to be with Waaboo. Cork had been seen, the damage to his face, a swelling around his right eye and a darkening bruise there, had been treated and X-rays taken of his ribs—nothing broken. The ER doctor had run him through a gauntlet of questions designed to ferret out possible concussive effects from the kick to his head. He'd been cleared to leave the hospital, so long as he didn't go to sleep right away, and when he did sleep, Rainy was to wake him every so often and question him to be certain he was still thinking clearly.

"But whoever it was, they told you to stay away from Aphrodite?" Dross said. "Did you recognize the voice?"

Cork was holding a gel ice pack to his swollen eye. "It was a whisper, growly. Male, I think."

"Are you sure it couldn't have been Aphrodite disguising her voice?" Dross said.

"I wouldn't put it past her," Jenny threw in.

"You told me Moonbeam Boshey was at Shangri-La and was antagonistic," Dross said. "Could it have been her?"

"I'm pretty sure the boot that delivered the kicks was steel-toed. Doesn't sound like standard footwear for a young woman. Or for Aphrodite, for that matter. I saw someone else at Shangri-La, a guy lurking in the background."

"Did you recognize him?"

"He was wearing a mask."

"Build?"

"Easily six feet tall, probably a little over two hundred pounds. Wearing a red plaid flannel shirt, jeans." Cork thought a moment. "And boots."

"Eh, voilà," Jenny said. "Our assailant."

"I think I'll have a talk with Aphrodite," Dross said.

"Not without me," Cork said.

Rainy put a hand on his arm as if in restraint. "You're going home, mister."

"She's right," Dross said. "You've been warned to stay away. I don't want you going near Shangri-La or Aphrodite McGill until I have this all sorted out." She glanced at her watch. "It's late and I have an incident report to write up. I'll interview Aphrodite in the morning and let you know how that goes." She eyed him sternly. "I know you, Cork, and I'm going to say this one more time. Don't go near that woman."

He'd been given ibuprofen and advised to continue icing his bruised face and ribs. He walked without any problem to Jenny's Forester. They drove back to the house on Gooseberry Lane. Waaboo had long ago gone to bed, but Daniel was waiting up for them. Per the ER doctor's instructions, Rainy wanted Cork to stay awake a while, so she made herbal tea and they gathered around the kitchen table, as they often did.

"Cookie, anyone?" Jenny asked.

From the jar on the counter, which was shaped like *Sesame Street*'s Ernie, Jenny took a chocolate chip cookie for each of them. Cork sipped his tea and munched on his cookie while Jenny quizzed him about what he'd found out since she'd abandoned him that afternoon in favor of her son.

Cork recounted his visit with Patsy Boshey at Sweetgrass, his talk with Ed Larson, and the question that had arisen in his mind about why Aphrodite would have lied about the phone call with her daughter.

"You think it was Aphrodite who killed Chastity?" Jenny said. "Dad, that's so, I don't know, so Greek mythish."

"She might not have done it herself," Cork said. Then he told them about the file he'd pulled at Sam's Place and the long-ago incident involving Aphrodite and a kid named Roger Sakala.

Rainy said, "So you're thinking that if Aphrodite seduced a kid into attacking a man, she might have seduced someone into killing her daughter? Oh, Cork, as a mother, that's too hard for me to believe."

"Maybe it wasn't supposed to go that way," Cork said. "Maybe it was just some kind of intimidation that got out of hand."

"Why the intimidation?" Daniel asked.

"Because Chastity refused to let Aphrodite near her grandchildren. Or maybe it was over a man. Patsy and Axel both are pretty sure Chastity was seeing someone. It's possible Aphrodite was interested in the same man. Axel told me Chastity accused her mother of stealing her boyfriends. Maybe Chastity turned the tables and stole someone from her mother. Aphrodite doesn't strike me as a woman who would tolerate that kind of theft."

"But killing her own daughter?" Rainy said.

"It's just one of the speculations."

"You've clearly whacked a hornet's nest," Daniel said.

"And Aphrodite sicced someone on you," Jenny said. "Probably that guy we saw at Shangri-La today. But who was he?"

"If what Cork tells me about Aphrodite McGill is true," Rainy said, "you could be looking at half the male population of this county." She studied Cork. "I think it's been long enough since you got that blow to your head. Why don't you try to get some sleep?"

"What about tomorrow, Dad?" Jenny asked. "Where do we begin?"

"Hold on there," Daniel said. "As I understand it, Marsha Dross made it clear you weren't to go near Aphrodite McGill. And given the beating Cork took tonight, I'm not at all sure that you should be involved in this, Jenny."

"You forget that I risked my life to pull our son from under a rock. This is nothing. And from now on, we'll only sleuth during the daylight hours. Yes, Dad?"

"I'll have to sleep on that and let you know in the morning." Cork rose from the table. "Thanks for the cookie," he said to Ernie.

Ernie just smiled enigmatically.

"I wasn't around when, apparently, Aphrodite went berserk after her daughter's death," Rainy said.

They lay in the dark of their bedroom, Rainy with her arm across Cork's chest. Although he knew he needed rest, sleep was eluding him.

"Across all my years as a cop, I saw what mothers and fathers and brothers and sisters were capable of doing to one another," he told her. "Family's a guarantee of nothing, certainly not of love."

He felt her fingers caress the undamaged side of his face. "It is for us."

"We're among the lucky."

"Marsha doesn't want you anywhere near Aphrodite. Are you going to go along with that?"

"For the moment. But that doesn't mean I have to stop my investigation."

"Where do you go from here?"

"To talk to a man who hates Indians. Maybe two men."

"You'll be careful?"

"Caution is my middle name."

"Don't I wish." She kissed his cheek. "Now go to sleep. I'll wake you in an hour or so to make sure you're still lucid."

CHAPTER 38

"What's the plan, Sherlock?" Jenny said the next morning when Cork stepped into the kitchen.

"That's getting a little old," he replied.

"Oh, grumpy are we? Not enough sleep?"

"And my ribs hurt like hell."

"That face isn't going to open a lot of doors," Jenny said. "Can I fix you some breakfast?"

"Where is everybody?"

"Waaboo's off to school, Daniel to work, and today is one of Rainy's volunteer days at the clinic in Allouette. Just you and me. And the game is still afoot."

"Drop the Conan Doyle stuff, okay? And I'd love something to eat."

While Jenny scrambled eggs with cheese melted atop and dropped a piece of whole-grain bread into the toaster, Cork sat sipping coffee, trying to gear himself up for the day ahead.

"Before she left, Rainy told me that you intend to talk to a couple of guys who hate Indians," Jenny said from the stove. "Got names?"

"Rocky Martinelli and Wild Bill Gunderson."

"Martinelli. He used to be a cop, right?"

"I fired him."

"I went to school with his son Drew. Kids used to call him Gruesome Drewsome, gave him a hard time because his mother had been, as kids put it back then, in the loony bin. Then she—oh, dear—she died in a fire, right?"

"That's right. The sanitarium where she was housed burned down. A tragedy, a scandal, really. It was run by some religious organization. Unorthodox methods of treatment, if I recall correctly. Arson was suspected. Several of the residents were killed, including Lucy Martinelli."

"And who's this Wild Bill Gunderson?"

"Martinelli's father-in-law. He was sheriff of Tamarack County before me. Keeps a low profile these days. Has a place out on Little Bear Lake. Works security at the Vermilion One Mine. Martinelli works security there, too."

"Vermilion One. That's where you found the bodies of all those Ojibwe girls."

"The Vanishings."

"I thought the mine was closed."

"Stories persist about the spirits of those murdered girls still wandering the area. People are always trying to get in. They have round-the-clock security."

"I'm just finishing up these eggs. If you want butter and jam on your toast, you'll need to get them yourself," Jenny said. "And silverware."

Cork got up, slowly because of his damaged ribs, and gathered the items. When he sat back down, Jenny put a plate of scrambled eggs and toast in front of him. "Want a little salsa with that?"

He said yes, thanks. She pulled a jar from the fridge, handed it to him, poured herself a mug of coffee, and sat down at the table.

"What does hating Indians have to do with Axel Boshey?" she asked.

"In his confession, Axel gave details of the murder, enough anyway to make the confession seem valid. Axel's claiming that Martinelli fed him those details during an altercation in his jail cell. Back then, I thought it was simply blind rage on Martinelli's part. But maybe the man had a different motive. I'd like to get a sense if it was just stupidity and prejudice or was there something more to it."

"Like what?"

"Not sure yet. Still working on that one."

"And what about this Wild Bill Gunderson?"

"He was pretty deeply mixed up with Aphrodite back then. One of her paramours. Maybe he still is. I'd like to know where he was last night."

"The plot thickens."

"Stop that."

"Eat up, Dad. Then let's get going."

They took Jenny's Forester, and their first stop was at Hensler's Tires.

"Slashed?" Mook Hensler said. He was a potbellied man, with a big beard and wearing a grease-stained khaki shirt with BASS PRO over the pocket.

"All four, Mook," Cork said.

"Sick Halloween prank, or did you really piss somebody off?"

"Working on that one. Can you get to it today?

"I'll send my boy over this morning. Want four of the same?"

"If you can."

"Will do. But I'd be careful if I was you."

"Exactly what my wife said, Mook."

Their next stop was the sheriff's department. Marsha Dross was with Chief Deputy George Azevedo, going over the duty roster for Halloween night. When they stepped into her office, she was saying, "You've got a good handle on this, George. Maybe we'll get lucky and it'll be a quiet Halloween."

"That'll happen when pigs fly," Azevedo said. "Cork, Jenny," he greeted them as he left the office.

"Halloween," Cork said. "Always troublesome back in my day."

"Hasn't changed," Dross said. She studied them and scowled. "You have that hunting look about you. I told you to stay away from Shangri-La."

"We're going nowhere near Aphrodite McGill. I want to talk to Rocky Martinelli and Wild Bill Gunderson today."

"Why?"

"Interested in why they hate Indians so much for one thing."

"I remember," Dross said. "I used to want to smack 'em both. And not just because they were disrespectful toward our Native community. What's that got to do with Axel Boshey?"

"You remember after I arrested Axel, Martinelli attacked him in his jail cell?"

"Yeah. Got Martinelli fired."

"Suspended first, then fired. Anyway, Axel claims that during the attack, Martinelli fed him details of Chastity's murder that he used in his confession. I just want to feel Martinelli out on that."

"He was always a cocky kid, good-looking and he knew it. But he's had his share of bad luck, particularly with wives."

"Wives?" Jenny said. "I knew about his first wife, Lucy. What about the other?"

"Others," Cork said. "His second wife died in a car wreck. Driving drunk. His third wife left him. He's on his fourth."

"Whoa," Jenny said.

"Why interview Wild Bill?" Dross asked.

"He was pretty heavily mixed up with Aphrodite back in the day. Maybe still is."

"Oh." Dross lifted her eyebrows. "You're thinking he might have been the one who gave you that bruised face?"

"I know he'd have been happy to kick me when I beat him in the election twenty-five years ago."

"But last night wasn't just about delayed gratification," Jenny said.

Cork said, "I think last night goes back to the spider at the center of the web."

Dross said, "I'll talk to her today, see what I come up with. How about we rendezvous back here this afternoon?"

Cork gave her a little salute. "Ten-four, Sheriff."

Rocky Martinelli lived in an old two-story house on Willoughby Street, on the west side of Aurora. In the long-ago past, it had been quite lovely, but neglect had eaten away at its beauty. The outside screamed for a new coat of white paint. The roof shingles curled up at the edges. Bushes battled one another for space. Fallen leaves lay in a moldering blanket on the lawn. In that season of ghosts and goblins, it looked like the perfect haunted house.

Greta Martinelli answered the door. She was, in many ways, like the wives who'd preceded her, pretty and docile. She looked a bit bedraggled that morning, dark brown hair hanging in strands over her forehead and along her cheeks, sticking to a sheen of sweat on her skin.

"Morning, Greta," Cork said, smiling.

"Oh, my," the woman said, squinting at his face. "What happened, Cork?"

"Just clumsy. Ran into a door."

"I'm so sorry." She looked at Jenny and offered her a wan smile. "I know you, don't I?"

"Jenny O'Connor." She nodded toward Cork. "The daughter."

"Oh, yes. I remember you from church. But you were so much younger." She gave a helpless little shrug. "It's been a while for me."

"I'd like to talk to Rocky, if he's home," Cork said.

"He's working today."

"I'll try to catch him at the mine, then. But a quick question. Was he out last night?"

"He and Bill were out drinking rather late. Again." Her words carried a hard edge.

"That would be Bill Gunderson?"

"Who else?"

"So they've been out together a lot lately?"

"Two peas in a pod."

"Has Rocky seemed upset recently?"

Her demeanor changed, a wary look coming into her eyes. "Why are you asking?" Then she seemed to understand. "That wasn't a door you ran into."

"No, it wasn't," Cork said.

"Why would Rocky want to hurt you?"

"Might not have been Rocky. More likely it was Bill."

"Look, I think we're finished here. And if you talk to Rocky, I'd appreciate it if you didn't mention this conversation."

"We never spoke," Cork said. "Thank you, Greta."

"I gave you nothing," she said.

"That's right," Cork said. "Nothing."

Back in the Forester, Jenny said, "She's afraid of Rocky."

Cork said, "Women always have been."

CHAPTER 39

On the way to the Vermilion One Mine, Cork drove through the nearly abandoned town of Gresham. At one time, it had been a bustling place where miners and their families lived. More than two decades earlier, the mine had shut down and the little community had become like a ghost town. Behind the high fence that surrounded the mine property, outbuildings could be seen, most of them abandoned, along with a headframe towering above a shaft that plunged nearly half a mile into the earth. A few years earlier, the tunnels deep underground had been briefly considered as a possible site for storage of nuclear waste, but that idea never got much traction. The land stood idle now. But the potential for trespass, for accidents, for lawsuits was significant enough that the parent company maintained security around the clock.

There was an unsavory history to the mine. A crazy man named Indigo Broom had once used one of the upper tunnels to hide the bodies of his female victims, young girls who'd gone missing over several years. Locally, folks had called them the Vanishings. It had been Cork who'd stumbled upon the dark sepulcher and the remains still inside.

The mine gate was monitored with cameras. Cork pulled up to the gate, rolled down his window, and punched the call button.

"Yes?" came the disembodied voice.

"Cork O'Connor. I'm here to see Rocky Martinelli."

There was a long silence, followed by a muttered "*Shit.*" Then, "Come to the security office. I'll be waiting."

The gate swung open and Cork proceeded to the gathering of buildings a hundred yards inside.

Martinelli wasn't alone. Wild Bill Gunderson was there as well, former father-in-law and son-in-law somehow still bound together. The security office had a bank of monitors that showed various sites around the mine property. There was also a central table on which now sat several brown paper bags with partially eaten food items around them.

"Early lunch," Martinelli said, when he caught Cork eyeing the mess. "We come on duty at six."

Wild Bill cocked his head and studied Jenny. "Who are you?"

"My daughter Jenny," Cork replied.

"Sign in," Martinelli said. He handed Cork a pen and a clipboard with a log sheet on it.

"What can we do for you?" Wild Bill asked. "You want a tour of the Vermilion Drift? That's where you found 'em, wasn't it, Cork? All those butchered girls."

Wild Bill Gunderson had always been a man proud of his physique. Although he was nearing seventy, he still looked to be in good shape. His hair had gone silver but was still lion's mane thick. The skin of his face was smooth, his cheeks clean-shaven, his eyes a captivating blue. He'd always been a ladies' man, and Cork was sure he still saw himself that way.

"Long time ago, Bill. Here for another reason."

"What the hell happened to your face?" Martinelli asked.

Like his father-in-law, he'd aged well. Still in good shape, still dark and handsome in a smarmy way.

"It had an altercation with a steel-toed boot." Cork glanced down at the men's footwear. "If I don't miss my guess, those are steel-toed Wolverines."

"Company policy," Wild Bill said. "All security personnel have to wear steel-toed boots and hard hats when they're out walking the grounds. Never know when you might have to poke into a dangerous area. We get a lot of damn kids who climb the fence on some kind of dare, looking, you know, for the spirits of those murdered girls. And there are sinkholes."

"What is it you want, O'Connor?" Martinelli asked.

"Just wondering where you were last night around ten."

"Drinking and watching football."

"With me," Wild Bill said.

"Where?"

"My place," Wild Bill said.

"Who was playing?" Jenny asked.

"Jets and Ravens."

"Good game?" she followed up.

"Not particularly."

"Who won?" she asked.

"What is this?" Martinelli said.

"Did you know that Axel Boshey has retracted his confession?" Cork said. "His son has asked me to look into the murder of Chastity."

"Hell, good luck with that," Wild Bill said. "A crime twenty-five years old. Where do you even start?"

"Axel Boshey's nothing but a murdering redskin and a goddamned liar," Martinelli threw in.

"You know, Rocky, a man said almost the same thing to me last night after he did this to my face."

"Everybody who knew Axel knew what kind of man he was," Martinelli threw back.

"And steel-toed boots, Cork," Wild Bill said. "You'll find those on every logger in this county."

"You asked me where do I even begin this investigation, Bill. I'll tell you where. With Aphrodite."

"You stay away from her," Wild Bill said.

"That's exactly what the guy last night said to me."

"Hasn't that woman suffered enough?" Wild Bill said. "Lost her daughter. Pretty much lost her grandson."

"But she's still got a granddaughter," Jenny said.

"That girl's got nothing to do with her mother's death. You leave her alone, too," Wild Bill said.

"Does it ever bother you, Bill, that Aphrodite shares her bed with half the men in Tamarack County?" Cork said.

"Why would I care?"

"You were pretty tight with her back in the day. Based on your reaction this morning, I'm thinking you still are."

"Think anything you want."

"And here's a question for you, Rocky. I've never heard you say anything that wasn't derogatory about Native people. What do you have against Indians?"

"We're done here," Wild Bill said. "Time you two got off this property."

Martinelli escorted them back to Jenny's Forester. He watched until they'd passed outside the perimeter fence.

"Pretty testy back there," Jenny said. "Hit a few nerves it seemed to me. That Rocky, I can understand why Greta might be afraid of him. He gave me the creeps from the get-go. And did you notice, they didn't answer my question about who won the game last night?"

"Nicely done," Cork said. Then added, "Watson."

CHAPTER 40

They lunched at home. As they ate peanut butter and jelly sandwiches with chips and spring water Jenny seemed unusually quiet.

"Penny for your thoughts," Cork said.

"Pretty far out there, but I've been thinking about something I found in the notes you made during your initial investigation of the murder."

"What was that?"

"You made a note about talking with the priest at St. Agnes. Father Jude Monroe. I remember him. He rode a motorcycle, right?"

"That was another priest who came a few years later, Tom Griffin. Him we called Saint Kawasaki. Jude Monroe drove a vintage red Jaguar and we dubbed him Saint Jag. So what are you thinking?"

"What did you talk to him about?"

"Nothing to do with Chastity Boshey's murder. Rocky's wife, Lucy, was losing it back then. I was concerned about her children, whether she presented a danger to them. She was seeing Father Jude for some counseling. Right after that, her father put her in that sanitarium down near Cambridge. And not long after that, she died along with several others when the place burned down."

"When you say she was losing it, how exactly?"

"She made some pretty strange comments to Marsha Dross. Claimed she'd experienced a miracle, had become a virgin again. She said an angel had given her a new name."

"What name?"

"Magdalene."

"What did Father Jude have to say?"

"He couldn't say much. Priestly confidentiality."

"I still see Patsy Boshey in church sometimes. Did Chastity and Axel attend?"

"Not regularly as I recall, but sometimes. Why?"

"People tell priests all kinds of things. Maybe Chastity did, too."

"Like what?"

"Who she was seeing behind Axel's back."

"You're grasping at straws, I think."

"It's like you often say, pull one thread and others unravel. Any idea what happened to Father Jude?"

"He was reassigned by the diocese. As I understand it, he went through a deep crisis of faith and eventually left the priesthood. But that was years ago. I haven't heard anything about him since."

"Mind if I try to track him down?"

"Be my guest."

Cork's cell phone rang. It was Mook Hensler letting him know the Expedition had been fitted with four new tires.

"She's sitting at Sam's Place," Mook said. "After you pick her up, come on by and we'll settle the bill."

When Cork stood up from the table, Jenny said, "You're still hurting from last night. Let me give you a ride."

"I'm not an invalid. I'll walk."

"Okay," Jenny said. "I'll clean up here, then head to my computer and get started."

"On what?

"Tracking down Saint Jag."

After he left Hensler's, Cork drove slowly through town. It was the day before Halloween, and Aurora had prepared with great enthusiasm. From the window glass of the stores along Center Street, the faces of witches and goblins and the monsters of Hollywood's darkest imaginations eyed Cork as he passed. Until the Halloween when, as a kid, he'd sat at a hospital bedside watching his father's life slip away, Cork had loved this bewitching season. Even after nearly fifty years, the sting of his father's passing was still there, not so sharp as it once was but enough that it continued to take away the joy and excitement he'd felt as a child.

Sheriff Marsha Dross was in her office. She didn't look particularly happy when Cork walked in.

"I went out to interview Aphrodite," she said after Cork sat down.

"Did you come up with anything useful?"

"She didn't seem particularly surprised that you were attacked. Called you a meddling has-been. But her granddaughter vouched for her whereabouts last night. In keeping with the season, they spent the evening watching *Halloween*. You know, Michael Myers?"

"Got it. Did you see anybody else at Shangri-La?"

"Just those two. Also BCA got me a result on the DNA sample I sent to them, from the vaginal swab Sigurd Nelson took during his autopsy of Chastity Boshey."

"That was fast."

"Called in a favor. We have a match with Moonbeam Boshey.

Whoever Chastity had sex with the night she was murdered, he was also the father of Moonbeam. And here's another thing. He definitely wasn't of Native blood."

"No ID on him?"

"Nothing in the legal system."

"And I'm guessing nothing on Ancestry or it would have shown up when Moonbeam and Axel had their DNA tested."

"So, who did she see that night?" Dross said. "When you talked with Axel, did he give you any ideas?"

Cork shook his head. "Jenny had a thought about someone we might ask, but it seems way out in left field."

"Who's that?"

"Father Jude Monroe. Used to call him Saint Jag. The priest here years ago."

"I remember him. He helped calm down Aphrodite McGill after Chastity was killed."

"Jenny's wondering if Chastity might have talked to him."

"I haven't heard anything about him in forever. Any idea where he is?"

"Jenny's trying to track him down now."

"You're the private dick, aren't you?"

Cork pointed toward his bruised face. "Give me a break."

His cell phone rang. It was Jenny. She said, "I found him."

"Father Jude?"

"I got both a cell phone number and a business number. He runs a shelter in Duluth, a place called Open Arms. But when I tried calling, he wouldn't talk to me."

"What did you ask?"

"I told him we were looking into the murder of Chastity Boshey. He told me he had nothing to say on that subject."

"So there you go."

"Dad, he shut me right down. Didn't even give me a chance

to explain anything. The name Chastity Boshey came out of my mouth and he cut me off. Doesn't that tell you something?"

"So what do you propose?"

"I'm heading to Duluth to talk to him."

"Not without me you're not."

"I figured you'd say that."

"I'll be home in five."

He ended the call and explained things to Dross.

"I don't know exactly how it works," the sheriff said. "But he might still be under some priestly constraint and won't be able to share anything."

"It's a thread," Cork said as he stood to leave. "We've got to give it a pull."

CHAPTER 41

On their way to Duluth, Jenny stopped at a tobacco shop.

"What are you doing?" Cork said.

"Something Daniel turned me on to. An offering that might get people to talk to us. I'll be right back."

She returned with two packs of Newport 100 menthol cigarettes. "Street currency, Daniel calls it."

"We're talking to Jude Monroe."

"Who runs a shelter for unhoused people. Street people, Dad. You never know where information might come from."

Cork smiled broadly. "You're learning."

The shelter was located in an old elementary school in West Duluth. A small crowd, dressed mostly in clothing that had seen better days, milled about the front of the building. As Cork and Jenny approached, a young couple sitting on the steps of the shelter eyed them intensely.

"Got a cigarette?" the young man asked, rising. He had a beard that trailed down his chest like a flow of brown water.

"I don't smoke," Cork said.

"Neither do I. It's for her." He nodded toward his companion, who sat hugging herself and watching with fearful eyes. "She'd ask but she can't talk."

"Here." Jenny broke open one of the Newport packs and handed him four cigarettes.

The man glanced down at the young woman, who smiled, touched her chin with her hand and signed *thank you* to Jenny.

As soon as the others saw the exchange, they gathered around. Jenny distributed all the cigarettes from both packs amid thanks, given both heartily and in mumbles.

Inside the building, Cork said, "Where did that get us?"

"Maybe we'll find out when we leave."

Cork and Jenny followed a sign that read OFFICE with an arrow pointing down the corridor. When they stepped in, two women looked up from desks strewn with paper. They both held phones to their ears.

"Send them over," one of the women said into her phone. "We'll get the paperwork done here."

The other woman shook her head and said into her phone, "We don't have the medical capability for that. Send them to the ER at St. Mary's."

The first woman, early forties with dark hair cut in bangs straight across her forehead, hung up her phone and gave Cork and Jenny a welcoming smile. "Can I help you?"

"We're looking for Jude Monroe," Cork said.

"May I ask what for?"

"I'm an old friend. He used to be the priest at our parish."

"Back when he was Saint Jag?"

"That's right. How'd you know?"

"We're mostly Catholic here. Word gets around. And he still drives that Jaguar. He's with kitchen staff right now. Down the hallway and to the left. Follow your nose."

Farther down the corridor, they passed a large room that must have been a school cafeteria at one time, and beyond that, they found Jude Monroe in a clean kitchen that smelled of savory soup broth. Two women and a man were at work, all in aprons and wearing hairnets. Jude Monroe stood in front of an industrial-size refrigerator, studying the contents.

"I don't see any, Jasmine," he called over his shoulder.

"Then we'll have to order some," one of the women replied as she chopped carrots.

"Jude?" Cork said at his back.

The ex-priest turned, and the surprise on his face was in neon. "My God," he said. "Cork?"

"It's been a long time."

In the old days, Father Jude Monroe was so handsome Cork had heard the women of St. Agnes confess to having sinful thoughts about him. But that was a quarter of a century ago. From the lines etched deep into his forehead and at the corners of his eyes, Cork could see that the years had been hard on the man. His hair had thinned and he looked gaunt. But there was still a fire in his eyes that Cork recognized from the old days, the eyes of a man still passionate in his mission.

"And you remember Jenny," Cork said, nodding toward his daughter.

"Of course," Monroe said and smiled broadly at her. "You questioned everything in catechism class."

"I spoke with you briefly on the phone," Jenny said. "You didn't seem eager to talk to me."

"I apologize. We were having a bit of a crisis, and I really didn't have time to talk." He gave Cork a look of deep concern. "What happened to your face?"

"As nearly as I can tell, I pissed someone off. Not sure who at this point, but they jumped me last night at Sam's Place."

"You and trouble," Monroe said. "Always like two on a tandem bike. I guess nothing's changed."

"Quite an operation here, Jude," Cork noted.

"We offer limited overnight housing. We counsel. We refer. We feed."

"And pray?" Jenny asked.

"Just because I took off my collar doesn't mean I don't believe in the power of prayer, Jenny. Of course, we pray."

"Have you been here since you left Aurora?" Cork asked.

The ex-priest smiled wanly. "I went on a long journey first. I wasn't sure what I was seeking. The truth is that I'm still not sure. But until I find an answer, I'm doing my best to help those I can."

"This isn't your answer?" Cork asked.

"I think of it as a part of an ongoing journey."

Cork said, "Do you have a moment to talk now?"

"We're getting dinner ready, and we're down a couple of helpers. We're in the middle of making soup. Cliché, I know. Soup kitchen. But the nights turn cold and the soup is hot and hearty. Eh, Maggie?" he said to a woman wearing a hairnet as she approached them with her head down, eyes to the tile floor.

"We won't take long, I promise," Cork said.

"All right."

The woman Monroe had called Maggie slipped between them, heading toward the big refrigerator. "'Scuse me," she mumbled.

"Let's talk over here," Monroe said.

He moved a few feet away but kept an eye on the woman, who took a head of cabbage from the refrigerator, then shuffled back to a cutting board that lay on a stainless-steel counter. She picked up a big knife and began chopping the cabbage.

"You said this is about Chastity Boshey, right?" the ex-priest asked.

"Axel Boshey has recanted his confession, Jude."

For the second time, the man's face registered significant surprise. "Let me get this straight. After all these years, he's saying he's *not* guilty? I don't understand."

"Axel was seeing another woman. Bernadette Polaski."

Monroe thought a moment. "A librarian, right? Sang in the choir."

Cork gave a nod. "She was pregnant with his child. Axel thought Bernadette may have committed the murder. He says now that he confessed to keep her and his child out of prison."

"What's changed?"

Cork explained everything that had occurred recently, the essentials anyway.

"I don't understand how you think I can help," Monroe said.

"You were our priest. Chastity was Catholic. She baptized both her children at St. Agnes. People in the parish looked to you in a lot of ways, Jude, shared things with you. I remember, for example, talking to you about Lucy Martinelli back then, and you were helpful."

"I never shared a confidence given to me in the confessional, Cork." He said this in a loud voice, the kind he might have used delivering a homily from the pulpit. "I may not wear the collar now, but I still hold certain things sacred."

"It's clear that Chastity was seeing another man back then. He probably fathered Moonbeam Boshey. We just want to know if Chastity ever confided his name to you. A long shot, we understand."

"You think he might have killed her?"

"That's certainly a possibility."

The woman called Maggie shuffled to the refrigerator, pulled out another head of cabbage, shuffled back to her cutting board. In passing, she glanced up at Cork. There was something about her that felt familiar to him, but he couldn't place it. Monroe had said that they hired from among those who sought his help, so maybe it was just the beaten look Cork had seen on the faces of so many who walked the streets and had no place to truly call home.

"I can't say anything about the conversations I might have had with Chastity in the confessional. But I will tell you this. Any problems Chastity had were almost certainly a result of the environment she came from. Shangri-La. And I'll share something else with you as well, as evidence. Aphrodite once tried to seduce me."

"What?" Jenny said.

"I believe I was a challenge to her. Could she get the priest to break his vow of celibacy."

"How did she try to seduce you?"

"She approached me one day, in the sanctuary, if you can believe that. Ostensibly, she wanted to talk about the upcoming christening of Moonbeam. I'd been working with Chastity and Axel on that, but Aphrodite wasn't a part of it. We sat in a pew. She shared with me that she'd grown up Catholic but had some pretty bad experiences. Actually she claimed that she'd been molested by her priest. So she didn't go to church anymore. She said she was heartbroken that Chastity didn't want her at the christening. She began to cry and put her arms around me as if for comfort. Next thing I know, she's kissing me, and her hands are going to places they should never have gone. When I pushed her away, she laughed, as if it had all been a game. Then a week later, she came to the baptism despite Chastity's objections and behaved as if nothing had happened. I've dealt with lots of troubled people, but that woman was like nothing I'd ever seen before."

"If Chastity was seeing someone outside her marriage, could he have been a member of the congregation?" Jenny asked.

Monroe offered nothing in response to this suggestion.

"Jude?" Cork said.

"I told you that although I don't wear the collar now, I still feel bound by the Sacramental Seal. What was shared with me in confession remains confidential."

"So you do know something," Jenny said.

"Not anything that I believe would help you in this."

"Maybe we should be the judge of that."

"You haven't changed," Monroe said. "Still ready to push against a gale. I need to get back to dinner prep. It was good seeing you both. Good luck with your investigation."

He left them and returned to where all the chopping was being done. The woman he called Maggie said something to him, gave Cork a last furtive glance, then returned to work with her knife.

Outside, they found the bearded young man and his mute companion standing near an old, rusted Ford Escort parked on the street not far from the Expedition. Cork hadn't taken much notice of it before, but now the young man lifted a hand, beckoning. When Cork approached with Jenny, he saw the interior of the car stuffed with belongings and figured this was probably where they slept when they didn't have beds in the shelter.

"You cops?" the young man asked.

"No."

"Come on. My granddad was a cop. I know cops when I see 'em. You after someone?"

"Just trying to get to the bottom of a situation up north."

"Where up north?"

"Aurora."

"Hell, we know Aurora. Just came down from International Falls three weeks ago. Paper mill I was working at downsized, lost my job. We hoped I could get work here."

Cork glanced at the cluttered inside of the Escort. "I'm guessing you haven't found anything yet."

"Still looking. In the meantime, we hang out at the shelter.

Free meals, and occasionally a bed and shower. Got a car, as you can see, so sometimes we supply rides."

"For free?" Jenny asked.

"Gas money usually. Or cigarette money. But if somebody's really desperate, Rosie insists we do it for free. Heart of gold, this girl." He touched his companion's arm tenderly and she gave him a loving smile in return. She signed to him, and he said to Jenny, "Got any more cigarettes?"

"All out. Sorry."

"'S okay."

When they climbed into Cork's big Expedition, Jenny said, "I should have brought more cigarettes."

"That's not going to solve their problems," Cork said.

"God bless people like Jude Monroe," Jenny said.

"Who clearly knows things."

"I have a sense we'd never get him to spill. So what now?"

"Home," Cork said. "Enough sleuthing for one day. That soup smelled wonderful, and I'm starved."

CHAPTER 42

It was nearing dark when they walked into the house on Gooseberry Lane. The air was redolent with the aroma of chili peppers and garlic and sage. Cork's stomach immediately began to growl.

Waaboo raced down the stairs to greet them. "I won!" he cried.

"What?" Jenny asked.

"Scariest Halloween picture. Mrs. Landvik let us draw in class today and it had to be a Halloween picture. I won."

"What did you draw?" Cork asked.

"The Windigo. I made it really scary. See?"

He held out a sheet of manila paper. The drawing was in bold crayon, a beast with horns, fiery red eyes, long fangs and claws, a brown, furry body. It was pretty good, Cork had to admit.

"Other kids drew pumpkins and jack-o'-lanterns and ghosts and witches, but I drew the Windigo."

"Why the Windigo?" Jenny asked.

"Because it's here."

Waaboo had been gifted. He was in touch with the world in a way that allowed him to sense things others didn't. Two years earlier, it had nearly got him killed.

Jenny glanced at Cork then said to her son, "Come sit with me."

They nestled together on the living room sofa. Cork saw Rainy step from the kitchen doorway. She had a big wooden spoon in her hand, which she held up as a sign of greeting. He waved back. They both stood listening as Jenny quizzed Waaboo.

"What do you mean the Windigo is here?"

"Bad things are going to happen. It's the Windigo."

"What kind of bad things?"

"Well, Baa-baa got beat up." He looked at Cork.

"I'm pretty sure a bad man did that," Cork said.

"But what was inside him?" Waaboo said. "Something was eating his heart."

"Are there other bad things that will happen?" Jenny ran her hand soothingly over her son's hair.

"I think so. Until it's gone."

"Are you afraid?"

Waaboo shook his head. "It's not hungry for me. Or us."

"Do you know who it's hungry for?"

He shook his head. "Unh-uh."

Jenny held the drawing up. "It certainly is scary. You drew it well, little rabbit."

"Can we put it on the refrigerator?"

"It might eat up all our food," she cautioned.

"It only eats people," Waaboo said.

A bit later, after Daniel had come home from his shift with the Iron Lake Tribal Police, they sat around the dining room table eating the chili Rainy had made. Cork added sour cream and cheese and chopped onions to his bowl, and he sipped from a bottle of Leinie's as he ate. Jenny filled them in on much of what had gone on that day. Because Waaboo was at the table, she kept her comments general.

"All that in just one day?" Daniel said.

"Jenny was insistent," Cork said. "A real bloodhound once she had the scent."

"It must be in her DNA," Rainy said and winked at Cork.

"Gil Young told me you can get worms in your blood," Waaboo said, then put a big spoonful of chili in his mouth, the last from his bowl.

"How do you get worms in your blood?" Daniel asked his son.

"Eaaing ish," he said.

"Finish chewing," Jenny said.

"Eating fish," Waaboo clarified when he'd swallowed.

"Eating fish?" Daniel said.

"There are sometime worms in some fish," Rainy said. Then to her grandson, she said, "But not in what we eat. And we cook our fish correctly so that even if there were worms, they wouldn't get in our blood."

Waaboo drained his milk glass and said, "Can I be excused? I want to draw some more Halloween pictures."

"Take your plate and glass to the sink, please," Daniel said.

When Waaboo had gone upstairs to his room, Rainy said, "I get the feeling there's more to what you found out today. Wild Bill and Rocky aren't cooperating and this ex-priest, this Saint Jag, knows more than he's saying. Is that about right?"

"That's the gist of it." Cork glanced toward the stairs where Waaboo had gone. He wanted to make sure his grandson wouldn't hear. "But it gets weird."

"How so?" Daniel asked.

Cork nodded to Jenny, who said, "Jude Monroe told us Aphrodite tried to seduce him. Just to see if she could make the priest shatter his vow of celibacy, sounds like."

"Talk about a dysfunctional woman," Rainy said.

"So, where do you go from here?" Daniel asked.

Jenny wiped her mouth with her napkin. "More and more

we're thinking that Aphrodite is at the center of all this. So, tomorrow we're going to shake her web a bit and see what happens."

"How?" Rainy asked.

"First thing in the morning, we're going to hit the Ben Franklin store and buy Halloween costumes."

"What for?"

Jenny looked to her father, who said, "We're going to crash Aphrodite's Halloween party."

Cork woke in an instant. It was the dead of night. He glanced at the clock on his nightstand. A few minutes after midnight. Silver light from the moon, which was heading toward full, illuminated the room. He glanced at Rainy sleeping peacefully beside him. He tried to grasp what had yanked him from his own slumber.

Then he heard it. The creak of the swing on the front porch, faint but constant. He rose from the bed, put on his slippers, grabbed his robe, and headed downstairs. The front door stood open, and through the storm door he could see the front yard so white under the moon it looked glazed in ice. Stepping outside, he found Daniel in the swing.

"Everything okay?" he asked.

"Couldn't sleep," Daniel replied. "Didn't mean to wake you."

"Want company?"

"Have a seat."

The air was chilly. Cork pulled his robe tighter around him, plopped down beside his son-in-law, and the two men rocked a bit in silence.

"The Windigo," Daniel finally said. "He's sensed the Windigo."

"But it hasn't come for him," Cork said. "He's not afraid."

"And that worries me. He should be afraid. Any normal seven-year-old who senses such things should be afraid." Daniel turned to him. "Just look at you. It's like you battled the Windigo. You could have been killed. And now Jenny's poking into things with you. You should both be afraid. We all should."

"You wear a cop's shield. You face the threat of God-knows-what every day. Do you live in fear?"

"That's me. I'm talking about the people I love."

"You think Jenny doesn't worry about you out there dealing with guys high out of their minds or people so confused they don't realize what they're doing or someone who just hates anyone wearing a badge?"

"She knows I can take care of myself."

"You think she's any less capable?"

"I carry a gun. She doesn't."

For a while, the night was quiet, except for the creak of the porch swing. Then Daniel said, "I can't help wondering what if it had been Jenny out at Sam's Place instead of you."

"But it wasn't. And it won't be. In all this, I won't let Jenny out of my sight. I won't let any harm come to my daughter, I swear."

"This from a man who walks like he battled a bear."

"You know you can't keep Jenny out of this."

"I know." Daniel stood up, walked to the porch railing, leaned into the white moonlight, and became like a man carved from ice. On the lawn, the skeleton and the witch and the ghost that had been erected on poles, and the jack-o'-lanterns the family had carved in the kitchen, all seemed frozen in the icy light as well.

"It's chilly out here," Cork said. "We should go back inside."

But Daniel didn't move. "What if it all goes south, Cork? For Jenny or you or me or Waaboo? The Windigo's out there. It's hungry." He turned and gave Cork a cold stare. "And God alone knows who it's come for."

CHAPTER 43

"Halloween!" Waaboo hollered coming down the stairs. He flew into the kitchen, where Cork was flipping pancakes at the stove while Jenny was frying bacon beside him. "Can I wear my costume to school?"

"Sit," Jenny said. "And no, you can't wear your costume. Against school rules."

Waaboo's shoulders slumped and he made a sad face. Then he brightened. "But tonight!"

"Tonight, indeed," his mother said. "You and all the other ghosts and goblins."

Rainy came in. "Breakfast under control?"

"As soon as the bacon's done, I'll scramble up some eggs," Jenny said.

"And pancakes'll be up soon," Cork said. "If you want to help, you can pour orange juice for our little rabbit."

Rainy headed to the refrigerator as Daniel walked through the kitchen door, dressed in his tribal police uniform, but yawning.

"I wondered when you'd get up," Jenny said. "You must not have slept well."

"I was awake awhile last night. But I'm okay."

"You better be. You're taking our son trick-or-treating tonight."

"Yay!" Waaboo yelled, lifting his arms as if in triumph. "Are you gonna wear a costume, Dad?"

"I think I'll go as a police officer," Daniel said.

"That's not a costume," Waaboo said.

"Maybe not, but it'll scare people," Daniel said. "At least anyone who's up to no good."

Waaboo babbled on happily during breakfast until Jenny sent him upstairs to dress for school. Then things took a more serious turn.

"I'm not going to mince words," Daniel said. "That Waaboo has sensed something dangerous here concerns me a lot."

"But he doesn't feel threatened," Jenny pointed out.

"I'm not worried so much about him. I'll be with him tonight, in full duty gear. Frankly, I'm worried about you and this plan to infiltrate Shangri-La with Cork."

"*Infiltrate* has such a cloak-and-dagger connotation," Jenny said. "We'll just be observing."

"Take a look at your father's face. That's what came of his last visit to Shangri-La."

Cork had been sipping coffee. He put his mug down and said, "I'm fine going alone."

Now Rainy weighed in. "I'm with Daniel on this one. I don't like the idea of either of you in that place with God knows what going on there."

"Drinking, deviltry, probably some drug use, some slinking off into dark corners," Cork said. "That's what will probably be going on there. I don't think anyone will be wearing steel-toed boots and having a go at me again, especially with so many people around."

"Safety in numbers," Jenny said.

"What do you hope to accomplish?" Daniel asked, a hard edge to his words.

"I won't know until it happens," Cork said.

"*We* won't know until it happens," Jenny said. "I'm going, Daniel, and that's that."

Rainy gave a deep sigh and said to her husband, "And I know it's useless trying to get you to back down. But for God's sake, promise us that you'll both be careful."

"We will never be out of one another's sight," Cork said. "Okay, Daniel?"

"I'm still not happy about this." He looked steadily at Jenny. "But if you make that promise, I won't keep badgering you."

"Promise," she said.

Cork and Jenny cleaned up the breakfast things while Daniel took Waaboo to school on his way to the Tribal Police office and Rainy headed to Zupp's to pick up some groceries. Then the two of them made their plans for the day.

"A stakeout of Shangril-La?" Jenny said. "Why?"

"It might be interesting to see who comes and goes without a costume."

"You'll just sit and watch all day?"

"That's pretty much what a stakeout is."

"Sounds boring."

"Can't argue with you on that one."

"It shouldn't take two of us. Here's what I'd rather do. After we pick up our costumes at the Ben Franklin store, I'll go back to the Property Room and have another look at the notes from your original investigation. Maybe we missed something."

"I think that's a great idea. If you stumble across anything, let me know."

"And if you see anything interesting between naps, you let me know."

* * *

Halloween wasn't just a day. It was an atmosphere, a sense of sinister possibilities, of the potential transformation of normal people who, safely hidden behind masks, might give their dark side, the Mr. Hyde in them, freedom to come forth, at least for a night. Cork could feel a tingle as he drove through Aurora, past houses where witches and ghosts and devils had become front lawn sentinels, just as they had at the house on Gooseberry Lane. When he'd been sheriff, Halloween had always been a law enforcement nightmare. He didn't envy the job Marsha Dross and her deputies had ahead of them that night. As for him, despite his bruised face and sore ribs, he was rather looking forward to being inside Shangri-La, deep in the spider's web. What he'd told Daniel was true. He didn't know what might come of that infiltration, but it was an opportunity too enticing to pass up. And although he wasn't concerned about any danger to him or to Jenny, he would make certain they never lost sight of each other.

He parked his Expedition in a copse of poplars near the turnoff to Aphrodite McGill's home on Apostle's Cove. He could see Shangri-La from there, rising against the steel blue surface of Iron Lake. He'd brought the Leupold binoculars he used for hunting so that he could observe the details of anyone who came and went. It turned out, there were lots of those.

As the sun rose to its zenith, deliveries began. First came a van from Zupp's grocery store driven by Kelly Nelson, a kid who'd worked for Cork at Sam's Place and who, grown now, was in charge of the deli at Zupp's. Kelly, along with a kid Cork didn't know, made several trips into the sprawling house, carrying white boxes of what Cork assumed were the catered eats for the party. They hauled in some equipment as well, stainless-steel-looking apparatus whose purpose Cork couldn't even guess at.

Next came a pickup with MORTENSON'S LIQUORS printed on the side. From the pickup bed, the driver, Mark Ireland, whom Cork saw every Sunday at St. Agnes, dollied in three hand-truck loads of boxes containing various alcohols.

A man from Geary's Electric arrived, took a toolbox inside, and came out an hour later. As soon as he drove off, another pickup, black and shiny, turned in to the drive that led to Shangri-La. The man who got out was huge and wore dark pants, a dark sport coat, and mirrored sunglasses. When the glasses came off, just before the man headed to the front door, Cork was surprised. He recognized Arlo Hornsby, a former Tamarack County sheriff's deputy who now operated a security firm that was sometimes a competitor for the kind of PI work Cork did.

Security? Cork wondered.

Near two p.m. Cork's cell phone rang. It was Stephen.

"Just checking in, Dad. How're things going up there?"

"I got my face kicked in a couple of nights ago but, aside from that, all's well."

"What? Did it have to do with your investigation?"

"Pretty sure."

"Who did it?"

"They jumped me at Sam's Place, but it was too dark to see who."

"Any idea why?"

"I think I woke a spider."

"I'm not sure I understand."

"Give me a little more time and I might be able to offer a better explanation. How's Axel doing?"

"He's still not fully on board with all this. I know that some guys who've been incarcerated a long time are reluctant to leave prison because life on the outside is alien to them. I don't know if that's part of the issue or if, as Axel continues to maintain, his work at Stillwater is too important for him to leave it. Would you do me a favor?"

"Name it."

"Talk to Henry, get his take on this. They're both healers. He might have some insight to offer."

"I'll get back to you on that."

The stakeout became quiet. Cork called Jenny to see if she'd discovered anything more of value in the notes. She yawned and told him she was looking them over. As they spoke, Cork saw a black SUV pull onto the lane to Shangri-La.

"Guess who just arrived," he said to Jenny.

"Who?"

"Wild Bill and Rocky."

"Of course," Jenny said.

As Cork watched, Arlo Hornsby stepped from the house and shook their hands, then they all went inside.

"Lots of security at Shangri-La tonight," he said. "We might have more trouble slipping in than I thought."

"But we like a challenge, don't we, Dad?"

On that point, Cork was beginning to be a little less certain.

CHAPTER 44

Before he abandoned his stakeout, Cork called Jenny again. She'd found nothing in the old notes that furthered their investigation. Although Waaboo typically walked the four blocks home from school alone, considering her son's sense of the lurking Windigo, she told her father that she wanted to be with him. So Cork headed to Crow Point by himself. It was late afternoon, the path through the woods deeply shaded by tall evergreens and nearly leafless birch and aspen. Cork's thoughts were just as dark as the shadows that fell across him as he walked.

It was Halloween, the anniversary of the day Axel Boshey had been sentenced to prison. For more than twenty-five years, Axel Boshey, like most convicted Native Americans, had experienced a life behind bars at the bottom of the brutal social strata inside the correctional system. That he'd found a way to maintain his dignity, to heal himself even, didn't make Cork's guilt any less onerous. Axel had missed out on years of knowing what it was to watch his children grow, to see grandchildren born and to be a part of their lives, to have had the chance to build a loving relationship with another woman. All this had been among the blessings Cork counted in his own life. As he broke from the trees and began across the meadow toward the two cabins, he walked like a man more pained by his thoughts than by the beating he'd recently been given. In the late sunlight, he cast a long, black shadow, a companion that made him think of the evil entities given freedom to roam at will on All Hallows' Eve.

Prophet stood in front of Meloux's cabin, watching as Cork approached.

"He's waiting for you at the fire ring," the man said.

They followed the path silently as it threaded through the outcrops to the fire ring on the far side. Meloux—or more likely Prophet—had built a fire, which, in the calm afternoon air, sent flames straight toward the blue arch of the sky.

"Sit," the old man said without looking at him.

Prophet took another length of wood, added it to the fire, then stood back, arms crossed as if he were a sentinel now. Cork wondered what he might be watching for.

"The Windigo," the old man said.

"You've sensed it, too?" Cork said.

"The Windigo and I are old enemies." The Mide touched his long flow of white hair. "It has been this color since I first battled that creature as a young man."

"I'm going to do my best to make sure Waaboo never does."

"I know you worry, but he has the heart of a warrior, that little rabbit."

"He says it's not here for him."

"Even so, it will not leave until it has feasted."

"I wish to God I knew who it was hungering after. But I'm here about something else, Henry. I'm here about Axel Boshey."

The old man had been staring into the fire. Now he turned his almond eyes on Cork but said nothing.

"Stephen tells me that Axel doesn't want to leave prison. He thinks part of it may be that Axel's been inside so long he's not sure he'll fit in the regular world. Which may be true. He's created a place for himself among the inmates. They look to him in much the same way the rest of us look to you."

The old man thought on this for a good long while. As Cork waited for Meloux's response, he watched an eagle take wing from the top of a pine along the shore of Iron Lake, then drop precipitously to the water, and rise with a fish in its talons. He thought again of the Windigo.

"I spoke to Axel Boshey only once after he went to prison. He was a man in need of much healing, both his body and his spirit. It seems that across these years, he has become a different man, a healer." Meloux nodded as if acknowledging to himself some truth. "In healing, we are often healed. What is it you want from me, Corcoran O'Connor?"

"If I can prove Axel is innocent, his son would like him to leave prison, but as I told you, Axel is reluctant to abandon the life he's created for himself. Is there something you can offer that might guide him in that decision?"

"Guide him toward abandoning those who might still benefit from his presence, you mean?"

"That's the gist of it, Henry."

The old man closed his eyes for a long time, and although Meloux's posture didn't change, Cork wondered if he'd fallen asleep.

"Prophet," Meloux finally said.

"Yes, Henry?"

"I would ask a favor."

"What's that?"

"Go with Corcoran O'Connor."

This surprised Cork and he could see that Prophet was surprised as well.

"To what end, Henry?"

"The Windigo is hungry. Although our little rabbit doesn't believe the monster is here for him, I would like to be sure he is safe."

"All right," Prophet said.

"And, Corcoran O'Connor, tell this to Axel Boshey. He may think of himself as old now, but I am still his elder. There is healing to be done everywhere. In my work here, I could use the help of someone who is on the same path but younger. Tell him that I would welcome his presence."

"*Miigwech*, Henry." Cork stood, but before he left, he said, "I'm feeling pretty old myself. Got any advice for me?"

The Mide looked up at him. "When it comes to aging, I know of only one cure."

"I'm not ready to take to the Path of Souls, Henry."

"But there are dark winds at your back, urging you toward that end."

"Dark winds?" Cork said.

"Guilt and regret. They are more painful to you than anything done to your damaged body. Think on this."

Cork gave the old Mide a final nod, then he and Prophet walked away from the fire.

By the time Cork and Prophet reached Gooseberry Lane, dusk had settled over Tamarack County. Cork parked in the drive next to Jenny's Forester and they came into the house through the mudroom door. The place was deathly still.

"Anybody home?" Cork called. When he received no response, he tried again. "Hello?"

He glanced at Prophet, then headed through the kitchen toward the living room. Prophet followed. They moved cautiously into the heart of the home. There were no lights on, and in the gloom of dusk, the house took on a threatening feel. Cork paused and tried once more.

"Anybody home?"

Still nothing.

He gave Prophet a gesture, indicating for him to head toward the hallway and check the office. Cork took the stairs. He mounted slowly, listening intently, hearing nothing. He reached the second floor and crept to Waaboo's room. The door was closed. He leaned, put his ear to it, then reached for the knob.

At that instant, the door flew open. Waaboo, wearing a scary clown mask, leaped at him and cried, "Boo!"

Adrenaline shot through Cork. Every muscle of his body tensed and filled with fire. It was only with great effort that he kept himself from leaping at his grandson. Waaboo laughed and said, "Got you, Baa-baa."

Cork mustered a smile. "You sure did."

Jenny stepped up behind her son. "He insisted, Dad. You okay?"

"Clowns have always scared me," he said. "I thought he was going to be a werewolf."

"That would take Daniel to do the makeup. And he won't be here before we go trick-or-treating."

"Something bad's happened on the rez," Waaboo said, taking off his mask.

"What?"

"A fatality," Jenny said. "I don't know any of the details. Daniel just called to say he'll be tied up and could I take Waaboo trick-or-treating."

"Guess I'll be going to Shangri-La alone then."

"Not necessarily," Prophet said, stepping up silently beside Cork.

"Prophet!" Waaboo cried with delight. He quickly donned his mask and threw a "Boo!" at the tall man. When Prophet didn't respond, Waaboo said, "I didn't scare you?"

Prophet replied, "I grew up in a Catholic residential school. Nothing scares me, little rabbit."

"What did you mean 'not necessarily'?" Jenny asked.

"Henry assigned me guard duty tonight." Prophet nodded toward Waaboo.

"Is it a good idea for you to be wandering around town?" Jenny asked.

Prophet was a Canadian citizen, in the country illegally, flying under the radar of the white authorities. He said, "It'll be dark. And maybe there's a mask lying around that I could wear?"

"I've got an old Frankenstein mask somewhere," Cork said.

Prophet looked at Jenny. "Waaboo will be safe with me, I promise. Go and do your sleuthing."

"Okay?" Jenny said to her son.

"I'm okay with Prophet," Waaboo said.

"That's settled," Cork said. "Any idea where Rainy is?"

"She didn't think we had enough candy to give out," Jenny replied. "She made a last-minute trip to the store."

"All right," Cork said. "We'd better get some dinner going. Lots to do tonight."

"Waaboo, I put the candy we have and a big wooden bowl on the dining room table. Would you go down and fill the bowl?"

"You betcha!"

Her son was gone in an instant, and Jenny said quietly but hopefully, "Maybe the Windigo was here for whoever died on the rez." She eyed Prophet. "But you take care of our little rabbit tonight. Promise?"

"I'll guard him with my life," Prophet swore.

CHAPTER 45

Before they all went their separate ways after dinner, Rainy insisted they gather in the living room and smudge with sage. It was a ritual that cleansed the spirit, and on that night especially she said she wanted to be certain there was nothing in them that would call to evil.

Before Waaboo and Prophet took to the streets, Waaboo in his scary clown mask and Prophet in his borrowed Frankenstein mask, looking as imposing as the real thing, Jenny asked her son, "Do you still sense the Windigo?"

"I don't get anything. I'm too excited." He squinched up his face in apology. "Sorry, Mom."

"That's okay. You and Prophet have a good time."

"Let's go!" Waaboo said and grabbed Prophet by the arm.

"We'll be fine," Prophet promised as Waaboo tugged him toward the door.

It was dark by then, and they'd already had their share of very young trick-or-treaters. Cork and Jenny were dressed for the Shangri-La party but hadn't yet donned their masks—Cork was the exaggerated face of the killer from the Scream movies, and

Jenny the face of the evil queen Maleficent from *Sleeping Beauty*, horns and all.

Rainy said, "I'm still not sure what you hope to accomplish, but for God's sake be careful, both of you."

"I won't let him out of my sight," Jenny said.

Cork said, "Ditto."

"Let me know when Waaboo and Prophet are back safe and sound, okay?" Jenny said.

"Of course," Rainy promised.

The doorbell rang, as it had more than a dozen times already, and little voices chimed out, "Trick or treat!"

Rainy went to answer while Cork and Jenny left the house through the mudroom.

The streets were alive with creatures of the season—miniature devils and witches and ghosts and superheroes—all in the company of adults, some of whom themselves were dressed in costume. They raced in and out of the illumination of streetlamps or porch lights, and Cork drove carefully, mindful of the danger of a child who, blinded by excitement, might run into the path of his Expedition.

"What exactly are we looking for tonight?" Jenny asked as they rolled out of Aurora and south along the shore of Iron Lake toward Apostle's Cove and Shangri-La.

"Aphrodite will be in her element," Cork said. "The belle of the ball, relaxed, probably with the help of alcohol and maybe some illicit substances. Her guests will be in the same state, I'm sure. We might be able to catch her, or one of her minions, off guard."

"Ambush them, you mean?"

"Question them while they're a little off balance, at any rate. I'm hoping that under the influence of everything Aphrodite's offering tonight, their tongues might loosen a bit."

"Any idea who we should focus on?"

"Wild Bill and Rocky for sure. I'd like to keep an eye on Moonbeam as well."

"What could she have to do with what happened to her mother?"

"Nothing, but I feel a responsibility to her grandmother to make sure she's safe in that place."

"By her grandmother, you mean Patsy Boshey?"

He nodded. "I know she's worried about the influence Aphrodite wields over that young woman. I'd be worried, too, if I were her. Aphrodite's appetite for the bizarre seems bottomless."

"What makes a woman like her do what she does?" Jenny said.

"Her past probably. But I don't know her history before she came here, so it's hard to say. You're a writer. What kind of background would you create for a character like her?"

"Complicated as hell, and full of mistreatment."

"So there you go."

"Are you saying we ought to have some sympathy for that woman?"

"Know your enemy. First rule of warfare."

"We're going to war?"

"Look at my face. I didn't get this playing checkers."

Lights that had been set on the great lawn of Shangri-La for the occasion cast eerie, floating images across the odd structure with its horizontal lines and sudden upthrusts of pagodas. The circular drive was lined with vehicles, as was the lane that led to the great house. Cork parked well back, and they stepped from the Expedition. He and Jenny stood a moment, scoping out the scene.

"That's Arlo Hornsby at the front door," Cork said. "He was a deputy here when I got elected sheriff. Just a kid, really. Wild Bill hired him, never should have. Some guys go into law enforcement because they think it'll be a golden pass for roughing people up. That was Arlo. Complaints from the get-go. After I dismissed him, he worked for Duluth P.D. for a while but got the boot from there for the same reason. Worked a few more jurisdictions, then opened his own security business operating mostly on the Iron Range. I've had a run-in with him now and again, stepping on his toes or him on mine. I'm guessing Wild Bill brought him on for tonight and, among other things, he probably has instructions not to let us pass."

"So, what do we do?"

"Follow me."

They walked to the edge of the cove and followed the shoreline, keeping just inside the growth of poplars that lined the lake. In that way, they approached the house from the rear. It wasn't difficult to see their way. The terrace was brightly lit, and the moon, nearly full, was on the rise. It hung over Iron Lake like a great, white, all-seeing eye, and the long, brilliant reflection it cast across the black water was like the righteous sword of Gideon.

Although there'd been a light snowfall only days before, the weather had turned pleasant again and the night was unusually warm for so late in the fall. While they crossed the lawn to the broad back terrace, they donned their masks. They could hear music pounding through the double-paned windows. As they mounted the steps, they caught another sound, furtive laughter, coming from a shadowed corner of the terrace and a woman's husky voice saying, "You devil. Do it again."

Cork knew that voice. It belonged to Cissy Koskinen, who worked at Zupp's as a cashier. She was a redhead, a grandmother, though a young one, and as she rang up his groceries, she and Cork had talked many times about children, grandchildren, mutual friends, things going on in Aurora. Her husband was a trucker, often gone on the road, but Cissy never complained, at least to Cork.

He heard a man's low reply, "There? Like that?"

Cissy's response was a little moan.

Cork said in a loud voice, "I didn't see it out there. Maybe you dropped it inside the house."

From the shadowed corner came a sudden silence. Cork and Jenny walked to the terrace door. As soon as they swung it open, the night was filled with a blast of music and voices and laughter, and they entered.

Inside Shangri-La, they found themselves in a small sea filled with clashing currents. Flows of costumed bodies shifted among the many rooms, most faces concealed beneath makeup or masks, hands clutching liquor-filled glasses. Dance music blasted from a large cleared area near the terrace doors where bodies writhed together like snakes in a den. As he made his way through the chaotic throng, the smell of overheated bodies made Cork think of gymnasiums and high school dances, except that here the miasma was overlaid with the scent of burning pot. In one far corner, under a psychedelic light display, a woman whose face was hidden behind a kitten mask danced topless on a table. Cork and Jenny were both constantly jarred by guests drunkenly stumbling against them, spilling drinks. Behind the safety of anonymity, every human temptation seemed embraced. Like almost everyone in Tamarack County, Cork had heard stories of the bacchanalian gatherings at Shangri-La, but he'd never been a part of one. This gaudy display of abandon, especially in an area dominated by staid Scandinavian stock, felt like an assault against all the sensibilities he'd developed in his years as a cop. Every nerve in him cried trouble.

Jenny leaned to him and spoke close to his ear to be heard above the din. "My God," she said. "I thought I saw some wild blowouts in college. They were tea parties compared to this."

"I don't see Aphrodite," Cork said.

"She could be behind any of the masks."

"I don't think she cares about hiding her identity. She's like the queen bee in the hive. I don't see Moonbeam either. But there's Wild Bill."

He was dressed exactly as his moniker dictated, in western gear, replete with a ten-gallon hat, a holstered revolver—a real one, it appeared to Cork—and spurs. He sauntered à la John Wayne among the throng. Zorro followed not far behind him, duded up in a black cape, black hat, and black mask, with a rapier hanging at his side. Rocky Martinelli, all swagger.

Cork and Jenny wove among the milling guests. Not everyone had chosen to mask their identity, and Cork recognized a face here and there. Cy Cedarholm who owned the Howling Wolf bar in Yellow Lake, a bear of a man whose business catered to bikers and loggers and who, considering the number of times Tamarack County law officers had been called to his establishment to quell a fight, didn't give a tinker's damn about being seen at a gathering that he probably considered on the staid side. Erik Amundsen, who'd left Aurora out of high school to pursue a career in Hollywood and had been cast in minor roles in a few slasher movies, before returning home to open a tattoo parlor and bask in the glow of being a minor celebrity. But most of those who showed their faces were strangers to Cork, probably not from Aurora or even Tamarack County, friends or acquaintances of Aphrodite who were, perhaps, holdovers from the days of her infamous solstice parties.

They finally located Aphrodite, holding forth among a small group near the open bar, which had been constructed as if it were the inside of a crypt, caskets on either side and a backdrop of cobwebs and skulls. She was dressed again as Cleopatra—gold dress, asp tiara, eyelids darkened with kohl. In addition, a small scabbard hung from a gold chain around her waist, and from it protruded a jeweled knife handle. Moonbeam wore the devil's costume Cork had seen her in a couple of days before. Still, in that place of wild abandonment, he thought she looked surprisingly subdued.

Jenny leaned to him and said, "She's pissed."

"Who?"

"Moonbeam."

"Drunk, you mean?"

She shook her head. "Angry. Look at her eyes."

Jenny was right. Moonbeam's eyes shot fire. Her brow was furrowed as well. And she was staring at Aphrodite, as if her anger were directed there.

They stood at the outer edge of the little gathering, but Aphrodite spoke well above the din of the party, so Cork could hear her words clearly. She was wildly animated in face and gestures, so much so that Cork guessed she was high on something, which didn't surprise him.

"And of course, I told him 'It's all real, sweetheart. But don't touch the merchandise unless you're ready to pay for it.' And he did." She held out her right hand, displaying a ring on her finger set with an emerald the size of an acorn.

There was general laughter. Polite, Cork thought. But Moonbeam, clearly, was having none of it.

"Darlings," Aphrodite said, sauntering to the table of catered food. "You really must try the tête de veau. It is to die for." She drew the knife from the scabbard that hung from her waist. With the knife tip, she stabbed a meat slice and slipped it into her mouth. After the meat was devoured, she said, "For those peasants among you, tête de veau is calf's head." She ran her tongue along the blade as if tempting fate, then smiled and said, "What is life all about if you don't live on the edge, darlings?" She slid the knife back into the scabbard.

Definitely high on something, Cork thought. Dangerously high.

Then Wild Bill muscled his way to her and spoke into her ear.

"Darlings," she said to the small gathering around her, "I'm needed elsewhere. Now, go and enjoy yourselves."

She turned and walked away, saying over her shoulder, "Come, my little Hot Stuff. We're needed."

Moonbeam followed, though she didn't look at all happy with the idea, and the little gathering dissolved into the greater mass.

"I think we should stick with Cleopatra and Hot Stuff," Cork said to his daughter.

"Hot Stuff?"

"An old comic book character. You're too young to remember."

They turned to follow the two women, but before they could move in that direction, the meaty fingers of a huge hand wrapped themselves around Cork's arm in a death grip, and a deep, menacing voice growled, "Got you, O'Connor."

CHAPTER 46

Cork tried to pull free, but the grip was a human vise. He turned and looked straight into the surly face of Arlo Hornsby.

The man was twenty-five years older than when Cork had fired him. He wore his hair in a crew cut and the six-pack abs he'd been so proud of as a young man now sported a bit more padding. But from the iron in his grip, Cork understood that Hornsby was more than capable of dealing out a significant beating, if it came to that.

Hornsby ripped the mask from Cork's face. "How the hell did you get past me?"

"How the hell did you know it was me?" Cork shot back.

"A little birdie told me you bought yourself a Scream mask at Ben Franklin this morning. This is the only Scream mask here." He looked at Jenny. "And the wicked witch. I've been watching for you, too. Let's see your face."

Jenny removed her mask. Cork was impressed that Hornsby knew about the purchases at the Ben Franklin store, but he suspected the information had come as a result of the web Aphrodite had spun in their small community.

"Let's go, you two." Hornsby grabbed Jenny's arm in a crushing grip as well.

"You're hurting me," she said.

"Your own fault, missy. Trespassing."

"Let her go, Hornsby," Cork said.

"Happy to do that outside. Like I said, you two are leaving this party, and leaving it now!"

Although there was general chaos going on in the great house, the altercation had drawn a decent audience.

"Hey," a man wearing a half mask like the Phantom of the Opera's said. "No need for violence."

It was another voice Cork recognized, one that belonged to Gunnar Miza, principal of the high school and a regular customer at Sam's Place.

"Interfere with this at your own risk, buddy," Hornsby warned.

"You harm these people and there will hell to pay, I can promise you," Miza said in the authoritative voice of a principal.

Hornsby let go of Jenny, reached out, and grabbed Miza's arm. "You're leaving, too, buddy."

"Stop that, you cretin," said Catwoman, who stood next to Miza. His wife, Cork realized. She was a regular customer of Sam's Place as well.

Guests had been drawn from other corners of the great house, and Hornsby cast a cold eye across the growing crowd near the bar.

"Let them go, you brute," a woman's voice called out from the gathering.

Cork felt the grip on his arm tighten even more, but Hornsby didn't move. He seemed uncertain how to proceed. Then Wild Bill and Martinelli appeared.

"O'Connor," Wild Bill said. "Figures you'd be at the heart of trouble."

"Just enjoying the party, Bill," Cork said. "Then your goon here spoiled things."

"Tell him to let my husband go," Catwoman said.

Wild Bill nodded to Hornsby, who complied. But he didn't release his hold on Cork.

"Please escort the O'Connors to the front door," Wild Bill said to Hornsby, then to Cork, "Best go quietly."

Hornsby finally let go of Cork's arm but shoved him ahead and nodded for Jenny to follow. "Let's go."

They'd taken only a couple of steps when shrieks broke out above all the other noise of the party.

Hornsby spun around and he and Wild Bill and Martinelli pushed their way through the crowd toward the source of the screaming. Cork and Jenny followed in the path the two men cleared. They made for the dance floor and then for the terrace, whose doors stood wide open now. By then, the screaming had stopped. Outside, the moon had risen higher and cast a hard white glare across the brick of the terrace, where Moonbeam stood, her red Hot Stuff costume stained with even deeper rubicund patches. She looked down at the bloody knife in her hand as if she couldn't quite figure out what it was. On the bricks at her feet lay Cleopatra in a spreading pool of blood that reflected the silver glow of the moon. Moonbeam lifted her eyes to the gawking crowd.

"Somebody help," she said, then she fainted.

CHAPTER 47

"She said it was sticking out of her grandmother's heart and she couldn't just leave it there, could she?" Cork reported to Daniel and Rainy at the house on Gooseberry Lane.

It was late by then, the streets empty of trick-or-treaters, Waaboo long ago gone to bed. Cork had called Oliver Bledsoe, a Shinnob attorney who handled a lot of cases for folks on the rez and asked him to advise Moonbeam, who was being held and interviewed at the sheriff's department. He'd called Patsy Boshey, explained things, then offered to give her a ride to be with her granddaughter. Finally, he'd swung by home to drop off Jenny.

"My God," Rainy said. "Do you think Moonbeam did it?"

"She was in shock," Cork said. "But she was clearly upset about something before Aphrodite was killed. So who knows?" He looked at Daniel. "What happened on the rez, the fatality?"

"Not a fatality as it turned out. Travis Anderson shot himself while he was cleaning his gun. He'll live."

"So the Windigo was all about Aphrodite?" Rainy said.

"It seems like it's been fed," Daniel said.

"It's still hungry."

They turned and found little Waaboo standing on the stairs, rubbing his eyes as if to get the sleep out of them.

"You should be in bed," Jenny said, then went and cuddled him.

"You made too much noise and woke me up," he complained.

Daniel said, "What did you mean about the Windigo?"

"It's still here and it's still hungry." Waaboo yawned. "But not for us."

"Do you know who?"

"Unh-unh."

"Let's get you back to bed," Daniel said.

"Can I have a Kit Kat?"

"Not now. In the morning." His father gently lifted him and carried him upstairs.

"It's still here," Jenny said.

"And still hungry," Cork added. "I need to pick up Patsy. Don't wait up for me," he told Rainy.

"You're not going without me," Jenny said.

Clouds scudded across the face of the moon as they made their way to Sweetgrass Assisted Living in Allouette, where Patsy Boshey was waiting for them. Jenny got in the backseat and Patsy rode up front with Cork while he gave her the full lowdown on the evening.

"What a horrible, horrible thing," Patsy said. "Poor little Moonbeam. I knew the moment she moved in with that woman there would be trouble. She just wouldn't listen to me. Oh, Cork, this can't be happening, not again."

"We'll get to the bottom of it. Promise."

Patsy was quiet for a long moment, then said, "Just like you did before with Axel?"

Which felt like a knife plunged into Cork's heart.

* * *

Despite the late hour, the Tamarack County Sheriff's Department was a hub of activity. When Cork, Jenny, and Patsy Boshey walked in, Deputy David Foster was on the contact desk dealing with a couple whose backs were to the door. Two deputies were on phones at their desks in the common area, both dressed in street clothes, which told Cork they'd been called from home at a moment's notice. Dross stood at the door to her office, deep in conversation with Chief Deputy George Azevedo, her major crimes lead investigator. Bledsoe and Moonbeam Boshey were nowhere to be seen.

Cork caught Foster's eye and nodded to the security door. The deputy buzzed Cork and the others through, then went back to the couple in front of him.

"Hello, Ms. Boshey," Dross said.

"Where's my Moonbeam?" Patsy asked. "Is she okay?"

"She's still a bit dazed. She's in an interview room at the moment with an attorney, Oliver Bledsoe."

"Can I see her?"

"When we've finished interviewing her."

"Are you going to arrest her?"

"We haven't made a decision yet."

"She couldn't have killed that woman," Patsy said.

"We're working on getting to the truth of what happened," Dross said. "Why don't you have a seat. It may be a while. Jenny, will you stay with Ms. Boshey? Cork, can we see you in my office?"

Cork followed her in, and Azevedo brought up the rear.

"I thought I told you to stay away from Shangri-La," she said the moment she'd shut the door behind them.

"Like asking a mouse to stay away from the cheese. Has Moonbeam said anything?"

"Her account of the evening has been a bit disjointed. The shock, I suspect."

"What has she said?"

"She claims that a woman approached Aphrodite and spoke to her a moment, whispered something in her ear. Moonbeam didn't hear what was said, but apparently it caught Aphrodite by surprise. Aphrodite told Moonbeam to wait and followed the woman toward the terrace."

"What did this woman look like?" Cork asked.

"Older, medium height, medium weight, wearing a red fright wig," Azevedo said. "That's all Moonbeam was able to give us."

"She waited, as instructed," Dross said, picking up the story, "but when Aphrodite didn't come back, she went out onto the terrace to check on her. That's when she found the body."

"And pulled the knife out and started screaming," Azevedo added. "Although she claims not to remember that."

"She seemed upset about something before Aphrodite was killed. Did she say what?"

"Drugs," Azevedo said. "Moonbeam watched Aphrodite consume a whole cocktail of things. She said she tried to talk her grandmother into being reasonable but got nowhere."

"Did any of the guests see the woman in the fright wig?"

"There were nearly two hundred people at the party," Dross said. "We haven't finished interviewing everyone. We took names and contact information and let them go. BCA is sending up a team from Duluth to help us on that front and with forensics. They won't be here for quite a while. To answer your question, a few of the guests believe they remember seeing her, but only that. Nothing useful."

"What about Wild Bill and Rocky?"

"When they heard the commotion Hornsby was raising with you, they split off from Aphrodite and returned to the bar. Neither of them saw the woman in the fright wig."

"Hornsby was supposed to be checking the guests on arrival. Didn't he see her?"

"Claims ignorance. But he pointed out that you and Jenny got by him, so she probably found a way, too."

There was a knock at the door, and one of the deputies in street clothes poked his head in. "I've got Agent Leary at BCA on the line. She wants a word with you."

"Coming," Dross replied.

Cork and Azevedo followed her out. While she took the call, Cork glanced at Foster on the contact desk, who was still dealing with the couple who'd been there when Cork arrived. He'd only glimpsed the backs of the couple, but now he saw their faces and recognized them. The young man caught sight of Cork at the same moment.

"Cigarette dude from Duluth!" he called out. "I knew you were a cop!" Now Jenny turned from where she stood with Patsy Boshey, and the young man saw her, too. "And cigarette girl!"

Cork approached Foster. "What's going on, David?"

"They're claiming their car's been stolen."

"Maggie," the young man said as if it were a cussword.

"Maggie?" Cork thought a moment and remembered the woman in the kitchen with Jude Monroe. "From the shelter?"

"That's her."

The young woman with him, who Cork recalled was mute, gave an enthusiastic nod.

"What's the story?" Cork said.

"She paid us to give her a ride up here. We stopped at a gas station a couple of miles outside town. Rosie went in to use the bathroom. I went in to get a pack of cigarettes. Maggie said she was cold and could I leave the car running with the heater on. Then she drove off. That bitch stole my car."

The young woman touched his arm and signed something.

"Okay, that *woman* stole my car. We've been walking practically all night."

"Any idea why she wanted to come here?"

"Didn't say. Just offered me a hundred bucks."

Jenny had joined her father, and now Dross, who'd finished her phone conversation with BCA, joined as well. Foster filled her in.

"Do you have the make, model, and plate?"

"Got it," Foster said.

"Put it out there. Let's see if somebody on patrol can spot it." To the young couple she said, "So what does this Maggie look like?"

"I don't know. Fifties, maybe." He glanced at his companion, who signed something. "About your height and probably weight," he said to Dross.

"Hair color?"

"Brownish."

Jenny touched Cork's arm. "Fiftyish. Medium height and build." To the man and woman she said, "She didn't happen to be wearing a red fright wig?"

The young woman signed something.

"She says she saw what she thought was a snarl of red yarn in the big handbag Maggie brought with her," the young man said. "Could have been a fright wig, I suppose."

"Who is this Maggie?" Dross said.

"I have no idea," Cork said. "But I think I know someone who might."

CHAPTER 48

Jude Monroe sounded alert, as if he were used to being awakened by phone calls in the dead of night. Cork explained the situation and asked what light the ex-priest might be able to shed.

Monroe was quiet for a long time, until Cork finally asked, "You still there, Jude?"

"I need to check on something, Cork. Can I call you right back?"

"I'll be here."

The young couple had been buzzed through the security door and now sat at one of the empty desks in the common area.

"Okay to smoke in here?" the young man asked.

"Not in any public building in Minnesota," Dross told him.

"Your names?" she asked.

"Lonnie Perpich," the young man said. "This here is Rosie."

"Rosie Perpich?"

"Tolgaard. We're not married."

"Can you tell us anything at all about this Maggie?"

"We've never had a lot to do with Maggie. She helps in the kitchen, serves up the dinners, that kind of thing. Never says much. She's one of the folks who live there pretty much full time. But after being in the car with her for a couple of hours, I can tell you for sure that she's got problems. Kinda moaned the whole way up here."

The young woman signed.

"Yeah, real sad sounding," the young man added, nodding in agreement. "Like she was in pain or something. Not her body but, you know, like, her soul."

Cork's cell phone rang. It was Jude Monroe, calling from his own cell phone. Cork put the call on speakerphone, so Dross and Azevedo could hear. "Yeah, Jude?"

"Has anyone checked on Bill Gunderson?" The ex-priest sounded deeply concerned.

"I don't think so. Why?"

"Check on him. Do it now. And does Rocky Martinelli still live in Aurora?"

"Rocky? Yeah, he's still here."

"Check on him, too."

"What's going on, Jude?"

"Too much to explain on the phone. I'm on my way."

"Jude—" Cork began. But the ex-priest had ended the call.

Dross said to Azevedo, "Did you get numbers for Gunderson and Martinelli when you interviewed them tonight?"

"I did."

"Give them a call."

Azevedo made the call to Wild Bill's cell phone. When he got no answer, he tried the man's landline. "Both go to voicemail," he reported.

"Try Martinelli."

Azevedo got an answer this time, but it was clear he was speaking with Martinelli's wife. When he hung up, he said, "Martinelli received a call a while ago and went out to Gunderson's place."

"I have no idea what's going on, but, George, head out and check on Gunderson. See if Martinelli's there, too. Foster, you go with him."

After the two deputies had left, Dross said, "Nothing makes sense here." To the young couple, she said, "Can either of you tell us anything more about this Maggie?"

They both looked clueless, then the door to the interview room opened and Oliver Bledsoe stepped out.

"We're ready," he said.

Moonbeam still wore the bloodstained devil costume. She sat, shoulders slumped, looking beleaguered, aged beyond her years. Cork was there "as a consultant," Dross had put it. Under questioning from the sheriff, Moonbeam had gone over the early part of the party and had admitted that she was unhappy with Aphrodite for all the drugs she was taking. She'd also admitted that the whole affair felt overwhelming to her, the gathering so much more chaotic than she'd imagined.

"Let's take it from when you and Aphrodite left the bar," Dross said. "Bill Gunderson spoke to her. Do you know what that was about?"

"Some guy from the Twin Cities, one of what she called the 'old gang,' was acting up in some ridiculous way. Bill wanted her to talk to the guy before they threw him out. We were making our way through the crowd of guests when we heard the commotion back at the bar. Bill and Rocky left us. That's when the woman in that crazy red wig accosted my grandmother."

"Accosted?"

"Grabbed her arm and said something."

"Did you hear what she said?"

"No. Aphrodite just looked kind of shocked and told me to

wait and then she and the woman went off together toward the terrace."

"She looked shocked, you said."

"Really surprised. Not in a good way."

"Were you concerned?"

"It was Aphrodite. I figured she could handle anything. But when she didn't come back, that's when I went out to the terrace."

"Did you see anyone else?"

"Just my grandmother. Lying there."

Cork said, "Marsha, you might want to talk to Cissy Koskinen. She was on the terrace earlier."

Dross made a note, then asked Moonbeam, "And the knife, it was in your hand. How did it get there?"

"I don't remember. I don't remember anything after I saw her dead."

"And you have no idea why someone would want to kill your grandmother?"

The young woman looked completely bewildered. "She was so much larger than life. She didn't give a hoot what people thought of her. She lived exactly as she wanted to. She offended some people here, sure. They're so . . . provincial. But is that any reason to kill her?"

A knock came at the interview room door.

"Come," Dross said.

One of the deputies in street clothes poked his head in and said, "Call from Azevedo. The stolen car is at Gunderson's place. Martinelli's car is there, too. And, Sheriff, there's a woman inside who's got a shotgun trained on both of them."

CHAPTER 49

"I'm going," Cork said once again.

"You're staying here," Dross said. Once again.

"I've been in on this from the beginning, Marsha. I'm not standing down now."

"A woman's been killed. And it sounds like the killer is at Gunderson's. That changes everything."

"I'm the one in touch with Jude Monroe. He's the only one who might be able to explain all this. You need me."

"Give me his cell phone number."

"Not unless I go."

"And me, too," Jenny said.

"I don't have time for this," Dross said.

"Then quit arguing," Cork said.

Dross seemed ready to continue the discussion but said instead, "Gooding, two more vests."

Deputy Randy Gooding, one of the two deputies in street clothes, had already grabbed a vest for himself and a scoped rifle from the department armory. He left the common area now and returned with two more Kevlar vests. Dross had assigned Kent

Nelson, the other officer in street clothes, to dispatch, and he was in the process of contacting off-duty deputies and the State Patrol to request assistance.

Patsy Boshey sat with her arm around Moonbeam, who'd come from the interview room with Oliver Bledsoe.

"Can I take her home now?" Patsy asked.

Dross shook her head. "Until we understand what's going on, I'd like her to stay here. For all I know, she may be a target as well."

"What about us?" Lonnie Perpich asked.

"You're free to go."

"Where? We don't have a car?"

"Then stay. I'm sorry, but I don't have time to figure this out for you. Let's roll," she said to the others.

Wild Bill Gunderson had lived forever in a cabin home on Little Bear Lake, five miles west of Aurora. Dross drove her department cruiser, with Gooding in the passenger seat and Cork and Jenny in the rear. The moon, nearly full, was just rising above the eastern horizon at their backs. Once the town was behind them, the cruiser's headlights tunneled through dark. But Cork, as he sat thinking about the complex puzzle of all that had occurred, finally began putting pieces together in a way that was making sense.

There'd been chatter on Dross's radio, Deputy Nelson communicating with other agency units, but in the cruiser, no one said a word, until Jenny asked, "What's Wild Bill Gunderson to this Maggie?"

"No idea," Dross said. "But I suspect that if she's living in a shelter, she's been a street person and so there could be significant mental issues involved. We don't always take care of people like we should."

Cork said, "I've been doing some fast thinking here, Marsha. I know this will sound crazy, but I have an idea who Maggie might be."

"I'm all ears," Dross said.

"Do you remember after Chastity Boshey was murdered, you had a conversation with Wild Bill's daughter?"

"Lucy Martinelli? That was twenty-five years ago, Cork."

"It was at the Pinewood Broiler. She told you she'd experienced a miracle. She'd been made a virgin."

"Oh, yeah. A really bizarre conversation."

"She also told you, I believe, that an angel had given her a new name. Magdalene. And your comment was something like 'very biblical.'"

"I do remember. Then Wild Bill committed her. And then she died in the fire at that sanitarium."

"Did they ever recover her body?"

A long silence descended in the cruiser. Finally Dross said, "You're saying this Maggie could be Lucy Martinelli?"

"I think Maggie could be short for Magdalene. When I saw her at the shelter with Jude, I thought she looked vaguely familiar. I'm thinking now that was because, even twenty-five years later, I could still see Lucy Martinelli in her face."

"You're right, it sounds crazy." She drove for another minute, then said, "Why would she kill Aphrodite?"

"I don't have an answer for that one. Maybe Jude will."

"Get him on your cell and tell him to meet us at Gunderson's."

The cruiser drew up to the cabin. Azevedo and Foster were waiting for them. Both held scoped rifles.

"Status?" Dross inquired.

"She's in there, still wearing that fright wig," Azevedo reported. "Gunderson and Martinelli are sitting together on a couch. She's got a shotgun trained on them. I advised her to put the weapon down. She said she had a lot to get off her chest, and if I came into the cabin, she'd shoot them. I've checked the side window." He lifted the rifle he held in his hands. "I can get a clear shot, if it comes to that."

"Let me try talking to her," Dross said. "But go ahead and position yourself at the window. Gooding, check the back of the cabin. But if there's a door, don't go in. Foster, stay with Cork and Jenny. Don't let anything happen to them."

The inside cabin door stood open, and a long rectangle of light fell across the porch. Dross mounted the steps, careful to stay outside the light, and spoke through the screen door.

"Lucy, this is Marsha Dross. You remember me?"

A long moment, then, "Yes."

"I'm the sheriff here now. I'd like to talk to you."

"You stay where you are or they both die."

"Don't come in," Wild Bill said. "She means it."

"What's this all about, Lucy?"

"Magdalene. My name is Magdalene. And this is between them and me."

"We can sort it all out, I promise. You just need to put that shotgun on the floor."

"No."

"Jude Monroe is on his way. Will you talk to him?"

"Maybe. If I haven't already done what I came for."

"Just be calm, Magdalene. He'll be here soon."

There was a long stretch of silence, then, "I'll wait."

Dross descended the steps and joined the others. "Any idea of Monroe's ETA?"

"Should be here momentarily," Cork said. "Is it Lucy?"

"Yeah," Dross said. "She was troubled when I knew her back in the day. But I never thought she was dangerous."

"I'm hoping Jude can shed some light."

The sound of a powerful little engine cut through the quiet of the night. A minute later, a pair of headlights appeared on the lane leading to the cabin. Jude Monroe pulled up in his red Jaguar and parked.

"You made good time," Cork said.

"Pretty much doubled the speed limit. Where's Maggie?"

"You mean Lucy?"

"So you know?"

"Finally put two and two together," Cork said. "She's inside, pointing a shotgun at her father and her ex-husband."

"What's going on?" Dross said.

Jude Monroe looked toward the cabin door. "Let me talk to her."

"What's going on?" Dross said, this time not a question but a demand.

"There's a lot of confusion in Lucy's thinking about the past, most of it because of her father. Among other things, she believes he killed her mother," the ex-priest said.

"I thought that was a boating accident, a drowning," Dross said.

"Maggie—sorry, Lucy—swore to me that she saw it happen. She'd repressed that memory, but during her treatment at the sanitarium, the memory resurfaced. On one of the few visits her father made while she was there, she confronted him. He denied it. But then he made threats to her and told her something terrible. He claimed Lucy had killed Chastity Boshey."

"What? Did she believe him?"

"I visited Lucy at the sanitarium twice. The second time was just before the fire destroyed it. That facility was old, pretty run down. Didn't surprise me when I heard it burned. Lucy told me there were so many dark places in her memory, deep wells of forgetfulness. But during her therapy, some things were coming back to her. The memory of her mother's death, for one. When she accused her father of murder, he told her she was crazy. That's why she was in the loony bin, as he put it. Then that heartless man convinced her that she'd killed Chastity Boshey and that he'd covered it up. He threatened that if she didn't stop repeating the crazy story about him killing her mother, he'd make sure they put her in a straitjacket forever."

"Did she remember anything about Chastity's death?"

"She told me she had a vague memory of Chastity lying on a floor, covered in blood. But that was it. No memory of killing her."

"Did you believe her?"

"When I counseled her years ago as her priest, she told me she suspected there was something going on between Rocky and Chastity. It was clear that she was becoming more and more confused. When I heard that Chastity had been killed, I wondered if it might be possible that Lucy was responsible. But then Axel confessed, and I admit, I was greatly relieved."

"What about Bill and killing her mother?"

"Lucy told me that she'd been abused much of her life by her father. Sexually and psychologically. That was something we talked about when I was her priest. Sometimes it was clear to me that she was confused in her memories, in her thinking, out of touch with reality. Honestly, when I visited her in the sanitarium, I thought she was probably struggling with some sort of psychosis."

"How'd she get to your shelter?" Cork asked.

"In the confusion of the fire, she slipped away. For the next twenty years, she lived on the streets in Duluth. Not long after I opened the shelter, she showed up. I took her in. She's been on medication for years now. I didn't think she was a threat so long as she took her meds. But when you and Jenny came the other day, something you said set her off."

"What?"

"She heard you talking to me about Aphrodite and Chastity,

and everything came rushing back. Incredible anger at her father, deep guilt for what she believed she'd done to Chastity. We talked but I couldn't comfort her. I suspect she stopped taking her meds. I didn't even know she'd left the shelter until you called me, Cork."

"I'm pretty sure she killed Aphrodite," Dross said.

"I need to talk to her, before she does any more harm."

"Foster will get you a vest. But you're not going inside. You talk to her through the open door but stay well away. Understood?"

"Understood."

"I'll be up there with you."

Deputy Foster went to the cruiser and came back. In one hand, he held a Kevlar vest, which he gave to Jude Monroe. In the other hand, he still held a scoped rifle. "I might be able to get a straight shot at her through the doorway, Sheriff, if I stand outside the light."

"I can talk her down," the ex-priest said. "I know I can."

Dross said, "Take your position, David."

"Ten-four, Sheriff."

"You do what you can, Jude," Dross said. "But I need to be ready if worse comes to worst."

The priest donned his vest and started toward the cabin porch, Dross at his side, her firearm drawn.

Jenny said, "Do you think he can get through to her, Dad?"

"That depends."

"On what?"

The moon cast a glaring white light over the scene as Cork stood watching Dross, Monroe, and Deputy Foster move to their positions as if they were the final chess pieces in an endgame.

"Whether the Windigo has finished feeding," he said.

CHAPTER 50

Cork and Jenny moved to a place near Deputy Foster, who'd positioned himself outside the long rhomboid of yellow light that pushed through the door of the cabin. They could see Wild Bill Gunderson and Rocky Martinelli, both sitting on a sofa, and Lucy standing a few feet in front of them with the shotgun pointed in their direction. Wild Bill had an arsenal of weapons in his home, and Cork figured Lucy had gotten her hands on one. Gunderson dripped with so much sweat that even from such a distance, Cork could see the glisten of it as it poured down his brow. He couldn't see Martinelli sweating, but he could see all the man's facial features pulled together as if anticipating at any moment to be obliterated by a load of searing buckshot. Jude Monroe stood on one side of the doorway, Dross on the other. Backing the cabin, the calm surface of Little Bear Lake reflected the glow of the moon so powerfully that it was as if, instead of water, the lake was filled with white-hot fire and the little structure that sat on its rim was ready to be consumed by flames.

"Magdalene," Monroe began. "It's me."

"Father Jude?" She sounded relieved but didn't turn her head to see. She kept her focus and the barrel of the shotgun on Wild Bill and Martinelli.

"Can we talk?"

"Go ahead. But it won't change what I'm here for."

"Which is what?"

"He killed my mother."

"That's a lie," Wild Bill said. "I did no such thing."

"I saw you do it."

"She was always a clumsy woman. She fell off the damn boat and hit her head. There was nothing I could do. And, hell, you were just five years old. You don't remember anything."

"You argued. I heard you. About me. About what you were doing to me. She knew."

"Don't listen to her," Wild Bill called toward the door. "She's crazy. She killed Chastity. She butchered that girl."

"Ask him how he knows?" Dross said to the ex-priest in a low voice.

"How do you know she killed Chastity, Bill?" Monroe said.

"She came to my place afterward, covered in that woman's blood."

Dross said in that same low voice, "Ask if he tried to get rid of the evidence at the Boshey cabin? Did he wipe away the prints and try to frame Axel Boshey?"

Monroe relayed the question.

Wild Bill didn't respond. Lucy took a step forward so that the barrel of the shotgun was only a few feet from her father's face. "Tell them the truth."

"All right, all right. Don't shoot. What was I supposed to do? My daughter, a goddamn murderer? Think I'd be able to live here after something like that?"

Lucy spoke as if stumbling into a memory. "She . . . she was a Jezebel. She was going to steal my husband, ruin my family, hurt my children. And . . . and after that the angel came. She called me Magdalene. She said I had cleansed the wicked and had prepared the way to be purified."

"You never told me this," Monroe said. "I never knew why you called yourself Magdalene."

"After he put me in that place, I began to remember. The way my mother died. How he used me as a child. And then you came, and you were such a comfort to me there. After you'd gone, I began to remember. An angel had spoken to me. I'd been born again. I was Magdalene. Clean, a servant of the Master and of the light." Now she turned her head slightly to see the door, where Monroe stood. "And I have been that, haven't I, Father Jude?"

"Yes, Magdalene. But the shotgun, that's not serving the Master. His way is the way of peace. Will you put the gun down?"

"Not until he admits he killed my mother."

"Okay, I killed your mother. Now put that damn shotgun down."

"Those are just words. You don't mean them. Maybe when you're on your way to hell you'll confess truly." She laid her cheek against the stock of the shotgun and sighted.

"Don't, girl!" Wild Bill cried. "I swear, I'm sorry for whatever it is you think I've done to you."

"And my mother?"

"Her, too. I didn't mean to kill her, I swear. It just . . . we argued, see . . . and things got out of hand. She was going to tell everyone I was a goddamn pervert. I swear I didn't mean for it to happen. Please, you've got to believe me."

"Why? My whole life you've done nothing but hurt me."

She swung the barrel of the shotgun toward Martinelli now, who jumped as if bitten by a snake.

"And you," she said. Tears began streaming down her cheeks, and for a few moments, she seemed unable to speak. When she did, her words were punctuated by sobs. "I killed Chastity because of you."

"Jesus, Lucy, don't listen to Bill."

"I did it because of you. You and that Jezebel. You made me a killer." She curled her finger around the trigger of the shotgun.

"Wait, Lucy, wait!" Martinelli held up his hands as if trying to stop the spray of buckshot about to tear him wide open. "You didn't kill Chastity!"

"Shut up, Rocky," Wild Bill snapped.

"I don't want to get shot, Bill."

Lucy said, as if in disbelief, "I didn't?"

"Who did kill her, Rocky?" Dross called from the porch. "You?"

"Hell, no. It was Aphrodite."

The silence that fell over them all at that moment was a thing of contradiction, bringing with it such weight that no one could breathe, but at the same time offering Cork a profound sense of release. It quickly became clear that Lucy felt the same way.

"I didn't kill her?" She spoke like a woman who'd just sprouted wings and had been lifted on the hands of a redeeming wind.

"Put the shotgun down, Lucy," Martinelli pleaded. "I swear I'll explain everything,"

But the avenging angel inside her returned immediately, and once again, Lucy trained the shotgun on her father, her finger on the trigger. "You! You monster! You need to pay."

"Magdalene, our Lord knows all the sins of this man," Monroe broke in, speaking in a calm, loving voice. "If there's to be punishment for what he's done, it will be meted out justly when he stands before God, whose faithful servant you are. I have seen you minister to the hungry and the homeless and the lost. I have seen you work with a pure heart. It's time to put the gun down and return with me to that path of peace. I swear, I will not desert you. You will never be alone."

"I want him punished in this life."

"Magdalene." It was Dross speaking now. "I promise you we will get to the truth of what happened to your mother. We will put that man behind bars. You and I, we were friends once. As a friend, I give you my word."

"Magdalene, sweet Magdalene," Monroe cooed. "Put the shotgun on the floor."

Lucy didn't move. Cork saw that both Foster and Azevedo had their rifles to their shoulders, sighting through the scopes. There was nothing but silence now, not a breath of wind. In the moonlight, which lit everything as if with white fire, nothing moved. It was, Cork understood, the fatal moment of decision. Her life or Wild Bill's or the both of them, in the balance.

"Please don't, Lucy," Jenny whispered.

"Please, girl," Wild Bill whimpered.

"Magdalene, sweet Magdalene," the ex-priest intoned.

And Lucy's finger finally left the trigger. Slowly the shotgun barrel came down until it pointed toward the cabin floor.

The instant he was out of danger, Wild Bill leaped from the sofa, yanked the shotgun from his daughter's grasp, then swung it, caught her with a hard blow to the side of her head, and she fell to the floor.

"You little bitch!" he screamed, standing over her. "You always were the bane of my existence."

Jude Monroe was inside the cabin in a flash, well ahead of Dross. He delivered a right cross to Wild Bill's jaw that sent the man sprawling. The gun clattered to the floor. Monroe knelt above Lucy, who lay dazed. Slipping his hand under her, he gently pillowed her head.

"Get an ambulance," he said to no one in particular.

Dross had picked up the shotgun and spoke to Azevedo as he came through the front door. "You heard him, George. Get on the radio. Now."

Along with Deputy Foster, Cork and Jenny had entered the cabin. Martinelli still sat on the sofa, watching the proceedings as if he were now simply a spectator. Wild Bill slowly began to get up from where Monroe's punch had thrown him. He made it to a sitting position but was having trouble rising further. Cork walked to him, and the man lifted his hand as if for help.

Cork said, "God as my witness, Bill, if you get up, I'll be the one who knocks you down this time."

Wild Bill eyed him fiercely.

Then Jenny, who'd joined her father, added, "And if he doesn't, I will."

Wild Bill considered his situation and finally chose to stay put. He rubbed his jaw, sat looking surly, eyed Jenny, and under his breath, in a harsh rasp, as if it were a curse word, said, "*Women.*"

CHAPTER 51

Lucy Martinelli was examined at the ER of Aurora Community Hospital. Except for a deepening bruise on her left cheek, she was deemed to be in no danger, physically. However, in the interview room of the sheriff's department later, she rocked back and forth and let out little groans as if in pain, in the way Lonnie Perpich and Rosie had described she had when they drove her up from Duluth. She'd waived her right to an attorney, but she'd asked for Jude Monroe to be with her while she was being questioned. He sat beside her, holding her hand as she suffered. Dross had allowed Cork to sit in on the interview.

"I didn't go looking for *her,*" Lucy said. "I went after *them.*"

"Them?" Dross asked.

"My father. And Rocky."

"Why?"

She moaned a little, then said, "To make them understand."

"Understand what?"

"Everything they did to me. They made me like I am." She'd been looking down at the hand Monroe held. Now she looked into his eyes. "Crazy."

"Not crazy, Maggie," the ex-priest said with great gentleness. "Terribly hurt."

"But you did kill Aphrodite, yes?" Dross said.

"I didn't mean to. There were so many people. I didn't see Rocky or him. But I saw her."

"You approached Aphrodite and then what?"

Lucy rocked back and forth. "Told her who I was. She looked at me like I was a ghost. I told her we needed to talk. About Chastity. I told her we needed to talk somewhere private."

"The terrace?" Dross said.

"Her suggestion."

"What happened out there?"

Lucy stopped rocking, but a long, sad mewling came from her throat.

"It's all right," Monroe said. "I'm with you. What happened, Maggie?"

"I wanted to tell her that I was sorry for what I'd done. I thought maybe it would take away this heavy rock that's been sitting on my heart ever since my father told me I killed Chastity."

"And did you tell her?" Dross asked.

"Yes."

"What happened then?"

Her face took on a bewildered look. "I watched her change. Not like me after the angel spoke. Not forgiving. She became this . . ." Lucy paused and thought. "Like this blizzard of cold hate. She pulled out a knife from her belt and screamed that she was going to cut my heart out, like I'd cut out hers. Then she came at me. But she wasn't very strong. She never had to live on the street." She looked again at Monroe, as if for understanding. "I wasn't there to kill her, but the knife ended up in her."

"And your father?" Dross asked.

"I wasn't there to kill him either. That's not why I went. I just wanted to get the truth from him. I just wanted to hear him say that he killed my mother. Then after what happened with Aphrodite, I figured . . . I figured I was damned. And if I was going to go to hell I might as well take him with me."

"What about Rocky?" Cork asked. "You said you were looking for him, too."

"Him? I just wanted him to know that I killed Chastity because of him. He was a faithless man. I wanted him to admit what kind of man he is. I've always known the truth of his spirit, that he's a worm. I wanted to hear him admit it. And . . ." She leaned forward and took to moaning again. "And I wanted to know about our children. I haven't seen them in decades."

"They're fine," Cork assured her. "They left Aurora years ago, made lives of their own elsewhere. If you ask me, they knew the truth of their father's spirit, too."

"They're fine?" She looked at him and smiled through tears that began to stream freely down her cheeks. "They're fine. Oh, they're fine. Thank God for that."

Jude Monroe said to Dross, "Is that enough for now, Marsha?"

She nodded. "For now."

Whether it was because, as Rocky Martinelli maintained, all the events surrounding Chastity's death were so long ago that the part he'd played was well past any statute of limitations, or just his general overblown view of himself, he said he didn't need a lawyer. And as he began to tell his story in the interview room, he had a cocky grin on his face.

"I'd been seeing Chastity for years. It began when she was in high school. Even then, Chastity gave me all kinds of things my wife could never begin to imagine."

"You're talking about Lucy," Dross clarified.

"That's what I said. So, then Chastity goes and gets herself pregnant. Maybe it's mine, maybe not. I know Chastity's seeing other guys. Lucy's clingy as a leech and strict Catholic to boot. There's no way I'm giving the kid my name. So Chastity marries that Indian, Greensky."

"Just to give Sunny a father?"

"That and to piss off her mother. Greensky had a job at the resort, a place to live so that Chastity could get away from Shangri-La."

"She had a problem with living there?"

"Yeah, and her name was Aphrodite."

"Go on."

"So, doesn't matter she's married, we keep up what we've been doing all along. After Greensky gets himself killed in the hunting accident, she gets herself pregnant again and marries her second Indian, Axel Boshey. Like before, the kid could've been mine."

"You kept up the affair while she was married to Boshey?"

"You bet. Hell, she told me both guys screwed like damn preachers, all delicate and such. She liked it rough, let me tell you."

"How'd you manage the affair?"

"We had a signal system. If the flag was up on the mailbox out there at the cabin, it meant the coast was clear. We used it when she was married to both Indians. Those two dumb redskins were clueless."

It was clear how proud Martinelli was of this system that had facilitated his adulteries. Cork couldn't help thinking that Lucy had grasped the true spirit of the man. A worm.

"The flag was up that night. Chastity and me, we did some coke, drank some Jack, got down to business. We're having a good time, then we hear the cabin door open. Next thing you know Aphrodite waltzes into the bedroom. And I'll be damned, she's got this camera and is snapping pictures. Chastity yells what the hell does she think she's doing. Aphrodite laughs like some kind of crazy woman and says something like 'You think you can keep my grandchildren from me? Who's going to believe a cheating wife is any kind of mother?'"

"You say Aphrodite was acting like a crazy woman. High on something? Drunk? What?"

"Probably both. That woman loved her vices."

"Go on."

"So Chastity leaps out of bed, tries to get the camera, they stumble into the other room. I follow them, try to be reasonable, tell them we can talk this through. But they're both wasted. Like I said, Chastity and me had been doing coke, and God only knows what Aphrodite was on. They're screaming at each other. The baby's screaming in the back room. It's a real shit storm. Then Chastity goes berserk, grabs a knife, threatens her mother. Aphrodite grabs the poker from the fireplace. Chasity lunges. Aphrodite swings that poker, catches Chastity on the side of the head. Chastity goes down, just lying there on the floor. Then, God knows why, Aphrodite starts going at Chastity with the sharp end of that poker. Again and again, I mean absolutely out of her mind. I grab her, pull her away. She's still screaming, tries to get me with the poker. I hit her a good one to the jaw, knock her out cold."

He stopped his account, then shook his head at the memory and said to himself, "Christ, it was a nightmare."

"What did you do then?"

"I'm standing there naked as a jaybird, still not thinking real clear but thinking I can't handle this shit alone. So I get dressed, head up to Grady's, the all-night truck stop, use the pay phone there, call Bill."

"Why Bill? You were being unfaithful to his daughter."

"There was never any love in his heart for Lucy. And he always told me I wasn't just a son-in-law. I was the son he never had. Also, I knew him and Aphrodite had a thing going for a long, long time. So Bill comes and we decide we have to get Aphrodite out of there. We carry her out to Bill's truck. He drives her back. I follow in her pink bug."

"What about your cruiser? What if Boshey came back or someone saw it there?"

"We thought of that. I parked it behind one of the empty cabins."

"Go on."

"We get her inside Shangri-La, get those bloody clothes off her, get her into bed. Then I tell Bill we have to hightail it back before Boshey shows up. But Bill's real cool, tells me not to worry. If Boshey's not there, I call it in like I just discovered it on patrol. If Boshey's there, we blame the mess on him. Anybody who knows Boshey would believe it. So we go back. And I'm surprised as hell to see our station wagon parked in front of the cabin and Lucy standing in the doorway."

"Lucy? What was she doing there?"

"We'd been arguing for a while, Lucy accusing me of seeing someone else. She asked me about Chastity, because we'd been a hot item in high school. And hell, everybody knew Chastity's reputation. Lucy'd been threatening to confront Chastity, but I didn't believe she had the guts for it. She was such a wet rag of a woman. That night of all nights she proves me wrong. God or some demon must've had it in for me."

"What did she say?"

"Nothing. She's just standing there, staring, like she's catatonic or something. Hell, our kids were still in diapers and she left 'em. So maybe she was already nuts before she got to the cabin or maybe what she saw there just pushed her over the edge. It was like a goddamn slaughterhouse. It'd send anybody over the edge."

"Could she have been high on something?"

"I don't think so. She'd been having these episodes. She'd go off somewhere in her head. She'd get this look in her eyes like she wasn't really seeing me. Then when she came out of it, she'd tell me all this weird crap. She told me one time she'd talked with the Virgin Mary. Another time, she *was* the Virgin Mary. She was nuts. I talked to Bill about it. He told me she'd had that kind of thing going on all her life. When she was, like, twelve or thirteen, he had to put her in the loony bin for a while."

"You didn't think maybe she needed psychological help?"

"I figured you can't cure crazy."

Cork could see Dross working at containing her anger, probably her disgust. "So what did you and Bill do?"

"I get Lucy into our station wagon. She just sits there, staring straight ahead but mumbling now like she's talking to someone. I leave her and go back inside. Bill's already wiping down anything Aphrodite might have touched. The poker, the doorknobs. Then he tells me to get some of Boshey's clothes and some gloves. The clothes are easy, but I can't find any gloves. So I go out to the woodshed and there's a pair of old pigskin work gloves. I bring 'em back to Bill. He's already got Chastity's blood all over Boshey's things. He puts a little blood on the gloves. He says we gotta hide that stuff somewhere it'll be found. I tell him the woodshed's a pretty good spot, so we do. Then we go back to the station wagon. And Lucy's looking different now."

"Different how?"

"Real calm. She looks at me and Bill and she says something about talking to an angel. I'm just thinking the woman's really gone off her rocker. And thinking, too, that maybe it's not a bad thing. I drive the station wagon home. Bill's following me. I check on the kids. They're sleeping. But I don't want to leave Lucy alone with them. Bill tells me he'll take her back to his place. We load her in his truck and one more time, go out to Boshey's cabin. Bill drops me off and heads back to his place. I get in my cruiser, go home, give my ma a call from the house, tell her Lucy's left me, she needs to come and watch the kids. When she gets there, I go back out on patrol, like nothing's happened. It's morning by then. Not long after that, I get the call on the unit radio requesting me to head to the cabin. I think everything's falling into place until I get there and Aphrodite's sitting beside Chastity's body."

"Why do you think she went back?"

"She told Bill she had a nightmare while she was blacked out, saw her daughter dead. So she went out that morning to check on Chastity. Whatever she was on the night before, it blew her mind. Complete blank, except for that nightmare thing. Bill and me, we decided we'd never bring it up. And when Boshey confessed, well that just sealed the deal."

"You fed him the details of Chastity's murder that he used in his confession."

"And he just ate 'em up and spit 'em out."

"You and Bill, you've always been pretty tight," Cork said. "Did you know he abused Lucy as a child?"

"Knew there was something wrong with her. No idea what that was. Bill, huh? That man's a lot of things. Guess you can add pervert to the list."

"Why did he call you out to his cabin tonight?"

"Lucy had the shotgun on him, made him call me. So I guess coward's another thing you can add to the list."

"Do you have any idea how many laws you broke?" Dross said.

"Like I told you before, statute of limitations was up a long time ago, Sheriff."

"We're talking covering up a murder. No statute of limitations there, Martinelli. I'm going to see you go down for everything."

The grin he'd worn through so much of the interview died. "I want a lawyer."

* * *

It was nearing daybreak. Cork, Dross, Jenny, and Jude Monroe sat in the sheriff's office drinking bitter coffee from department mugs.

"All Hallows' Day," the ex-priest said, looking out the window at a red dawn. "The day we honor all the saints who have attained heaven."

"Any chance Chastity and Aphrodite made it there?" Jenny asked.

"They were human," Monroe replied. "Shaped—or maybe misshaped—by forces they couldn't defeat. My own belief is that our Lord's grace has embraced them, as it does us all."

"Lucy included," Jenny said.

"Absolutely."

"She suffered so much in her life, and so often at the hands of men who were supposed to take care of her," Jenny said.

"But there was so much she didn't remember," Cork said. "So much she repressed."

"My guess is dissociative amnesia," Monroe said. "I've seen it in people who come to the shelter, people who've suffered greatly, suffered trauma. It's a way the mind tries to protect us. What will happen to her?" he asked Dross.

"She's confessed to killing Aphrodite."

"That seems to have been accidental," Cork said. "Maybe even self-defense."

"We'll leave it to our county attorney to sort things out," Dross said. "But Axel Boshey has been cleared. He'll be a free man soon."

"If that's what he wants." Cork sipped his bitter coffee. "I broke my promise to him."

"What promise?" Jenny asked.

"I told him that if I found the truth, I'd share it with him first so that he could decide what to do with it."

"Not his truth to handle," Dross said. "Wasn't from the beginning."

Jenny put her hand on her father's arm. "How are you feeling, Dad? I know you've been carrying around a lot of guilt since Stephen first contacted you about Axel."

"He lost twenty-five years of his life," Cork said. "It happened on my watch."

"Not lost," Monroe said. "From what I understand, he found himself."

"A hard journey," Cork said.

"There are no easy journeys," Jude Monroe replied. "Believe me, I know."

EPILOGUE

It was a cold, dark night when Cork and little Waaboo accompanied Henry Meloux from the cabin along the path through the two rock outcrops to the fire ring beyond. Cork held a lantern. Meloux made his way slowly in the circle of light, using his walking stick, which was topped with the carved head of an eagle. The breath that came from their lungs sent white puffs into the light. Earlier, Prophet had told Cork that he'd prepared a hearty bean soup for the lunch meal that icy winter day and that the old man had eaten like a hungry bear. Which made Cork think of the black sky in the same way, a hungry bear that had filled its belly with a million stars. As they made their way to the fire ring, Meloux's digestive tract was well at work on the bean soup, so much so that it wasn't only his lungs sending forth air into the night.

"Your wolves are howling, Mishomis," Waaboo, who walked beside to the old man, said.

"Little rabbit, when you are more than a hundred years old, your wolves will make a ruckus, too."

"They already do," Cork said. "We won't let him eat cabbage anymore, Henry."

Waaboo said, "If you fart by the fire, Mishomis, you might explode us all."

"And if you continue to make fun of this old man, little rabbit, you might receive a knock on the head with a walking stick."

"Henry is an elder," Cork reminded his grandson. "Show respect."

"I'm sorry, Mishomis," Waaboo said. "But you always tell me to speak the truth."

"Only when it will do some good," the old man said. "And only when my walking stick is not in my hand."

The wheels of justice, as always, had moved slowly. It wasn't until the first night of the new year that Axel, as a free man, sat at the fire ring on Crow Point, where Prophet had a fine blaze going. Sunny Boshey had come up from the Twin Cities, and Marianne Polaski from Chicago. Patsy was there. And Moonbeam, though she looked uncomfortable. Patsy had shared with Cork that Moonbeam felt tremendous guilt for all those years she thought of Axel only with deep shame. She was also struggling with the understanding that Rocky Martinelli, a man she'd come to loathe, was her biological father. And she was sorry for all the concern she'd caused Patsy by choosing to live under the sway of Aphrodite. But Axel offered her the true spirit of a father, forgiving and embracing, and he'd invited her to sit next to him at the fire ring that evening.

All the O'Connor clan was there—Rainy, Jenny, Daniel, Waaboo, Stephen, and Belle. Meloux had set sage smoldering in a clay bowl, and he gave it to Waaboo, who circled the fire, offering the smoke to each of those present so that they might cleanse themselves through smudging. When his duty was done, he sat with his father and mother and warmed his hands by the fire, his eyes shining in the light of the flames.

Through all that had occurred in uncovering the truth of Chastity Boshey's death, Cork had come to an even greater appreciation of the blessing of family. As he watched Axel and Patsy and Sunny and Moonbeam sitting together in the warm glow of the fire, he understood the gift of the Creator in that bond that was about so much more than just shared blood.

Meloux offered tobacco, then a prayer, beginning, "*Miigwech, Kitchimanidoo,*" thanking the Creator in Anishinaabemowin for the beauty of the day, the gift of freedom, the love of family, and the strength to seek the truth. He closed by asking the blessing of the Great Mystery on all who were present that evening.

Then he said, "It is good to have you among us once again, Zoongide'e-makwa. Brave Bear. That is the name I dreamed for you and gave you in the naming ceremony long ago. You have lived that name. Through great difficulty, you have come to understand that even though the body may be locked behind stone walls and iron bars, the spirit can still be free. You have gifted this knowledge to your imprisoned brothers, and a great gift it is. I welcome you here. I invite you to share this place where others come to seek healing from the wounds of life. Is this what you wish?"

"It is," Boshey replied.

"Then it is done."

No sooner had he spoken these words than a long, low growl emanated from Waaboo's rear end. Meloux grinned and said, "Now whose wolf is howling, little rabbit?"

Cork laughed and said to his grandson, "Lucky we didn't all explode."

"Sorry," Waaboo said, then gave a little shrug. "But wolves do what they want to do."

Around the fire, there was a good deal of laughter. It was a night for embracing what was human, for offering gratitude for the blessings of Kitchimanidoo, for forgiving what was past, and, on that first day of a new year, looking with hope toward all that lay ahead.

And Cork thought, not for the first time, how blessed he was. How blessed were they all.